POSTWAR CHILDREN

TWO NOVELLAS

MICHAEL HARRIS

CANYON

by

Michael Harris

1.

Maybe John was the only one to remember it, because Annie, who sat beside him on the couch as they watched the Mallet through the window, was only four then. He was six. And even then, he couldn't remember all of it. They must have been making noise, because otherwise their father, sleeping into the afternoon after a night's work on the railroad, wouldn't have come out of the bedroom. But all John remembered was silence. This was in their old, rented house on Sacramento Avenue. The far side of the street had no houses; behind it, the land dropped off in a slope of wild blackberry bushes to the hidden tracks. The huge black cab-forward locomotive was steaming toward the turntable and roundhouse in the center of town. It seemed to glide as smoothly and quietly as a sled against the white mountainside beyond the river, through the falling snow. The flakes had their own silent, dreamlike speed. They made him sleepy. Maybe it all *had* been a dream. But he remembered it so clearly: how when their father came out, wearing just his Jockey shorts, he looked as broad and white and cold as a snowbank, and how in the dim light of the window the shadows of the real flakes fluttered down over his chest and arms like moths, and how the folds of the sheets he'd slept on had left strange creases in his skin, like marks chiseled into rock. Their father was silent too. He took the boy and the girl both by the hair and cracked their heads together so hard their ears rang. Then he went back to bed.

* * *

Now it was 1954, and John was ten. It was summer. They lived in a different house, on Shasta Avenue, a house they owned. But his father was sleeping again, behind an unfinished wall whose raw Sheetrock and two-by-fours gave off the smell of pitch. Maybe not sleeping, because of the pain where the boxcar had hit. But silent still. John had caught a glimpse that first night, around the side of his mother's body as she unhooked the straps of the overalls and sucked in her breath, of the great bruise over his father's butt, upper legs and back: a pool of purplish blue as dark as ink. She hadn't dared touch it. Who had ever seen a bruise like that? His father had had to lie on his stomach for two days now, yet the men from the railroad had begun calling, urging him to go back to work. His father swore — but not over the phone. Afterward. John didn't understand. Why did they call more than once, after his father had already *told* them? It hurt too much. They ought to be scared to make him mad, John thought — and couldn't they hear what was in his father's voice, the size of it, the size of the biggest bruise in the world? It was anger that pushed out through the wall and crowded the air now so that John could hardly breathe.

It made no sound, but it was part of every sound he *did* hear: the dog, Cleo, scratching her ear; the click of each dish his mother and Annie stacked in the kitchen.

He went outside.

What happened later, John knows, couldn't all have happened in one day, but that's how he remembers it, will always remember it: their five or six years on Shasta Avenue poured into twelve summer hours or so, brimful, but not a drop spilling over.

* * *

He was lying on the back porch with Cleo when the phone rang.

He heard his mother's footsteps going into the hall. Then her voice answering, though he couldn't make out her words. Then her voice, reluctant, calling his father.

So he knew it had to be the railroad again.

Silence. John found that every muscle in his body was taut as a bowstring. He heard a floorboard creak inside, as if his father had put his weight on it, getting out of bed, and then stood still in his pain before moving again. John laid his cheek down on a board of the porch, as if it were the same one. A bare pine board. It felt cool. This was the west side of the house, under the cutbank, still in mid-morning shadow.

His father moved. John listened to the steps. Three, four... six. Then his father's voice, a rumble.

Why don't they leave him alone? he thought. *Don't they know...* But how could they? How could they know they were putting *him* in danger?

3

He held his breath. Another silence. Another rumble, longer. And a silence.

Then a ringing thud as his father slammed the phone down.

His mother cried out.

John flinched, even with two walls between them. He scrooched over to the edge of the porch and looked down; Cleo ducked beside him, her tags jingling. He could see the boulder wedged against the beams that held up the porch. Speckled granite, dim in the shadow and dull with mud. The spring rains had loosened it. The bank was always sliding, oozing red clay and rocks. But nothing so big before. It had smashed into the porch in the middle of the night, shaking the whole house; Cleo had howled in terror, just as she had howled once when a bear came down the mountainside and rummaged in the garbage cans. John thought of that howl now — stroking Cleo's head, listening.

His father didn't go back to bed, as John expected. His father and his mother both came into the kitchen, where he could hear them arguing.

"— you think you're *doing?*" his mother said, angrier than he had ever heard her sound.

"— a man's own wife won't support him, ain't *that* a hell of a note?"

"Don't use that kind of language with me."

Where was Annie? John wondered.

"The old man told me once, and I didn't listen. How there'd come a time when you had to stand without a soul to help you. Not a solitary soul. And by God —"

"Frank, call him back. Please. Right now."

Maybe she wasn't angry, John thought. Maybe she was scared. And that was worse; that was even harder to believe.

"What's it take to make you understand?" his father said, and his voice seemed to take on the dark and ugly color of the bruise. "You think life is all pretty grammar and church socials? You think that's how the SP runs? They ran the whole state of California for forty years, you know that? This is *it*, Connie. If I knuckle under now, I'll never... they'll *have* me. Don't you see? They'll have me right —"

John buried his face in Cleo's warm side.

"Call him back. Please."

"Even my own wife. I thought I'd never see the day."

The thing is, John's mother had never been scared. She had always acted as if there was nothing to be scared *of.* This didn't keep John and Annie from tiptoeing around the house when their father was in a bad mood — but in another way it helped. There was a promise in her calm, bright voice. When they grew up, they felt, they had a chance to be like her. Unafraid, even sitting at the same table with him.

But not now.

Cleo's dusty brown hair tickled his nose. Suddenly he was about to sneeze — and was twice as frightened. They'd know he was here.

A coward. A sneak.

"— think of the *children*," his mother was saying, "if you can't —"

But then Annie's voice chirped up; she had come from somewhere else in the house. John heard her abruptly go quiet, as if she realized what was happening. But when his mother and father started talking again, their voices were normal. They weren't arguing anymore, not in front of her.

Holding in the sneeze, he slipped off the porch and ran.

* * *

John was stunned. He was used to the silences, but he had never heard his parents argue like this before. Almost fight. He wondered what it meant, what it meant for *him*... but he almost forgot about it when he left the house.

That summer he was two boys. One was the coward and sneak he felt he was becoming. But the other was still an ordinary kid. He became that kid now, and he might have remained that kid all day if his father hadn't been hurt — had been called out on a trip on the railroad. It all depended on Frank Hiller's pickup truck. A big maroon Chevy. Nobody knew for sure when a trip would end. If John came home and the truck was there — he remembered this half a lifetime later — he would change, inside his Keds and T-shirt and jeans, right where he stood on the street.

2.

The ordinary kid had a gun.

Gary Grissom was telling him, "You've gotta be a Jap."

"I don't want to be a Jap," John said.

"Somebody's gotta be," Gary said. "You and Freddie be Japs."

He looked at Freddie Ordoñez. Freddie didn't want to be a Jap either, he could tell. But Freddie was two years younger than John and Gary, a year younger than Gary's brother, Jimmy. So he had no choice. Besides, Freddie was half Mexican, so he looked more like a Jap. Whatever a Jap looked like.

"*Somebody's* gotta be a Jap," Gary said.

John hesitated.

They were huddled under the front steps of the Grissoms' house. It was cool and shady there. The masses of leaves on the oak trees swayed outside, and sunlight flickered through the cracks in the boards. Flecks of white paint stuck to Gary's bare back. It was tan, the way John's back never got. Tan and smooth and hard. And Gary's elbows were pebbly and rough, as if he'd rubbed them on sandpaper. John had tried to rub his own elbows, once or twice, but they just got red and sore; the skin didn't change. It wasn't fair, he thought. How just the kind of skin Gary had seemed to give him the right to decide who had to be a Jap. And all of them knew it.

"Then you be a Jap next time," John said.

Gary thought about that. "OK," he said finally. He took out his pocket knife and flicked it; it stuck in the dirt. He looked up, squinting. "Then you guys get on out of here. We gotta plan some strategy."

"Let's be Germans," Freddie Ordoñez said. "I don't want to be a Jap either."

"Japs or Germans, what's the difference?" John asked.

But he knew, or thought he did. Nobody could say Freddie looked like a German.

"The Germans were tougher," Freddie said.

Gary wouldn't give in. "The Japs were tough too," he said. He picked up his knife and wiped the blade on the legs of his jeans. "C'mon, I'm tired of fighting Germans. You be Japs this time."

Then Mr. Grissom called from the porch. His sons leaned their heads out.

"Jimmy. You do what I told you?"

"Yes, Pa," Jimmy said.

"You git them toys picked up out back?"

Mr. Grissom talked different. It was a twang, John's mother had told him. An Oklahoma twang. The Grissoms were Okies. A lot of Okies had come to California during the Depression, when she was a girl. "They had a hard time," she said. Still, John got the feeling that she didn't think they were quite as good as the Hillers. The Grissoms were new in Dunsmuir, for one thing. Mr. Grissom worked for the Commercial Garage downtown. He wore jeans and a faded blue work shirt, and as he clumped down the steps he carried a heavy toolbox that made the muscles in his arm stand out like ropes. He was strong, like John's father. But where Frank Hiller was solid and fair, Mr. Grissom was lean and dark and stringy, as if the sun had baked everything else out of him. His pale eyes squinted, just like Gary's.

"Yes, Pa," Jimmy said.

"You help your ma when she asks. She's got cleanin' to do... Gary, you hear? We got church tonight." He stared at Jimmy. "You *sure* you picked up them toys?"

"I... I will, Pa. Just a minute."

"You'd better," Mr. Grissom said. "If I find out any different, you'll wish I hadn't."

He hitched up the toolbox, so that muscles moved all down his back, under the shirt. He tossed it one-handed into the trunk of his car, a dusty black '49 Ford, and drove off slowly, bumping over the tree roots in the yard. Jimmy watched him, open-mouthed. *He's scared too*, John thought. Maybe he ought to be nicer to Jimmy from now on... though usually he thought Jimmy wasn't very smart. But Gary didn't even blink. He just folded the knife and put it back in his pocket. John wished he could be that brave. Then he thought: *Maybe his skin's so tough it doesn't even hurt when he gets whipped.*

"You go to church on Wednesdays?" he asked.

"Yeah, ever since we joined up here. Sundays, too… We're Southern Baptists." Gary gave him a quick look, almost shy. "You want to come?"

"I don't want to miss the Lone Ranger." It was on the radio at seven.

John grinned, then wished he hadn't.

"I mean it. C'mon. I'll ask my folks… It'd be OK."

"I don't know."

"Are you saved?" Gary asked. Now he wouldn't give up on this either.

"I don't know… I guess so."

John didn't want to make Gary mad, but nobody had ever talked to him this way before. Maybe the Jehovah's Witnesses who came to the door sometimes, but not just another kid.

"No guessin' about it." Gary shook his head. "You're either saved or you ain't. And if you ain't, you're goin' to Hell, sure as shootin'."

"Maybe I'd better ask *my* folks."

"Tell 'em," Gary said. "Tell 'em those other churches might be churches of God, but this is the church of Jesus Christ."

He looked so serious, squatting under the steps in his naked skin, repeating words some grownup — a preacher? — had told him. John felt embarrassed — for himself or for Gary, he wasn't sure. He tried to imagine himself asking somebody if he was saved. He couldn't. But Gary was brave. That was why he could tell them what to do. It must be hard, being brave like that. Awful hard… Suddenly John was sorry that he'd tried to argue.

And he thought of something else, remembering the muscles in Mr. Grissom's back as he'd tossed that toolbox into the car so easily: Who would win, if Mr. Grissom and John's father had a fight? It was strange. He'd never asked himself that question before — never had any doubt.

"OK, we'll be Japs," he said. "Just give us a head start. OK? Ten minutes."

* * *

He remembered a time at a Cub Scout den meeting when *he'd* told people what to do and they'd done it, like magic. They'd gone to a jamboree down in Redding and seen stuff other Cubs had made: wood carvings, baskets, rope knotted and lacquered and pinned to boards. One pack had made suits of armor out of cardboard, like knights had worn in King Arthur's time. John got so excited that he spoke up, for once. It all came jerking and tumbling out of him, how they ought to do it too. And they listened! That was the amazing thing. He expected them to laugh, but they didn't. Mrs. Garamendi, the den mother, smiled at him under her thick glasses, surprised… But that was the trouble. Why did Mrs. Garamendi have to be surprised? And why did John feel he was standing off to one side and watching himself, waiting for the laughter? Why did it seem like magic? Not real. He didn't think Gary ever felt like that. But John had tried to act as if it *was* real; he'd gone home and made his own suit of armor, begging cardboard boxes from the S&J Market, cutting out pieces and tying the joints with string, painting them silver. He'd made a fiberboard shield, painted yellow, with a black dragon on it and the words DEATH IS BETTER THAN DISHONOR. He'd made a wooden sword with an aluminum pie plate for a guard, punched with holes in intricate patterns. His mother had given him a pink-and-purple ostrich plume from her cedar chest to stick on the helmet. All he needed was a horse, and somebody to joust with… And then, at the next den meeting, he discovered that nobody else had done anything. He wasn't surprised. (That was the trouble again: that he wasn't surprised.) He supposed he ought to get mad, try to shame them, get them excited again… But his own excitement was gone, and so was the magic. Nobody cared as much about armor as he did. That was the truth. They might have thought they did, for half an hour, but they didn't. Now they just wanted to be left alone, the way he usually did. He understood that. It was too much work to pull them all, like a locomotive pulling a string of boxcars, with just his idea. Too hard…

He felt a terrible weakness, the way he felt when his father was angry at him. How could Gary fight it? he wondered. And he thought: *Well, if Gary wants to run a war, the least I can do is help him.*

* * *

By now he and Freddie were running through the Grissoms' back yard: wash flapping on the line, gnarled apple trees, tall grass with green-and-yellow foxtails.

They stooped, still running, and threw them at each other, but Freddie had his shirt off too: nowhere for the foxtails to stick. Then they reached the woods.

"Do I *gotta* be a Jap?" Freddie asked.

"It's just pretend," John said. "Don't worry."

"I want to be a German."

They were scrambling uphill, a rocky path of red clay. Something stubborn and whiny in Freddie's voice made John pause behind a big fir tree. "We gotta keep moving," he panted. "They'll catch up with us." And then, when Freddie shook his head: "Well, why don't you *be* a German? You don't have to tell 'em. Just let 'em think you're a Jap. It's OK with me."

3.

A joke.

That's what they all thought it was. Just because he got hit in the ass.

Even by a boxcar.

They couldn't help it, Frank Hiller thought during those days on his stomach, unable to sleep at night, only half awake the rest of the time, sweaty and feverish. It was human nature. Still, it pissed him off. He could eat only a little of the food Connie set on the floor beside his bed. Cleo ate most of it. She leaned her chin on the mattress and nudged him with her cold nose, curious. The kids peeked in through the door but came no closer. Once or twice, he staggered to the bathroom and squatted above the toilet without any skin touching the seat and still nearly passed out from the pain of bending his back and legs. The urine that dribbled into the bowl was bloody. Connie offered to bring something from the kitchen to use as a bedpan, but what good would that do? In bed or out, he'd have to move, raise some part of himself. Why couldn't she figure that out? Sometimes the woman had no sense. Though she *cared*, at least. Give her that much. His conductor, Will Jamison, had tried to sound sympathetic on the phone but couldn't keep a chuckle from creeping into his voice. *Hit in the ass. Jesus.* He could imagine Jamison fighting a grin on the other end of the line. *It can't be all that bad, can it, boy? Got plenty of padding back there.*

"Doc Reed check you out? Nothing broken?"

"No." *Except for damn near every last blood vessel I've got.* "He just said bed rest, give it time."

"Well, far be it from me to argue with Doc Reed. But still. How much time does he think you'll need? Just a ballpark figure, now."

"As long as it takes, he said."

"Well, that's fine, for him. Doc Reed ain't in the business of moving trains. But we can't have you making a vacation out of it, can we?"

A vacation? Frank Hiller thought. It puzzled him at first, what Jamison was getting at. No skin off *his* nose if he had to find another brakeman. It was Frank himself who lost money if he had to lay off. The way the Southern Pacific worked, a young brakeman was stuck on the Extra Board until he built up seniority. Anybody with more seniority could bump him off a job. A young guy got bumped all the time. He had to fill in, take the scraps nobody else wanted. Work was scarce enough so that he never laid off voluntarily if he could help it. Only now, with fifteen years in, was Frank able to work steadily with the same crew for weeks at a time. He was just getting to know Jamison — a man who looked as weather-beaten as a cowboy but who kept a chess set in the caboose and insisted that all his brakeman learn to play; a Mason who studied secret ritual from a little leather-bound book in his bib pocket. One of the old-school conductors, from the days when trains had no radios and a crew had to deal with everything from hotboxes to avalanches by itself. The old guys were masters, some of them. During the Depression, even a very smart man might never have a chance to go to college. He'd end up in overalls instead, with a sun-blistered neck and grease under his fingernails. Like Frank himself. The quality was falling off, Jamison complained. These days, a kid with any brains at all *went* to college and stayed off the railroad. Frank nodded. He liked to think Jamison saw him as an exception. But what was this phone call about?

A vacation? *Let it happen to you and see what you call it.*

But Jamison surely had been hurt himself, more than once. He knew how it was. He had helped Fred Ordoñez ease Frank into Fred's car for the ride to the doctor's office. Frank had to kneel on the passenger seat and face the rear so that none of the bruise touched the cushion. Jamison said, "Good look, son. Hope it ain't as bad as it looks," and seemed to mean it — then. This joke business — the hint of a chuckle — came later. Now it was as if Jamison was trying to tell Frank more than he was saying.

But what?

"Level with me, Will," Frank said the second time the conductor called. "You know I wouldn't stay out if I didn't have to." At least he hoped Jamison knew this — but then, how could he, on such short acquaintance?

"Somebody thinks I'm dogging it, goddamnit, have 'em come over here and look."

Look at what? he imagined Jamison thinking. *Your purple hind end?*

"That ain't necessary, Frank. Nobody questions you've been hurt. It's all in the incident report. I signed it. But there's some… well, just at this particular time, folks in high places, they see it as a *marginal* injury — that's the word they'd use, nothing broken and all. Not like the thing hit you in the *head*, right? Though if you ask me, you'd have been better off if it had. Gave as good as you got. A hardhead like you." Frank heard the chuckle now, but it wasn't as convincing as the silent one. Nor did Jamison usually chatter on like this. Frank was so furious at the word *marginal* that he didn't realize until after he hung up how embarrassed the man must have been. Passing on a message Jamison didn't agree with but had been ordered to give: "The safety picnic's coming up."

"That's it?" Frank asked.

"That's it."

The SP safety picnic was an annual event. Long tables of potluck at the Mount Shasta City park. Tubs of beer. Softball games. Railroad caps and buttons for the kids. Bigwigs from Shasta Division headquarters and even from San Francisco would brag about the company's near-spotless safety record: so few man-hours lost to injury in the average year that it was hardly worth the piddling effort to count them.

The safety record wasn't a lie, exactly, Frank thought, but nobody took it seriously, either. Maybe the government did, but not the men themselves, not the Brotherhood. If the SP wanted certain numbers, he had always thought, it would get them. So it was hard to imagine the company having to muscle *him*, now. Was this year worse than usual? He had no idea. Was the Shasta Division so close to some bad number that his bruised backside, if they counted it — and they'd have to count it if he laid off — was enough to push them over the line?

Maybe.

But then he thought: *This is crazy. I'm too small a fish for them to worry about. Connie's right. My temper's getting the better of me again. I must have misunderstood Will, that's all.*

It was the fever, Frank thought — the wooziness that came over him from the heat; from staring for hours on end at the pattern of bright new nailheads in the studs by the head of the bed, raw pine smelling of resin; from listening to kids playing outside, cars passing, the burp of somebody's chain saw, the grinding of the bulldozers on the freeway cut that was going to bury this house and all his work on it. No wonder the owners had sold it to him so cheap. Four thousand dollars. They'd probably known all about this Interstate 5 project and laughed at him all the way to the bank. The state would pay him, of course — the same four thousand. Market value. But it wouldn't pay a dime for all the hours he'd put in, all the hope and sweat.

Frank Hiller, who had learned what the exact freeway route was going to be only when the grading began, felt outraged all over again. It did a man no good staying indoors like this, he thought. Lying there helpless. Nursing grudges. The bruise felt as thick and stiff as a board, yet it burned at Connie's lightest touch, so now she just poured lotion out of the bottle. Lately he'd had the sensation that his body was trying to absorb the thing, suck all that dead, clotted blood back into itself. *That* was crazy.

Wasn't it?

But when Jamison called the third time, Frank could no longer ignore the truth. The SP really was trying to force him. He had thought he could work on Jamison's embarrassment — saying, *It isn't right, Will. You know that. Why don't they know that?* — but it came to him now that Jamison wouldn't have *been* embarrassed if the pressure from above hadn't been too strong to fight.

"Time's running out, son." The chuckle was gone. Somebody must have taken Jamison to the woodshed, Frank thought — told him to stop screwing around and get the message across or else. "We've been lucky so far. Schedule gave us a little slack. But any time now we've got to saddle up again. And you'd better be with us."

"Will —"

"I ain't got all day to jaw with you, Frank. You got a family, don't you? Sure you do. Nothing much you *can* do but suck it up. Better get used to the idea."

Frank clenched the phone, felt his pulse hammer at his temples.

"What about the Brotherhood?" he asked finally. That was the Brotherhood of Railroad Trainmen, their union.

"The Brotherhood," Jamison said, "has got to pick its fights, son. And this ain't one of them."

Not when it's only your ass.

* * *

The pain wasn't even the worst of it, Frank thought. The shock of being hit was. They'd been bringing a freight down from Klamath Falls, on the North End Pool, and at Cantara Loop, the steep grade north of Dunsmuir — the line doubled back on itself like a paper clip; he could see the caboose going in the opposite direction right above where he, in the middle of the train, was checking the brake hoses and couplings between cars — they jumped the tracks. Four boxcars, two flatcars, a tanker. It wasn't too bad, as derailments went. No cars actually tipped over and fell into the river. Thank God they were moving so slowly then. But it wouldn't have happened at all if the goddamned SP had kept up the track and roadbed properly. They'd rather save a buck or two in the short run, and what happened? Men got hurt.

Afterward, Frank remembered the banging and jolting and screeching, the red cutbank flashing by, cinders pulverized by the bouncing steel wheels, men yelling. But only afterward. The rear end of the boxcar behind him jackknifed out to the right and the swinging front end slammed into him. At a slightly different angle, he thought later, it would have crushed him against the flatcar ahead. It would have knocked him off the train, for sure, if he hadn't caught the ladder beside him and held on by instinct. Instinct was all he had going for him at that moment. Because the *weight* of the thing... how could he explain that to anybody? Connie? Jamison? *Dead weight.* Those words meant something to him now. Tons of steel, tons of whatever that boxcar was loaded with... all had tried to squash him like a bug. Less than that. Like nothing. The shock of being nothing, nothing at all, against so much force had driven every other feeling out of him. It had run right through him and shaken apart something inside — his bones, his atoms — that might never come together again. Even now, in the stifling bedroom, he felt a chill thinking about it. About how the world could kill you and not even blink.

Damn it, that's no joke.

But he knew they couldn't help thinking it was, all the same.

* * *

This morning he felt a little better, finally. He had an appetite for Connie's eggs and biscuits. He scratched behind Cleo's ears when she came to visit. He heard Johnny go out, heard little Tommy laughing with the womenfolk in the kitchen. He actually slept for a while and woke up at 9:51 by his railroad watch. He could feel the warm peace of the morning filtering through the walls, broken only by the barking of Thelma Hoffman's dogs next door. What was eating *them?*

Just another couple of days, he thought — if I lay off for just one trip — I'll be OK, maybe. He gingerly pushed up from the bed, and it didn't seem to hurt quite as much. He tried to look around himself, over his shoulder. The bruise, from what little he could see of it, had become spotty. More blue than purple, with a tinge of yellow around the edges of it. As if he *was* absorbing it, somehow, after all. Swallowing his own blood.

But when he put his feet on the floor and stood up to go to the bathroom, the pain clamped him as hard as ever.

Damn.

A couple more days at least, he thought, no matter what the bastards say.

Then the phone rang, and this time it wasn't Jamison but the division Trainmaster himself.

4.

Why is he so *angry*? Connie Hiller had begun wondering again.

That's what she could never understand. Her father hadn't been like that. A wide, calm man who never raised his voice, never laid a hand on his girls. He had no need to. They had only to sense that he was disappointed with them somehow. Then his voice got sad. That was more than enough. Her father had what Frank jokingly called a "great stone face" — a *graven* face, she thought to herself, as if it belonged on a dollar bill. He had lost most of his hair in a flu epidemic in Oakland in 1925, when her mother had died. Connie had been five then. She had only a vague, warm memory of her mother — a sleeve with lace on it, a caressing hand. A face shadowed by dark hair. But her father had taken care of them. He had remarried and, Connie remembered, never failed to praise her stepmother after every meal, even if the roast had been burned or the vegetables boiled into mush. "That was just lovely, Nellie," he would say. He had worked as a plumber and then as an industrial arts teacher at Tech High, and had never been out of work, even in the

Depression. He had sent both girls to the University of California (and would have sent their half-brother, George, too, if he hadn't caught encephalitis at eighteen). They rode the streetcar to Berkeley and both got their teaching credentials. Her sister, Henrietta, had taken a job at a school in Tupman, in the oil patch outside Bakersfield, and married a Navy man, even taller than Frank, from a big family of roughnecks. Connie had gone to Dunsmuir and married a railroader. Neither man had a college degree. Had the Weldon girls married *beneath* themselves, as some of their relatives hinted? It hadn't seemed that way. Frank and Wylie both were vital, ambitious young men; they blew into the girls' lives like a gale of fresh air. Frank was a reader, too. He had made her laugh, made her feel as safe as her father had…

But why so *angry*?

This thing about the Southern Pacific, now. They shouldn't be badgering him to go back to work — she was as indignant about that as he was — but he took it personally, in a way she couldn't. He *hated* the railroad, when it was just a company, out to make money. What else could you expect of it? When he hung up on the Trainmaster, it frightened her. She had stopped teaching to have a family. If Frank lost *his* job, how could they…?

"What do you think you're *doing?*" she cried.

Then they had the argument.

* * *

Frank didn't go back to rest, though she urged him to. He shuffled into their bedroom but stood beside the bed instead of getting in. He looked out the window, through the thin lace curtain. It bothered Connie — could somebody see him from the street, naked except for his Jockey shorts? She wanted to say something, but didn't. Frank just stood there. The back of his neck and his lower arms were tanned; the rest of him was white, except for the bruise. He held his head at an odd angle. The set of his face, turned away from her, was forbidding — and irritating, too. She waited a minute longer for him to speak — to apologize? — and went out.

It did no good, Connie had decided, to wish for one of Frank's moods to end before he was ready. But ever since his disappointment over the freeway burying their lot, the angry silences had grown longer. Last month she had decided to take them all for a picnic at Soda Creek, south of town, and Frank had almost refused to go. Maybe it would have been better if he had. Because he'd sat out in the car by himself, listening to a ball game on the radio, while the kids looked nervously back at him out of the corners of their eyes and she struggled with lighting the fire, roasting the hot dogs and marshmallows on sticks. All the fun had gone out of it. "Why are you acting like this?" she'd whispered, bringing him a paper plate of food, and he'd muttered something scornful about *togetherness*.

As if it was a stupid word for a stupid fashion — something that, by God, he wouldn't even pretend to follow.

But what was wrong with togetherness, anyway? Weren't they a family?

So fine, Connie thought now. *Just sulk.* Even though the sight of the bruise still made her wince, and she was still frightened. *But call him back, Frank, please, before he gets too upset.*

She decided to vacuum the living-room rug; the noise would drown out even her own thoughts. Tommy, who was four, played with blocks in a corner. Annie — still at the age when housework seemed a game — came behind her with a toy carpet sweeper. Annie wore a cowboy hat and a long-sleeved, red-checked shirt. She had freckles like her mother, and dimples. She made vacuuming noises: "Rum, rum!"

At least fifteen minutes went by. Then Connie turned off the machine, and that's when she heard him moving.

"Where are you going?" she said in alarm.

Frank was dressing himself. He had dragged on a pair of old brown slacks and a sport shirt, doubled over, huffing with pain; she sucked in her breath once again as he pulled the cloth over the bruise and buckled his belt. Then walked slowly into the living room. Against the light from the front window he stood, still bent, with his hands on his knees, glaring at her.

"Daddy, where are you going?" Annie echoed.

She clung to her mother's leg; Connie had to steer her along, gently, as she followed Frank.

"What do *you* care?" he muttered — not to Annie but to her.

"You should be in bed," Connie said. "If you aren't well enough to work, you shouldn't be going out anywhere."

"Ross thinks I should work." Ross was the Trainmaster.

"Call him back. I told you —" But Frank had turned away; he was walking again, toward the door. She could see the muscles moving in his back as if they were lines of pain radiating upward. "I'll call him myself. Please —"

But she was always conscious of Annie beside her, and she couldn't raise her voice.

"You going fishing, Daddy?" Annie asked.

Frank made a noise she couldn't describe — less a laugh than a bark. "Something like that, honey. More like hunting, maybe." He was out on the front porch now, still moving away. The boards creaked under him. "Hunting for another family, maybe. Somebody who gives a good goddamn."

"Frank!"

But even now she couldn't scream, even against the noise of the bulldozers off on the freeway cut to the north, and those dogs next door. She felt exposed out on the porch, where all the neighbors could see. Yelling like some trashy woman — Mrs. Sykes, maybe. Making a spectacle of herself. In front of Annie, too. But she *wanted* to scream. She had always told herself that she would leave any man who hit her — secure in the knowledge that no decent man, like her father or Frank, would ever hit a woman. But this was *like* being hit. Saying such a cruel thing in front of an eight-year-old!

She felt numbness spreading over her face, as if from the blow of a fist. He limped down the steps without looking back — except once, struggling into the cab of the pickup, when he raised his eyes at her, just a second. Still glaring. Then he slammed the door so hard that the truck rocked.

And drove off.

* * *

She couldn't call the Trainmaster — a man she hardly knew. It might make things worse. Unable to think of what else to do, she walked Annie back in to the kitchen and peeled her a banana, sliced it up and let her eat it in a bowl of milk and sugar. "Maybe he *is* going fishing," she said. "Maybe he'll bring us some nice trout."

"Where's his rod, then?" Annie asked. "And his creel?"

She sighed. "Maybe he'll come back for them." The girl was too sharp to fool for long. "Maybe he's just gone down to the crew dispatcher. To see how long till they call him." Connie still felt numb. She braced her hands on the drainboard and closed her eyes and tried to remember her first year in Dunsmuir, 1942, when she was a brand-new teacher at the high school, "batching" with two other young women in Mrs. Polonski's basement on Sacramento Avenue, next door to the house she and Frank would eventually rent. The town was full of excitement then. The war was on. Troop trains came through, and trains with tanks and artillery on flatcars. The Army posted guards at the tunnels to prevent sabotage — this was the main north-south rail route for the whole West Coast. On weekends Connie helped the Red Cross down at the depot, serving coffee and doughnuts to the soldiers. That was how she met Frank. She would never tell him — never in the world! — but first struck her as a homely man. He had a big nose and his ears stuck out; he rolled side to side when he walked, his arms swinging across his body. When he first asked her out, she was cool. That had been enough to discourage the few boys who had approached her in college. *Very* few. But it didn't discourage Frank. Not at all. He kept on asking, and joking with her, and Connie discovered that behind that first line of her defenses there was nothing.

Before she knew it, she'd let him take her to a baseball game. Frank played first base for the Dunsmuir Railroaders. His uniform was white flannel, a blue D over his left breast. He had his own big mitt and spiked shoes made of kangaroo leather. He let her touch them, feel how light that leather was, like the webbing of a bat's wings. He drove her to the ballpark in what would become the first of their Chevrolets, a tan '41 coupe, and never stopped talking — never gave her a chance to get nervous. He bought her a hot dog and an orange soda and led her up into the grandstand, its wooden seats soft and splintery with age. He pointed out the clay bank in left and center field, with the fence at the top of it and trees beyond that. Only one man had ever hit a ball out of the park in dead center, he told her — and that was Babe Ruth himself.

"Babe Ruth!" Connie said, smiling and shaking her head. The soda fizzed in her nose. This had to be another joke. "What could he have been doing here?"

"Barnstorming," Frank said. "He came out here in '24, him and Bob Meusel of the Yankees, and played an exhibition game. I've seen pictures of it. This old park looked just the same."

Somehow this made her laugh — she wasn't sure why. "Such a historic place. I'm honored," she said. Could this be her? Joking back? The grandstand offered shade, but she couldn't see him as well as she wanted through the screen that caught foul balls. Around the third inning she ventured out to the open bleachers behind first base, with the street at her back. She wouldn't remember what Frank did at bat. Maybe he was trying too hard. What she did remember was him standing crouched beside the base, yelling at the hitters on the other side, yelling at his own pitcher: *Hey baby, hey baby, just burn it in there, he's got nothin', got nothin', babe, just a girl up there, hum babe, hum babe!* Connie was amazed at this. She had grown up in a house full of women (except for George, who was so much younger). Her father had little interest in sports. She had never seen a baseball game before — not a game played by grown men with sunburned necks and stubble on their chins. They insulted one another terribly. One man on the other team chewed and spat tobacco. They yelled on the field, and they yelled in the dugout when it was their team's turn to bat. *Old lady up there, old lady, gotta roll the ball up there, he can't throw it, hey baby, got nothin' up there, you can hit him, got nothin' at all.* Connie had feared such loudness and crudeness all her life, but today she found it exhilarating. They were *boys*, she thought. Just boys, and having a wonderful time! She watched the Dunsmuir shortstop, Behnke — "that big dumb Dutchman," Frank had called him — with a gaze that seemed purified by the smell of grass, the cheers of the crowd and the slant of the sun over the western mountain, full in her face. Behnke, Frank had given her to understand, had a scattershot arm; he would throw at Frank's feet or a mile over his head — everywhere but where he was supposed to. This was true, she saw, though Behnke could hit. Twice he sent great cracking drives to thud into the bank in left field, lumbering into second as the outfielder scrambled for them up the steep red clay. And she saw, with the same sudden clarity, that Frank almost *wanted* Behnke to throw wild, just so he could rib him about it afterward. It was a kind of strange love that these men had. It shimmered around her in the Sunday afternoon light and warmed her like the sun, which already had begun to give her face and upper arms a painful blush. The very last enemy batter — for they were *her* enemies now — grounded hard into the hole between third and short, and Behnke lunged, caught the ball and threw off-balance into the dirt, and Frank dug it out neatly and stepped on the bag. It was a perfect ending. And then he *sauntered* — there was no other word for it — with the whole grandstand watching, over to where she sat, as if carrying a bunch of long-stemmed roses, and handed her the ball, scuffed by the dirt, with a round grass stain on it like a kiss.

* * *

It had seemed like an adventure at first, buying this house, Connie thought — in this quaint little town, in this beautiful country. It was a fixer-upper, of course, but *theirs*. And in those postwar years, when they could feel the steady upward surge of the economy under them, it was surely only a matter of time before they could sell at a profit and buy a lot and have a brand-new house built. Ranch style, with everything electric. Meanwhile, Frank sweated and strained on this one. "Look at these," he would say, showing her double joists and old square nails hand-hammered by blacksmiths. "You don't see workmanship like this anymore. They built things *right*." His enthusiasm made her giddy. Despite her fear of heights, she climbed onto the roof during the big snow of '52 to help him shovel while the kids tunneled in the drifts below. They sat around the oil stove in the living room — she loved that room: sixteen feet by twenty-four, the biggest she would ever have — while their boots and mittens dried. They ate cinnamon toast and drank hot chocolate and sang songs. Those were good times, Connie thought now as she vacuumed their bedroom — her first chance in days, with Frank out of it — and made the bed. But what had happened? The freeway thing was only part of it. He had worn himself out on this house. It was — let's face it, she thought — a shack. A dump. Just to make it weathertight had been an awful chore. Frank had to *fight* the house, just as he fought the railroad. And he got angry.

For Connie, finally, it wasn't the house that tried her patience, but the dirt. The back yard, with that bank, was hopeless. Nothing would ever grow there. It was just mud in the winter, dust in the summer. Dirty laundry without end. Not to mention that manure... and though she sympathized with poor Thelma, did anyone *have* to have so many dogs and cats? *Listen to them now, yapping!* That was another subject — the neighbors. There were some fine people among them, like the Ordoñezes. Rough diamonds. For a while it had been fun to get to know them — people she would never have met in Oakland, on a hill of neat stucco homes and tidy lawns. It made her feel broader — and, again, adventurous. But some of her neighbors, even by the most charitable reckoning, were characters. And a few... well, her father had a word for it. Two words: *Tobacco Road*. She had never read the book; she had no wish to read it. But it stood for everything she didn't want the children to grow up in. *Dirt*. Of course, they wouldn't be on Shasta Avenue forever — the freeway would make sure of that. But without any profit, would they be able to move anyplace much better?

No, Connie thought, an adventure was only temporary. It wasn't life. Life should be calmer and more comfortable. She deserved a better place, and so did the children. (Especially Tommy, who had been so terribly sick — infantile diarrhea — when he was three days old, and nearly died. Now he was strong and healthy, but slow. Brain damage, Dr. Reed thought. But how much, or what kind, nobody knew for sure yet.) And she missed having the other teachers — educated people — to talk to every day. Piling a batch of dirty clothes into the washer, trying to think about what to make for lunch — would Frank be back by then? In what kind of mood? Where on earth had he *gone?* — she made a promise to herself that she would carry out:

When the kids get a little older, I'm going back to work.

Once, after she visited the Ordoñezes, Fred had walked her out to the street. "Just want to let you know," he said. "Frank's a good man. He ain't like some I know. You see —" And Fred smiled and waved his hands, as if even to bring the subject up embarrassed him, though he had only good news for her. "— there's railroad men have two wives. One on the road, in Klamath Falls or Ashland. Maybe not *married*, but you know what I mean. They can get away with it for a while, the way the job is. What I mean is —" Fred smiled again and shook his head. "Frank ain't like that. You don't have to worry. He ain't the kind to be steppin' around."

This memory had always warmed her. It made her feel good about Fred — who hadn't *had* to say anything like that — and her husband too; it confirmed her sense of safety. But now, in the shock of Frank's leaving so suddenly, it did the opposite. Men had secret lives, she thought. Some men, anyway.

She shivered.

Did Frank, after all?

No. Of course not.

And his nickname for her: "Mouse." She'd always thought it was cute, and endearing. It meant he didn't care about the weight she'd put on, after three babies.

Frank had always insisted that he liked big girls. But maybe, she thought now, there was a nasty dig to it, too — a reminder that she hadn't kept her figure.

Connie realized that there had been another reason why she'd shrunk from yelling at him from the porch. It was more than just a woman making a fool of herself where everyone could see and hear. It was worse: a *fat* woman yelling.

"I want to go fishing," Annie whined.

The girl had been saying this over and over. She knew something was wrong. Otherwise, why would she have clung to her mother all this time instead of running out to play?

"Maybe your dad will be home soon. I can't have you going down to the river alone."

But Annie just looked miserable.

"If your brother were just a little older…" *Tuna sandwiches,* Connie thought. *That's enough. And Campbell's tomato soup.* She had no appetite herself. In fact, she was exhausted; first the argument and then Frank… it had worn her out.

"Johnny's no good. He throws rocks in the water and scares the fish," Annie said. Then she brightened. "You think Clyde'll take me?"

"Maybe Clyde will. Let's hope."

5.

There's only one chance, Frank Hiller's old man in Sacramento had said. *That's what your grandpa told me, and it's true. Just one chance for the little man to get hold of some land. And that's when the frontier's just passed but things aren't settled yet. Just a handful of years at most. Because after that, the big boys get hold of it all, like they did back East or in Europe or wherever the hell you came from in the first place. Your great-grandpa came out West just in time and picked out a hundred and sixty acres right from under their noses, north of where the American River runs into the Sacramento. Grew corn, mostly. Had a peach orchard. It was good, black bottom land. The best. We'd be landed gentry today if it wasn't for the goddamned SP and its freight rates. Oh, yes. That's what your grandpa told me. They squeezed him and squeezed him, and he finally had to sell out to the Farquhars, who were growin' hops all over that country, stringin' up vines, growin' hops to make beer with. They're doin' it still. Makin' a pile of money, I reckon. Because do you know who the Farquhars were? Pals of C.P. Huntington, that's who, who ran the railroad. They were just scratchin' each other's backs. And in those days, hell, son, the SP ran the Legislature too, and the newspapers. There wasn't anything your grandpa could do, though I know damn well he wanted to. I was twelve then. He wanted to shoot those sonsabitches, and I'd've helped him if he asked.*

Frank, who was fifteen at the time, must have looked skeptical. The railroad, by then, was just a railroad.

You don't believe me, there's a book about it. Man with the same name as you wrote it. Frank Norris. The Octopus. That's what he called the SP, because it had a whole bunch of arms that could rob you at the same time. Put it all down. It was a damn good book. Made up, you know, but true too.

Frank found it in the Grant High School library. It was thick and musty and old-fashioned, slow going in places, but the old man was right. The railroad strangled the wheat farmers of the San Joaquin Valley and foreclosed on some and threw their belongings out into their yards. The farmers tried to fight back, but they were many little forces against a big one; they wavered and split, and they lost. A few got killed. There was a blacklisted railroader, Dyke, who had a chance to shoot the big boss, but his pistol misfired. It *had* to, Frank thought. There was no stopping the SP. Even at the end, when the big boss wandered into the hold of a grain ship and was buried alive, suffocated, by tons and tons of wheat pouring down on him from a chute — what a scene that was! — Frank understood that Norris was just trying to make people feel better. In real life, that never happened. The big bosses died peacefully in their sleep, as rich as ever.

Your grandpa never was the same. He had him a bunch of little strokes, one after another, and wasn't much good after that. Sometimes I think he should've shot somebody. *It wouldn't*

*have turned out any worse for him. And it might have made…
hell, it might have made some of those sonsabitches* listen. *Just
once.*

The old man, Frank knew, had vowed to get the
farm back, but the best he could do was save for years
and make a down payment on inferior acreage in the
Del Paso Heights area — rockier land, too high to
irrigate, good only for pasture. And then the
Depression had wiped that out. Frank remembered
only what was left: the house and a half-acre behind it
where the old man still grew corn and his mother had a
vegetable garden. And kept chickens. The old man had
to work wherever he could and be grateful for it. He
drove a Top Hat potato-chip truck, wearing a white
shirt and a bow tie. His long brown hands — a farmer's
hands — hung out of the shirt; he grew a mustache, as
clownish as the tie, which Frank hated — it seemed to
be a sign of giving up.

*Your grandpa took me out there later to see those hopvines,
see the land we'd had once and watch the Mexicans the
Farquhars had working on it now. And he said: That's what the
sonsabitches want. To turn us all into Mexicans. Stoop labor. He
said: There's a time in every man's life, and it usually comes
sooner rather than later, and never when you're ready for it.
When it comes, nobody's gonna help you. I'm sorry, son, he told
me. That's just the way it is. There's nobody but you to say if
from here on out you'll be standing up or down on your knees.*

Frank hadn't wanted to be a farmer. Just cleaning
chickenshit out of those coops year after year was
enough to sour him. (He didn't even like to eat chicken
— though that didn't stop Connie from serving it.) But

he wasn't cut out for indoor work, either. Not like his older brother, Ralph, who was a sissy, no good at sports, uninterested in girls, who took what money the family had and went to Sacramento State and studied engineering. For a while, after high school, Frank didn't know what to do. He'd outgrown wanting to be Dyke. *My gun won't misfire, by God. I'll plug him right in his fat belly.* It was 1937. All he could find was part-time work in a gas station, cleaning windshields and patching tires. And he realized soon enough that the old man hadn't given up, really. Like his own father, he'd had no choice.

Then Frank's friend and ex-teammate Bud Jones got the cockamamie idea to drive down to Arizona State in Tempe and work out for the coach and talk themselves into baseball scholarships. Bud claimed he'd written to the coach, who'd said, "Sure, boys, come on down." So they piled into Bud's Model A Ford and, with twenty-five dollars to their names, headed into the desert. *My God! You thought the Central Valley was dry?* The Mojave was a whole different world. The Model A steamed on every grade. They scrimped on meals and slept in the car, the metal pinging as the heat left it, and by the time they got to Tempe they were sun-dazzled and dehydrated and in no shape to impress the coach anyway — not that he seemed to remember Bud's letter; not that he had any scholarships to offer. And even if he had, they couldn't afford to stay. They could barely make it back to Sacramento, chasing mirages up the two-lane concrete.

That was why Frank had ended up working for the SP a couple of years later. Like it or not, if you had nothing more than a high school diploma, nobody paid better than what used to be the Octopus.

* * *

Now, suddenly, his time had come.

Frank would never tell anyone exactly what the Trainmaster said to him. Just a few words. Short and brutal. Like he wasn't a human being at all but just a piece of machinery that had slipped out of place and needed to be hammered back.

He couldn't lie down again because those words had stung as bad as the bruise.

Sonsabitches.

And he had to get out of the house, finally, because he couldn't stand still.

Not with Connie running that damn vacuum in the living room, and Annie chattering along with her, as if what the Trainmaster had said didn't matter.

Nobody's gonna help you.

He'd told Connie the story, of course, about what had happened to the old man and *his* old man — told her how he felt he was carrying both of them on his back, trying to make up for their losses; how the freeway thing had made him feel like just another patsy — a sucker in a long line of suckers, outsmarted by the big boys. He'd told her more than once. And she'd smiled and frowned and sympathized, but all he had to do now was step out of the bedroom with his clothes on and look at her face to see that she hadn't really heard. *And what could I expect?* he thought. *None of her people ever had a hard day in their lives.*

Then he felt he was falling.

He knew deep down that he was acting like a kid — he would be ashamed of himself later — but he was furious enough to push out onto the porch, enjoying her flurry of alarm. *Now, damn it, maybe you'll listen. Just once.*

Then gravity seemed to take over. Frank stumbled down the steps as if somebody had shoved him. He hauled himself up, grunting with pain, into the cab of the pickup. He could barely let his hind end touch the seat; leaning over the wheel with his head brushing the roof, he felt dizzy; his legs were at the wrong angles to work the pedals. But he couldn't stop now. *Just this once, by God.* Awkwardly, he kicked the engine into a roar, snapped the brake. Then the street in front of him led downhill, and he drove — never mind where he was going.

At the bottom of the slope, where the street forked, he saw two boys up at the edge of the woods, crouching, as if trying to sneak up on somebody.

Grissom's kids. Okies. *Tough little guys.*

Then he drove up the hill past the Grissoms' house and down the other side. He thought of his own son: how Johnny never met his eye. Tried too hard to please most of the time; then, if you just looked at him wrong, he made himself scarce. *Is it too late already?* Frank wondered, thinking of his brother, Ralph, who had that same washed-out look to his face, who had still never married. *Something's wrong with him,* Frank thought —

41

though what exactly was wrong with Ralph, he would never come close to saying, even to himself.

Connie thought he was too hard on the kid. That was another bone he had to pick with her. Couldn't she see it was for Johnny's own good? *The world could kill you and not even blink.* Who would be there to help *him*, when his time came?

Nobody.

6.

Still, John had a gun.

It was a cap pistol from the local Sprouse-Reitz store. It wasn't as good as the Hopalong Cassidy pistol he'd gotten in Sacramento last summer, but that one had broken. He still had the holster, though. Black leather with thongs and a silver concho. He lay under the trees on the dead leaves and pine needles and acorns, thinking of the Weinstock-Lubin department store, around the corner from the Senator Hotel, where he'd ridden the escalators up and down while his parents were shopping. It had three floors and a mezzanine. The escalators were like stairs, but they moved all by themselves. The steps hummed up through gleaming metal teeth like a belt; then they separated into blocks and carried him smoothly, effortlessly, with a thrill in his stomach, as the rubber railings pulled his hands at exactly the same speed; then the steps flattened out again and threatened to drag him down through another set of metal teeth (he always felt a twinge of fright). He never got tired of it. Up and down. His parents — both had grown up in cities — smiled at him.

"You take care of that gun, now," his father said.

His mother added, "You have to remember, even toys aren't cheap these days."

"It's just like a real gun," his father said. "Or tools. You take care of things, put them back in the right place, and they'll last."

"I will," John said.

But the gun broke anyway. He'd known it would, the moment his father told him.

Just like a real gun…

But it wasn't real. It was just a cap gun, and he was tired of cap guns. When he turned twelve, his father said, he could get a .22 rifle and go hunting — "if you learn to take better care of it than this." But even a .22 wasn't the same as his father's .30-06 deer rifle, or his double-barreled 12-gauge shotgun — those smooth, varnished stocks and red-rubber recoil pads, the scope on the rifle, and the heavy, blued steel of the barrels, smelling faintly of oil and gunpowder.

A blue jay screamed above him.

He wondered if it was the same blue jay he'd shot with his BB gun on the hillside behind his house. Probably not. That one had just stood there, shifting its feet, on the dead, wirelike underbranch of a little fir. He'd zeroed in on it with his lever-action Daisy and pulled the trigger. A burst of feathers. Horrified, he'd started to run forward… and then seen the bird fly away, flashing blue and gray, apparently unhurt. So that he'd hardly had time to feel the horror before it changed into something else.

"Why didn't I kill it?" he'd asked at dinner, still disappointed.

"Well," his father shook his head, "you needed a little more ordnance there, I think. That's a pretty big bird for a BB gun. His breast feathers were too thick."

"His *feathers* stopped it?"

His mother said, "I don't think he should be shooting guns anywhere near the house. *Any* kind of gun."

"When I was his age, I was shooting rabbits out in the fields. Where all North Sacramento is now," his father said. "Didn't do any harm. Got some rabbits, too." And then, that rarest of blessings, he winked at John as if they shared a joke, and said, "Women."

* * *

Now Freddie Ordoñez whispered, "What do we do now?"

"Just lay low for a while."

"They're comin', I think."

"They can't see us here. If they don't move."

Then a second blue jay screamed, in another tree, and the first answered. He thought he could hear the crackle of footsteps. Darn birds might give them away.

"They're comin'," Freddie said.

"Look," John said. "You hold 'em here, OK? Lay low and ambush 'em. Then I'll sneak around behind 'em."

Freddie rolled his brown eyes. He didn't like that either. In the movies, they knew, it was always the sidekick, like Gabby Hayes, who had to hold the horses and cover the hero while the hero sneaked around behind. *In a little while*, John thought, *he'll get too big to do what I say.*

"Cover me," John said.

He couldn't resist saying it. Turning to run up the trail, he looked back for a second at Freddie scrooched around a black oak tree: the way his black hair shone and his back was brown and smooth too, in the sunlight and the shadows of the leaves. He wished he had skin like that. If he did, he thought, he wouldn't have to feel naked, even when he was.

7.

At times like this, Connie Hiller always thought of her father. In the years after her mother's death, he had never failed to come into the girls' room in the evening and listen to them say their prayers. First the Lord's Prayer, then "Now I lay me down to sleep." They had closed their eyes to see him still in their minds, silhouetted against the doorway, a reassuring, solid bulk. He never missed a night, no matter how tired or busy he might have been. It was a comfort to her then, just as the memory of it was now. How well he understood them! (If she could only say the same for her stepmother, who was small and quick and excitable and sharp-tongued.) When they enrolled at Cal, he had taken Henrietta aside, and Connie two years later, and told them, "Whatever happens, keep your chin up. You're as good as anybody else."

Their motto.

They believed him. How could they not?

And she remembered George getting sick. That was in '43, not long after she had married Frank. The fever, the weakness, the poor boy out of his head, almost completely paralyzed... her father and stepmother had needed Connie, because Henrietta was already pregnant and Wylie was shipping out soon with the Navy. So she went back to Oakland for the summer and helped care for George. They turned him over twice a night and rubbed his wasted body — his Adam's apple was so huge; black whiskers were just beginning to sprout on his chin — with mineral oil to prevent bedsores. He was sensitive to light and had to lie behind drawn shades. Meanwhile, Frank got a transfer to the Oakland Pier, loading baggage onto troop trains. That way he could spend two days a week with her, on average, in between trips to Klamath Falls and even Portland. It was hard on them — hard on their brand-new marriage, she thought now; they had no privacy in her parents' house — but what else could they have done? She had always loved George, and never more than in those dark weeks when she sat by his bed and moved his limbs to exercise them and read to him as if he were a child again. They all prayed, in their different ways. Frank liked her father, she knew, but also thought he was... what? Bland, unemotional. But here was a man who had lost his wife and now might lose his son, and what could be finer than the way he kept steadily, gravely on as before? *Chin up.* Some of the modern wonder drugs weren't available then, but thank God they had sulfa. George didn't die. The strength in his body slowly came back — except for his left arm and right leg, which would always be weak. Not like little Jackpot Sykes up the street; George had maybe half their use still. He could walk, shuffling along, his shoulders tilted, and go fishing with Frank on the McCloud River or the Klamath or at Box Canyon here on the Sacramento, if someone helped him over the slippery rocks. To that extent, their prayers had been answered.

Still, George (an accountant now, at a shipping firm in San Francisco) had never been able to marry. *And he was such a handsome boy.*

Connie thought of how good Frank had been with him, how much pleasure it gave George to come north on those fishing trips. And she was able, for a while, to calm herself.

This was just a quarrel, she thought. It would pass.

Nothing remotely as serious as what had happened to George. Nothing every couple didn't go through now and then.

If only he gets back before they call his crew. And apologizes to Mr. Ross.

And doesn't hurt himself any worse.

She smoothed her face, smoothed the front of her shirtwaist and knelt beside Tommy as he played with the blocks. They were educational blocks — a hollow wooden cube with holes in it, and blocks to fit those holes: a square, a triangle, a circle, a half-moon. "How's it going there?" she asked and nuzzled the close-cut top of his head, kissed him behind the ear.

He wiggled and made an impatient sound: "Ee-e-e!"

She bent closer. Sometimes the desire to teach was overwhelming, though she wasn't sure — maybe it was better to let him try on his own. "Do you know where that one goes?" she asked. He was holding the triangle.

Tommy slid it across the top of the cube. He paused it beside the half-moon hole and looked up at her.

"Is that it?"

But something in her voice seemed to tell him it wasn't. He slid it on to the square hole and paused again. Tommy's gray eyes were unusually deep-set; a sudden gleam came from them, and she wondered for an instant if he was teasing her.

"Is *that* it?"

But maybe not, she thought, because he tried to push the block in and it wouldn't go. Then he slammed it down on the floor and glared up at her (just as Frank had glared from beside the truck) as if its failure to fit was her fault.

"Well, that's not the one, you see," Connie said patiently. "This one's got three sides. Where's the hole with three sides?"

"Tree side!" Tommy said.

"That's right. One, two, three. Where's the hole with three sides? Here, try again."

And maybe — *probably* — it was luck, she told herself, but this time Tommy not only slid the block over the triangle hole but had it lined up perfectly, so that it dropped through in a flash and rattled on the bottom of the cube.

Tommy looked up, astonished.

"That's *it!*"

Then he looked unhappy — pushed his lower lip out — as if he had somehow lost the block. As if he would cry any second.

"No, you did it! That's *right!*" It took Connie a while to convince him, tipping the cube over and showing him the orange block, safe. "That's what you're *supposed* to do. You put it in the right hole, and *bingo!* There it went."

It took her a while, but his grin, when it came, was dazzling.

"Oh, you're a sweet, sweet boy," she said. "And a smart one, too." *That other doctor, the nerve specialist, said you'll never learn to read, but what does he know?* And indeed Tommy would grow up to read quite well, though numbers would always be hazy to him.

Connie kissed Tommy again — he still had a little of that clean baby smell the others had lost — but he struggled away, reaching for another block: the circle.

"OK, Mr. Grumpy," she said. "See if I care."

She went into the kitchen and started cutting bread for sandwiches. The washer rumbled. Cleo scratched at the back door. Connie let her in; the dog nosed at her food dish — empty already — and lapped some water, then went on to the edge of the living-room rug, circled and lay down.

Annie was still following her mother — stuck on this going-fishing idea, like a broken record. "Here," Connie told her, handing down a stack of four plates. "Don't drop these. You can help set the table." The girl usually was willing to do this, but now she dawdled and scraped her feet. This nagged at Connie, like her own worries. The house was beginning to heat up. She could feel sweat prickle under her bra straps, at her waist.

How much damage had Frank done, hanging up like that?

And why couldn't Mr. Ross be reasonable?

So that when she heard heavy, male footsteps on the front porch, she was flooded with relief.

"See! There's your daddy now. Just in time to eat."

She hurried to the door, not even thinking why Frank would bother to stop outside and knock, or why she hadn't heard the truck.

8.

It was better alone. John ran through the woods, first uphill, then across, at full speed, the holster slapping against his hip. He could duck the branches that whipped at him, hit a rock with each lunging step of his Keds, so he left no tracks. He knew these woods. All the branching trails — were they Indian trails? He didn't know, but he hoped so. Gary couldn't follow him here. Even the Japs and the Germans, if they ever came to Dunsmuir... they'd be in for a surprise, he thought.

But he didn't run far. Before long he circled back behind a little ridge to where he could see the roof of his own house, below the clay bank. Then he lay down inside what he liked to call the fort — a four-sided hollow of cedar logs that somebody had cut and stacked and left there a long time ago. It was too small to be a real fort, he knew, but it *looked* like one — just as the trails looked as if they might have been Indian trails, before the white man's boots rubbed out the tracks of the moccasins.

Nobody could see him.

But he could see to both sides through the chinks in the logs, and down below, and even what he couldn't see — the bulk of the mountain behind him — he could feel pressing up against his body, like an unmoving wave. It was called Mt. Bradley; the top of it, the fire lookout, was five thousand feet above the town. Halfway up the trees ended; the rest was dark green manzanita — tall as a man sometimes. "Rip the clothes right off you, try to walk through it," his father said. "Much less drag a deer down." Across the canyon was Girard Ridge, not so high, with trees all the way to the top. The air was so clear and the sky so deep a blue — almost purple — that the sky and the trees, blue and green, seemed the same distance away, as flat as a picture; and the trees on the far side were just as sharp and bright a mixture of greens as the trees overhead. A breeze stirred their branches, but on the ground where John lay it was still and warm. The logs had a dry, rotten smell. Ants crawled in the gray twigs by his hand. A squirrel started to run down the trunk of an oak, saw him, and stopped upside down, flicking its tail.

He felt almost sleepy.

The town itself was invisible — so were the river and the railroad — but from time to time he could hear rushing water, or a big truck groaning down the grade from Mount Shasta City, or bulldozers working on the freeway — they sounded like huge animals chomping — or the metallic bang and echo of boxcars coupling in the yards. Nearer, a toy wagon rattled, a kid yelled —

Gary?

No, somebody younger. Some little kid.

He listened for Gary and Jimmy sneaking up the trail. That was the trouble with hiding in the woods.

(He thought of real Japs and Germans again.) At first they didn't know where you were, and that was good, but after a while you didn't know where they were either...

And what about Freddie? He hadn't heard anything.

John held his breath. He could see just his own house, but he knew where everything in the neighborhood was, better than he would know any other place in his life — every crack in the sidewalks, every shortcut across a vacant lot, every picket in the fences he ran past with a willow stick, making a flapping noise like the playing cards they'd fasten with a clothespin to whir against the spokes of their bike wheels. Like the noise a quail's wings made, his father said, flushing from cover... It was all in his head like a map.

Just north of the Grissoms' house, on this side of the street, was a house with a tin roof and pale-blue asphalt shingles where, two summers ago, a new family had moved in. They had a daughter named Julie. Julie Land. She was eight then, the same age as John. She had blond hair and green eyes; he'd never seen a girl so pretty. She played in her front yard, by an apple tree, on top of a high concrete wall, so he had to look up at her. Her hair shone in the sun. She looked like a princess; he wanted to rescue her. (Maybe that was when he'd first had the idea of making a suit of armor.) But what — or whom — should he rescue her from? He tried to talk to her, and at first she'd been friendly, but later she wasn't so friendly anymore, and he (liking her just as much, but not knowing what else to do) had thrown green apples at her. It was almost funny to think about now. But when John was in high school, looking back, it would seem ominous — his first failure with girls in what had become a habit of failure, which he would understand no better than why he'd thrown those apples in the first place. Julie's father had come out into the yard and yelled at him, threatened to call the police. Before school started, even, they'd moved away.

Because of him?

John hoped not, but he couldn't help wondering.

Between that house and his own was Curly McPherson's house, set far back from the street in a grove of gloomy cedar trees. The sun never shone on it. Mr. McPherson didn't have a lawn; he just left the trees and the poison oak bushes underneath, with their telltale clusters of three shiny leaves that turned red in the fall. John wondered sometimes if Mr. McPherson was some kind of monster — a vampire, maybe — or a mad scientist who had a laboratory where, if a kid ever went in there, he'd do experiments on him.

"Don't be silly," his mother told him. "Curly's just a railroad man, like your father."

"But how come he never comes out?"

"He comes out whenever the crew dispatcher calls him, just like your father. At night, or when you're in school. You just haven't noticed."

"But I watched," John said. "He never comes out. And nobody goes in, either."

"He's a bachelor. He doesn't have a family, so there aren't a lot of people going in and out." Then his mother — she was ironing — had smoothed out one of his sister's blouses on the board, set the iron upright with a hiss of steam, and smoothed out her face the way she did when she was serious. "Now, I'm not saying Curly isn't a little *strange*, maybe. Living alone can make you strange. But you kids shouldn't talk about him like that. Children can be very cruel that way, without even knowing."

"Aw, Mom —"

"Well you *can*. And I don't want to hear you talk like that."

"He doesn't have a secret laboratory?"

"You have too much imagination." Then, no longer serious, she rubbed the top of his head with her knuckles so he giggled. "Remember what I said."

On the other side of his house was Thelma Hoffman's house. She lived alone too — a middle-aged lady with a swollen face and swollen ankles who wore only slippers and a bathrobe, even in the daytime. Something had happened to her, his mother said, without telling him exactly what. Her family had been rich; she was the granddaughter of one of the lumber mill owners who had started the town of Weed. But Thelma Hoffman was poor. She sent local news stories to the Sacramento Bee — John had heard her typewriter clacking — but his mother didn't think they paid her much, and he wondered how she found any stories to send, shuffling around in that old house with its gray, peeling paint and its smell. He didn't even want to go in there, the stink was so strong. She had six dogs, the kids figured — little, yappy dogs — and maybe two dozen cats. There was dog poop all over the yard. (That's what his parents called it. The solid stuff was poop and the water was pee. But other kids' parents taught them different words, like crap and taking a leak; that was strange. And then there were other words you weren't supposed to use.) It was all over John's family's yard too, because there wasn't any fence — new, sticky poop and old poop that had gone white and crumbly. Sometimes he shoveled it back into Thelma Hoffman's yard. Because although both yards looked the same — just bare clay, scooped out of the hill with a bulldozer — and his house was gray and peeling too, still, his family was different. Nothing bad had happened to *them*. His father was scraping the siding and planning to paint it a nice dark brown, with white trim; he'd bricked up the walk to the steps, built the porch in back and a retaining wall in front, and someday, he'd said, the place would look halfway decent. *So there ought to be a line*, John thought. *No dog poop on our side.*

His mother felt sorry for Thelma Hoffman — called her "poor Thelma" and sometimes took her a batch of cookies — but she didn't feel sorry for the Sykeses, who lived in the far house, where Shasta Avenue ended. "Because they don't try," she'd told John. "It doesn't matter if you're rich or poor, so long as you try." Mr. Sykes had been in the Army and brought back a war bride from Italy. "Ten years in this country and never learned to speak English," his mother said. Mrs. Sykes didn't often come out; she was fat and looked sleepy, or dazed; her face was dirty and so were the kids'; they had snot in their noses and rotten teeth. "I can understand being short of money, if he's out of work sometimes — though I don't know how hard he tries to *find* work - but there's no excuse for neglecting your children's teeth," his mother said. The oldest boy — there were two boys and a girl — had had polio; his left arm just hung from the shoulder, no bigger around than a broomstick. Yet the Sykeses were lucky, too; that same boy — called Jackpot, long for Jack — had been the first baby born in Siskiyou County that year. The family had received a pile of gifts, his mother said. "So maybe God looks out for those who *don't* help themselves. I don't know."

On the other side of the street, turning back south, was Dr. Malevich's house, also his office: a sooty concrete building with little, high windows of frosted glass that you couldn't see through. "Like a Nazi pillbox," Gary said. Dr. Malevich's name sounded creepy, and he wasn't a real doctor, like Dr. Reed downtown. "He's a chiropractor," John's mother said. "People who don't know any better, he does something to their spine — massages them, I guess — and they feel better. For a while." From her voice he knew she didn't approve of Dr. Malevich either, and the way his house looked, it was easy to imagine *he* might have a laboratory inside where he did terrible things. But Annie had gone inside once and nothing had happened. That was after she'd gotten into a rock fight with Hughie Williams and smashed one of the headlights on Dr. Malevich's car. Annie had a good arm, John had to admit. Good as a boy's.

Their father had whipped her then, with a willow switch, so red welts stood out on her legs. "This isn't for the headlight," he told her, and then to John: "Listen up. It's because it could've been Hughie's *eye* instead. You could've blinded him. His folks could've sued us for every cent we've got."

"He started it," Annie said. She sounded choked, but she wasn't even crying much.

"I don't care *who* started it. No more rock fights."

Then he sent her across the street with a five-dollar bill. "Tell him if that's not enough, let me know." John watched her go, walking with her legs apart — they must have been stinging still — looking very small, with her auburn hair in a ponytail, holding the money very carefully in her outstretched hand; and at heart he'd wondered if he could be that brave. But Dr. Malevich hadn't done anything to her. He hadn't even taken the money.

Lucky.

Hughie and his little brother, Walt, lived opposite the Hillers, but their house faced the other way, toward Florence Avenue, which also was Highway 99. Their back yard was as big as other people's lots. It had a clubhouse at the north end, in a cedar and willow grove, a wild blackberry patch in the middle, and then more woods, with a treehouse nailed between a couple of oaks. It was where most of the kids in the neighborhood played. Hughie had a sandbox next to the house; they filled it with water from a hose and floated toy boats in it — though sometimes Hughie's grandmother came out and told them to turn off the water; they were getting all muddy.

"Where's his mom and dad?" John asked once.

"Well, that's a long story," his mother said. "I don't know how much you can understand. But they got divorced. They don't live together anymore. And Hughie's grandmother... well, they had a big fight. She didn't like Hughie's mother, and she and Judge Williams wanted to take the children themselves. And they won."

"Why didn't she like Hughie's mom?"

"She wasn't... a lady," John's mother said. "I've probably said too much already. Don't talk to Hughie about it. It'd just make him feel bad."

South of the Williamses' back yard was the Knudsons' house, which was John's favorite in the whole neighborhood. Like most of the houses, it was old and needed paint, but it was three stories high and orange, with fancy carving — "a Victorian," his mother said, with a tower at one corner. The round tower room had a roof like a witch's hat and curved windows that fit the walls. John wanted more than anything else to live in that room and look out those windows at the street below... but the people who lived there were the Lorenzos, who rented the top floor from Mrs. Knudson. The father was a little, dried-up old Filipino man who cooked in a Chinese restaurant down by the tracks. The mother was a white woman, big and fat, a head taller than her husband. The kids — a boy and a girl — didn't look like either of them. They had blue-black hair and pearly skin and dark eyes with long lashes. The boy, Paul, knew a lot of dirty stuff, even though he was younger than John. He was the one who had taught him the other words — the ones you weren't supposed to say.

"It isn't poop and pee," Paul said scornfully, so that John felt, for the first time, embarrassed for his parents. "It's shit and piss, man, that's what it *really* is."

Mrs. Knudson was a widow. She lived with a much older brother, Clyde Carter, who sometimes took John and Annie fishing. Her son, Ronnie, had stayed with them last summer after he got out of the Marines. The Marines, he told all the kids — sitting on the front lawn in his khaki pants, drinking a can of beer, stubble growing on his thin yellow face — were a hell of a lot tougher than the Army. "We do all the fightin'," he said, "and they just come along afterwards and take the credit." Thinking of Mr. Sykes, John thought maybe that was true. His mother said Ronnie was still trying to "find himself" after being in the war in Korea. She sounded as if something was wrong with him. But Ronnie was OK. He made Gary, at least, want to join the Marines right away. He sold John's parents his old bike for John to ride — fifteen years old, covered with dust, but heavy and strong, with big balloon tires. And one day he'd told the kids he'd show them how the Marines tied up prisoners so they wouldn't escape.

"But first you try to tie *me* up," he said. "I'll get a rope."

He brought a clothesline. They wound it around and around Ronnie's long, lean body until he looked like a mummy. John wondered if he'd be embarrassed if he couldn't get loose — a Marine tied up by a bunch of kids. But Ronnie just grinned. Then he sort of shrugged his shoulders and the coils slid off him, like the coils of a Slinky walking down stairs.

"Now it's your turn," he said. "Any volunteers?"

John volunteered. Now he was the one who was embarrassed — Ronnie had gotten loose so easily. He vowed he'd get loose too. Maybe it *was* easy. He hoped so. But it turned out he didn't have a chance. Ronnie tied his hands behind his back, so tightly the rope hurt, and then tied his feet to his hands, so all John could do was wiggle on his stomach or flop on his side, like a trout somebody'd landed, while Ronnie stuck his face in close, smelling of beer and cigarettes and sweat, and grinned.

"Lesson number one," Ronnie said. "Never volunteer for anything."

John hadn't liked that much, but still, Ronnie was OK. He'd gone away and gotten married. Maybe that was what his mother meant about "finding himself" — it meant finding somebody else.

Next, finally, was Freddie Ordoñez's house, across from the Grissoms'. The hillside was steep there — so steep that the street split in a Y, cars going south ten feet above cars going north, with a bank and trees in between. Freddie's yard was below the street, and a bridge ran from the sidewalk to the second floor, which was really the main floor. Mrs. Ordoñez, a quiet, pale woman, usually would be inside, making soup. Her kitchen shone. The smell of onions blended with the smell of ammonia; John didn't know which was to blame for her red-rimmed eyes, the downward turn of her mouth and the way she would sometimes pause in mid-sentence and sniff, her nose pinched, as if the smell had stung her nostrils and made her forget what she wanted to say. Mrs. Ordoñez even talked through her nose. That was because she was French, his mother said. French people talked through their noses. "But don't you make fun of her. At least she *speaks* English," his mother said, comparing her with Mrs. Sykes. In fact, his mother seemed to have a special liking and respect for Mrs. Ordoñez, and not just because of her housekeeping.

One day she'd told him why.

"In the war," she said, "in France, she was in the Resistance. Those were just people, ordinary people like us, who wanted to keep on fighting the Nazis after their army surrendered. I don't know what Marie did — whether she sent messages or helped Allied airmen who'd been shot down, or what — but she was caught by the Gestapo. Those were the German police — but not like our policemen here; they were terrible people, they had concentration camps…" His mother sighed. "They tortured her."

"How?" John asked. He wanted to know, but then again he didn't.

"She didn't tell me everything. But she said" — and here his mother's voice was more than serious; it had a thrill to it, a catch in her throat, as if she wanted to make sure he never forgot this — "she said they put her in a bath so hot she fainted. And then, when she came to, they put her in a bath so *cold* she fainted. Back and forth, over and over."

"Oh," John said, a little disappointed.

"Think of it," she insisted. "How hot it would have to be to make you faint."

He thought of how hot bathwater could be — so hot he couldn't stand it. And that Nazi water must have been even hotter. He felt ashamed; his mother must have seen the disappointment on his face. And then, too, she might not be telling *him* everything — even as much as Mrs. Ordoñez had told her.

Because he remembered when she'd read him a Reader's Digest article about a Boy Scout who was arrested by the Nazis, somewhere in Europe. He'd carried messages on his bicycle. Maybe he was in the Resistance too. She'd read it with that same thrill in her voice, the same shining tension in her freckled face, as if she were reading "Evangeline" or "A Christmas Carol"; as if John ought to learn what being a Boy Scout meant, now that he was about to become one. His mother was nice, he knew — she wouldn't hurt anyone — but her ideas about what a boy should grow up to be were beautiful and fierce. *"They beat him,"* she read, and then stopped to explain: "And they aren't talking about when your dad spanks you. They mean *really* beat. With whips or clubs, maybe. *But the Scout was dumb."*

"Dumb?"

"He didn't tell them who'd given him the messages. He kept his oath."

"What happened to him?" John asked.

"They shot him. But he didn't tell."

So he figured they'd probably beaten Mrs. Ordoñez too, no matter what his mother said.

"Does she have any scars?" he asked.

"Outside, I don't know. She wouldn't show any-one, I'm sure... But inside is a different thing." His mother sighed again. "Fred told me —" That was Mr. Ordoñez: a short, stocky Mexican man, almost as dark as a Negro, who worked on the railroad too. With Mrs. Ordoñez so pale, that's why Freddie's skin was that nice medium brown. "— he was in the Army Medical Corps when we liberated Paris. That's how they met. He said she weighed less than eighty pounds when we rescued her. Just skin and bone.

"So that's why," his mother concluded, "you shouldn't ever make fun of her."

John promised he wouldn't. The next time he saw Mrs. Ordoñez, crossing the bridge to her house with a bag of groceries, he looked at her carefully. He saw no scars, but maybe they were under her loose, flowered dress. He offered to carry the bag.

"No, no, I don't need...," she said, surprised.

"Can I open the door for you?"

He followed Mrs. Ordoñez into the kitchen. She set the bag down on the table and turned to see him gazing up at her like a dog, with all the sympathy he could muster. He could feel it rise from his chest and pour out of his eyes, like some kind of science-fiction ray.

"What?" she said. "You want something to eat? A cookie, maybe?"

"No, ma'am. I just —" He wanted to tell her he was sorry about what the Nazis had done. But at the last moment he thought: *Maybe she doesn't want to be reminded of that stuff.*

"Why you look at me like that, with your mouth open?" She started to smile, but then — as if that ammonia smell had suddenly pinched her nose — her face turned suspicious. He could tell she thought he was one of those kids who *would* make fun of her. A smart aleck. "Eh? I do something to you? I sound funny, maybe? You think —"

"No, ma'am," he said desperately.

"You Mrs. Hiller's boy, no? She a nice lady. She no want you to make her ashamed. Go, go," she said, taking him firmly by the shoulders and shoving him out the door. "Go help your *maman*. Not me. You leave me alone."

* * *

Now, lying inside the fort, John wondered what it would feel like to be tortured. Suppose he'd been carrying messages on Ronnie Knudson's bike and the Gestapo arrested him, dragged him down into one of their dungeons.

He listened: still nothing.

Keeping his head below the top log, he peeled off his shirt. He rolled it up and stuck it under his belt.

Then he lay down again, so that the twigs and pine needles poked his back. With satisfaction, he thought of the ants crawling under him too. Already, the sun seemed to be burning the thin, milky skin over his ribs; the shadows of the branches overhead marked his chest, as thin as whip-slashes...

He shivered.

Then, out of the corner of his eye, through a crack in the logs, he saw something move far below. John turned. It was his father, clumping stiffly down the front steps, wearing regular clothes instead of overalls. Where was he going? *Not to work.*

His father stopped, opened the door of the maroon truck and looked angrily back up — toward the porch, which John couldn't see. Then he got in, slammed the door and, after a second pause, drove off.

John remembered the argument then, and felt several things at once.

He was relieved, as always, that his father was going — he felt muscles relax in his shoulders, in his jaw, that he hadn't even known were clenched — but he was puzzled, too, by the slacks and the seldom-worn Hawaiian shirt, a tan-and-green pattern of palm branches. And it hurt to see his father struggle like that, just to climb up into the truck. As if he was crippled — for good?

He thought again of how Mr. Grissom had tossed the toolbox.

How can Dad beat him like that?

9.

It wasn't Frank. It was Clyde Carter.

His wire-rimmed spectacles gleamed in the shadow of the porch. He carried a bamboo fishing rod and a wicker creel; he wore a khaki canvas vest with pockets in it, full of jars of salmon eggs and split shot and other items Connie could only guess at. A dozen trout flies hung from his shapeless canvas hat, and he'd folded a pair of rubber waders over his shoulder. Clyde was old — almost seventy — with skin all flaked and spotted and stained by the weather. He didn't smile — he rarely did. But he was just the man Annie wanted to see.

"On my way down to the bridge," Clyde said, "and I thought I'd see if any of these youngsters…"

"Fishing!" the girl shrieked, and ran to get her child-sized rod.

"Johnny's out somewhere," Connie said. "I don't know…"

"Never mind *him,*" Annie said. "Let's go!"

"But don't you think you should —"

"Let's *go!*"

"Hold your horses, young lady. You haven't had your lunch yet." To Clyde she said: "Would you like to come in? Can I get you something?"

Clyde waved the suggestion off.

"You sure? Even a glass of water?"

"Plenty of water down there," Clyde said.

"Well, I suppose that's true. Just wait a minute," she said to Annie, "while I make you a sandwich, at least." Connie returned to the kitchen and put the fourth plate back into the cupboard. She cut the bread, spread on tuna and celery and tomato and mayonnaise, wrapped it in waxed paper and brought it out. All the while, Tommy watched them. He had let his blocks spill and followed Cleo when she got up lazily to greet Clyde. "But how are you going to carry it?"

"Plenty of pockets," Clyde said, patting his vest. He smiled then, a little.

"Well, that's true too. You be careful," she told Annie.

"I'll take good care of her."

"I know you will."

"I'll bring her back by… say, two at the latest."

The girl was dancing with impatience, but Clyde waited a moment longer; Connie could see curiosity in him — his eyes slid toward the bedroom.

"How's Frank?" he asked.

"Oh, he's doing better," she said. "He's starting to move around now."

"Good. Glad to hear it."

Chin up.

10.

She was a peach, Frank Hiller had thought.

Just hanging there, full of juice, waiting for somebody to pick her off the branch, like one of the big freestones that grew on the tree in his back yard in Del Paso Heights. (Grafted from the original stock in his grandpa's orchard, they said — though you didn't see freestones so much anymore; the canners preferred clings.) A peach. Just hanging there, with the blush and fuzz on her, coppery hair and a prim expression that couldn't fool anybody who bothered to look. He'd come off the South End Pool from Red Bluff — a passenger run, for a change, so he'd worn the blue uniform and the silver-lettered brakeman's cap instead of overalls — and there she was, at the Red Cross table with the coffee urn and boxes of doughnuts, and a line of soldiers in front of her. Frank didn't mind the soldiers. They'd be gone tomorrow; he wouldn't. And neither would she — this Miss Constance Weldon. A peach. Almost *too* ripe from hanging there so long; almost ready to drop off the branch without anybody reaching for her. Built like a brick shithouse (Frank would never tell her that, of course) and unaware of it.

Well, maybe a little. She knew just enough to keep her curves covered up. But she had no notion, he was sure, of what those curves were *for* — which made her irresistible. A peach. The kind of girl you were *happy* to take home to Mama. A nice girl — a thoroughly nice girl — with a college degree, no less. Frank marveled at his luck. How come nobody else had picked her off? Guys must have been blind. Either that, he would come to think, or she had gotten them, somehow, to share her own blindness. So that those curves, if she didn't see them herself, didn't exist.

But she didn't fool him.

Hot damn.

Still, Frank thought now, after a dozen years, he'd been perfectly capable of fooling himself. Oh, yes. Maybe those other guys had seen something he hadn't — though if they hadn't married Connie Weldon, how could they know? It took a while to sink in. He'd thought Connie was shy, and she was, in a way. She had trouble disciplining the high school kids she taught. (As far as he was concerned, by taking her out of the classroom he'd done her a favor.) She didn't like to raise her voice, and even when she did, she didn't sound as if she meant it. Those teen-agers could tell. But what Frank hadn't seen at first was her stubbornness, her quiet insistence — bred into her, he thought, in that mission-style stucco house in Oakland, where only her stepmother raised *her* voice and the light always seemed dim and churchlike and there was hardly a speck of dust anywhere — that she knew what was right, what was proper, what was in good taste. Or maybe she got it from Cal, along with her diploma. As if that framed piece of paper with the fancy print on it meant she was smarter than he was, or knew more — not just that her family had more money.

Anyway, Connie *judged* things. And people. Every moment of every day, it seemed, she was passing judgment on somebody — on Dr. Malevich for being a quack and Ed Sykes for being a lazy bum (which he was); on Dunsmuir for being a backwater (which was true too, but still); and most of all on Frank himself, for his bad temper and dirty habits, for muddling through all the work he did on the house, for not being a crackerjack plumber like her father or an electronics whiz like her brother-in-law, Wylie Stone. She'd set out to improve him, and she never let up. Not that she'd order him to do this and forbid him to do that. Not Connie. That wasn't her way. She'd just look pained and long-suffering and tolerant. She *tolerated* it if Frank smoked or took a drink once in a while, but she wished he'd quit. Oh, yes. She *tolerated* it if he went hunting with Bob Chapman, but she thought by now he should have outgrown the need to camp out with other boys and come back unshaven and smelling of smoke, with something bloody and disgusting in the truck — something she'd have to cook, even if nobody particularly wanted to eat it.

And it wasn't the blood either, as you might expect. It wasn't the killing. That didn't bother her. Connie would help pluck the ducks and geese and even — a trick she'd learned from Bob's wife — melt paraffin in a saucepan and dip the birds in it and store them in the freezer. That way they kept for months. And when she wanted to roast one, she'd just peel off the wax and the pinfeathers with it. Neat. She would cook venison, though chewing that leathery stuff made your jaws ache. No, with Connie it wasn't the hunting. It was Frank's going away to do it — as if all those hours he spent on the trains and in Klamath Falls or Ashland weren't enough. "Do you *have* to?" she would ask, not expecting him to answer — for how *could* he answer? He was in the wrong. Somehow, with Connie, he was always in the wrong. *Togetherness* she wanted. That was fine. That was dandy. It was just... *No, I don't have to*, he thought, *but by God, I want to*. And why? *Because without it... without a little fun... it would be like eating potatoes every day, nothing but potatoes, like some of my mother's people had to do back in Ireland in the old days. Surviving. But not living.*

"Don't you enjoy being with us?" she would ask. "After all —"

"Sure I do," Frank would tell her.

But the truth was, he thought, there was a *deal*. A deal they'd made when they got married. And Connie had reneged on it.

He thought about it in cabooses and in hotels at the other end of the line. He thought about it walking the trains at night, under the stars. He thought about it when business was slow and his crew wasn't called for days at a time and he sawed and hammered on the house to distract himself from the lack of money coming in. He thought about it when business was crazy and he hardly had eight hours to sleep, any time of night or day, before they called him again. (The kids *had* to be quiet then.) He thought about it when he'd "died on his sixteen hours," as they called it — union rules said you couldn't work any longer at a stretch than that. So a crew that had "died" waited in place to be relieved and rode back to town on a passenger train, often too tired to sleep, their minds clicking away as relentlessly as the wheels underneath. Most of all, he'd thought about it in '44 and '45 when he was trying to enlist and get off the railroad and into the war like Wylie, who had been in some of the naval fighting at Leyte Gulf. He thought about the deal — the promises he and Connie had made to each other. Unspoken but no less binding than the vows they'd stood up and made in church.

I'll take care of the outside of the house. You take care of the inside. I'll fix the cars. You'll take the kids to the doctor. I'll work at a hard and dangerous job; that's OK. I'll bust my back, because this is a war too — the war every family fights on its own to survive, and to do a little better than survive.

Look at Tommy, Frank thought. All Connie saw was the cute little guy he was now. But what would happen ten years from now when Tommy put his hands on some girl because he didn't know any better? People in Dunsmuir would lynch him, crucify him. A small town like this had no mercy. They only hope was to put the fear of God into the boy, so that he never, never touched a girl. If that hurt him, so be it. It would save him from getting hurt much worse.

But if I bust my back, by God, you ought to…

There had been a time, not just after the wedding but a little later, before they went down to Oakland to take care of George, before Johnny came along and then Annie, before Connie put on weight and never lost it. A time when her clothes came off and she no longer felt ashamed or awkward, when those curves were bared for Frank to see — when she kissed him back, kissed him hard, and seemed to mean it. All those *noises*. The *smell* of her. Three times a day they made love, if they could. Connie would get up in the middle of the night — whenever he came home from a trip — and fix him something to eat. All the barriers between a man and a woman were down. Things between them were... he shied away from the words, because it wasn't *about* words. Tender, trusting. Why couldn't it have stayed that way? What put the barriers back up? Frank thought of his mother, disappointed over the loss of the farm in Del Paso Heights, not blaming the old man out loud but blaming him anyway, for sure; he thought of the old man's baffled face, of those long brown wrists hanging out of the white shirt. Had the same thing happened to *him*? Frank couldn't ever ask. And he couldn't blame Connie, really, and not be in the wrong again. It took a lot out of a woman, having a baby. Oh, yes. He'd seen it. Once she had the kids, she couldn't get up at ungodly hours to cook for him anymore. He understood that. And it was natural for her to put on a few pounds. *Hell, we all get old.* But it wasn't the weight, really, though she might not believe him. She was still a pretty woman. It was just that...

He still wanted it. What they'd had.

That was the deal.

Not *togetherness*, damn it, but the real thing.

And it was the one thing you couldn't ask for, Frank knew. You couldn't beg. You couldn't say a single goddamned word.

All you could do was wait. Wait for Connie to change her mind, to feel a little of the old itch herself — though that had hardly happened at all in the last few years. Wait for her to remember: *That's what it's all for. All of this…*

He hadn't fooled around, by God.

And if he lost his temper now and then, hell, he'd been tired. Exhausted. *You have no idea how often I've just stood there and gritted my teeth and taken it. I haven't yelled at you. I haven't slapped you around, and there's more men do that to their wives than you can believe. I could name you names, right in this town.*

When I stop talking and walk away, Frank thought, *that's the absolute, level best I can do right then. Don't you realize that?*

I'm trying to tell you something. Is it so hard to figure out?

I want you to act different. Be different, like you used to be. Stop all this complaining about stuff that isn't important. Then everything will be fine.

But that was the problem, Frank thought. *You have no idea.* Connie insisted on comparing him with her father, a man so calm he hardly had a pulse.

And as time had gone by and Frank looked around him, he'd seen that other men were in the same fix. Maybe not Fred Ordoñez; Fred always seemed happy, though Marie had a sour look to her. She had a right to it, poor woman, after what she'd gone through. Maybe she *couldn't* smile anymore, even if she wanted to. Fred didn't seem to mind. But Frank couldn't name more than two or three other men he knew who looked as if they still had what they'd gotten married for — and once you saw that, he thought, it made more sense why they acted as mean or stupid as they did sometimes. Why they got drunk or picked fights or made life miserable for the younger guys. It was something nobody talked about but everybody knew: a grim joke. Old Frank Norris knew it. He kept writing about how *forces*, not wishful thinking or morality, moved people. Blind forces, like Nature's need to get more babies born. You got married thinking it was one thing when it was really something else, simple and brutal, that had nothing to do with you. An old guy like Will Jamison — you couldn't go to him and complain about how things were at home, except in the most general way. *Hell fire, son*, he would say. *What do you think this is?*

A joke.

Like getting hit in the ass.

11.

Years from now, Connie Hiller would read newspaper stories about child molesters and murderers and feel uneasy about having let Annie go fishing alone with Clyde. What could she have been thinking of? How well did she know Clyde Carter, really? It appalled her. The things that could happen to little girls... *It was a simpler time*, she would tell herself. *More innocent. People didn't think about such things.* But was that true? People might not have *talked* about them so much, but weren't there just as many evildoers around in those days? Probably, she thought. Yet Clyde, as far as she knew, had never done anything bad. Annie had had a wonderful time. If Connie had been more suspicious — a better mother, maybe — she would have deprived her daughter of that, and Clyde too: the pleasure that young and old could have together.

What was the answer? She didn't know.

Today she was relieved to see Annie and Clyde go off together — the girl had been pestering her so. But once she was alone in the house with Tommy and the dog, the silence seemed to close in on her. She almost wished she had one of those television sets that her brother-in-law, Wylie, sold and repaired in Richmond. An "idiot box," Henrietta called it. But it would be something to listen to, at least. The nearest stations were in Redding and in Medford, Oregon, more than fifty miles away, and the mountains around Dunsmuir blocked all reception. She would have to wait a few more years for cable to be laid. Meanwhile, there was only one radio station: KWSD. Weather reports and polkas and sermons — each one beginning *The cosmic hour has struck, loved ones!* — by the widow of the founder of a religious sect that had bought the old Shasta Springs resort north of town and believed that little people, Lemurians, lived inside Mt. Shasta.

"Come on," she told Tommy and went out onto the porch in hope of a breeze. It was getting hotter.

She sat in the shade in a folding chair while he ran down the steps. "Don't go into the street!" she called. Tommy had been slow to walk — as with everything else — but now he was a regular monkey. He had a yellow toy bulldozer with a blade that moved up and down. He moved dirt with it, as he'd seen the real bulldozers doing. He pressed the back of his left hand to his mouth and trembled. He made noises — and not just bulldozer noises, either. If she listened carefully, she could hear him invent companions, voices that noted his hard work and cheered him: "Yay, Tommy!" His hand had an ugly callus already. It embarrassed her when other people saw it — saw him lost in his little made-up world — and then she felt ashamed of being ashamed. Wasn't this play-acting a sign of something?

Don't tell me there isn't a mind in there, he'd think. Some parts of him had to be undamaged. But which?

Cleo followed him. She sniffed the dirt he'd plowed up, sniffed at him, licked him behind the ear. Tommy giggled.

Such a good dog. *She seems to know*, Connie thought. *She knows he's a baby, he's special, she has to be extra patient.*

Just after Tommy was born, and before he got sick: this was Connie's secret. Her memories of her father she shared with Henrietta and George. This was hers alone. Tommy was her biggest baby — nine pounds, six ounces — and had caused her the most pain. The first baby she'd had not in Oakland but in the little hospital in Mount Shasta, with Dr. Reed attending. It had been early September. Just as hot. A forest fire was burning to the north, near Black Butte, and smoke blew into town. Ever since, when she smelled a forest fire, she remembered what it was like to lie in the recovery room, so exhausted that she seemed to float on the bed, to drift with the acrid smoke. She floated, she felt, into a starry night sky, to the farthest end of the universe. She could see everything, and she understood that everything was all right. She sighed and relaxed (in the body she'd left behind) all the way down to her bones. *Why do people worry so much? Why do we struggle? It's all so simple.* Connie remembered thinking those words. They were what God meant to her now — not the church service every Sunday, though she went.

It was strange, Connie thought. To have had such a feeling just once ought to last a lifetime. She shouldn't ever worry again. But she did.

Where *was* Frank? He'd never done anything like this before.

Hunting for another family, maybe.

She could still see him hobbling down the steps, hear the slam of the truck's door, feel the outraged numbness spreading over her face.

The dogs next door barked; Cleo pricked up her ears. Kids shouted somewhere down the street. Johnny?

And she found she couldn't sit still anymore. "Come on," she told Tommy. "Let's heat up the soup. Do you want a banana, like your sister?"

"Banana!"

"You want one?"

"Yes," Tommy said.

"What's the magic word? Yes, *please.*"

Before fixing lunch, Connie called the crew dispatcher. No, the switchboard girl said, Frank wasn't there, and he hadn't stopped by. His crew was fourth out. Maybe they'd be called as soon as dinner time. But you never knew for sure.

12.

Driving downtown, Frank felt as if he was kicking free of Connie and lunging at the Trainmaster all at once.

He imagined their faces recoiling as he smashed them. It felt sick — a shame and regret deep in his gut — but it felt good, too: this letting loose at last.

Falling.

The pickup bucked as he tried to work the pedals standing. His head bumped against the roof; the backs of his legs ached. But when he sat down for just a second — just brushed the upholstery — the pain of the bruise jerked him back upright. Sweat ran into his eyes. He was on Florence Avenue now, Highway 99, heading south, and the town *looked* different as he squinted and blinked at it — the way once, when he'd been hit in the head playing football at Grant High, the whole world turned a bright pale aqua color and he heard... not birds tweeting, like people said, but a kind of tinny music. Dunsmuir looked like a place he'd never seen. No, that wasn't it, Frank thought. Like a place he'd never see again, not the way he used to.

Because what he was doing now would change it forever.

And change *him*.

For maybe the last time, he drove past the elementary school and the Texaco and Union gas stations. It was a small town. *Damn* small. Already he was plunging down the hill into its center — between Dr. Reed's office and the Owls Club and Littrell's auto parts and Mannee's pharmacy on one side and the California Theater, the Masonic Temple and the Sprouse-Reitz on the other. He groped for the clutch, the brake. The truck jerked again. Nothing he saw looked real. All that mattered was this sick, terrible pressure inside him and the momentum of his fall. He screeched to a stop at the corner as one of Connie's teacher friends — he knew the woman's name, but he couldn't remember it now to save his life — crossed in front of him. She waved. Frank waved back. Why not? Her dress had pink flowers on it. Shiny grease spotted the asphalt where her feet stepped. None of it was real. He turned left on Pine Street by the Bank of America and plunged again. Down, down, the lumber and bricks in the bed of the truck rattling. Out of the corner of his eye he saw his neighbor Ignacio Lorenzo climbing the sidewalk to the bank. Little, skinny, coffee-colored old Ignacio, grabbing a break before the lunch crowd showed up at Motto's, where he cooked Chinese. And even at this moment, Frank thought the same thing he always thought when he saw Ignacio: *Better not let that woman of yours ever get on top, pal. Because there won't be anything left of you but a grease spot.*

Just a block to the bottom: then the street ended. Frank crossed Sacramento Avenue. He tried to park against the retaining wall and iron-pipe railing of the lawn between the crew dispatcher's office and the depot. There were benches, a clock on a tall pole, a fountain where speckled trout swam. But by now the sweat in his eyes was stinging him half blind. He braked too late. The front wheels hit the curb; Frank's nose hit the rear-view mirror. He yelled. Then the truck rocked back and he fell against the seat, tasting salty blood, and yelled a second time — like an echo — at the pain in his rear end. He lurched back up, yanking the handbrake. The engine shuddered and stalled. He picked up a rag from the floor and tried to wipe his eyes, but this only seemed to drive the sweat in deeper. He was crying.

Frank got out.

All this time, he realized, he'd been yelling at Ross in his head:

Didn't your mama teach you right? Huh? Didn't she tell you not to be an asshole?

Who the hell do you think you are? God?

You think you can do anything you want to people and you'll always get away with it? Huh? You don't think anybody'll ever fight back?

Well, this time...

But now he was dabbing at his eyes *and* his nose, dribbling blood over the stupid Hawaiian shirt he'd pulled out of the closet at random, trying to suck blood back into his nostrils while he flooded the stinging out of his eyelids with tears. Neither worked. To get to the Trainmaster's office he had to go down around the front of the depot and up a flight of stairs. But he couldn't *see*. He had to close one eye at a time while he squinted out of the other for a second or two, then switch eyes. Everything was wavery splinters of light: the turntable where one of the new diesels, painted red and orange — a passenger engine for the Shasta Daylight — was swinging slowly to line up with its stall in the roundhouse, like a bullet in a revolver clicking into place to be fired; the footbridge over the tracks to the engine shops; the two-story depot, yellow with brown trim; a couple of men in overalls lounging by the crew dispatcher who had looked up as the truck slammed the curb and now gawked at Frank as he stood there with blood and tears running down his face. He dabbed again with the rag — but the rag was filthy.

Was that Jamison?

Nothing had gone as Frank had hoped. No way he could burst into Ross' office now and face that icy little man behind the desk when he looked like an idiot who'd been in a bar fight. Because even if he could haul himself up those stairs — and the bruise was hurting like hell — wouldn't Ross just turn it against him?

You made it this far, Hiller, haven't you? And you want me to believe you're in such bad shape? Well, I'll tell you something. What you don't want is for me to run out of patience.

Ross wouldn't blink, either. Even though he was five-seven, tops, and pushing sixty.

The Trainmaster scared Frank a little. That was the truth.

But Frank didn't let himself realize that yet. He just thought of how ridiculous he looked. *All this blood. Jesus.* Nobody would let him get anywhere close to Ross without stopping him and asking questions. He struggled again to see. Yes, he thought, that was Jamison coming out onto the porch of the crew dispatcher, lighting a cigarette, and he recoiled from that as fast as his tires had bounced off the concrete.

Mindless.

Frank jumped back into the truck. He started it, backed up with a squeal of rubber, yelled again at the pain and headed south on Sacramento, willing the big hunk of maroon steel to vanish into thin air like a mirage on the Mojave, willing Jamison not to see it. That seemed possible. It was still like that moment on the football field: the pale-green tint of shock, the music. None of it real, including himself. So maybe he could escape. He passed the pool hall and Byrd's barbershop and Motto's. But then, as if the truck were steering itself, he turned right on Cedar Street, and somebody else he knew was standing at the entrance to the S&J Market — Dino Bastiani, wearing his butcher's apron. Dino waved. A good guy. Again Frank waved back. *Who next?* All these people seemed to be reaching out to grab him, hold him back. The street rose steeply to City Hall. One of those godawful Dunsmuir grades where you had to ride your clutch at the stop sign. His hamstrings screamed. His nose still dripped blood. The Commercial Garage, across Florence, was dead ahead — and was that Charley Grissom he saw in one of the service bays, setting down a tool to look? *Damn.* Frank wrenched the wheel, heading back north.

Escape. That was it.

What the hell had he thought he was doing, trying to punch Ross out? He'd end up in jail.

Screw him. *Just get out of here, by God.*

Leave this town.

Now.

Why not?

And once again Frank had that sick, thrilling feeling in his gut. Once again Dunsmuir faded and became unreal. He passed Tallerico's shoe repair and Lockart's hardware, the Traveler's Hotel and the Big Liquor, the bakery and the flower shop — Connie's friend just turning into it. That pink-flowered dress. Jesus. Did she wave *again?* Had he gotten a good look at him, bleeding like a stuck pig? He gunned the engine to take the hill past the theater. His legs cramped even worse. Then he glanced down and saw the needle of the gas gauge bouncing on empty. He wasn't going anywhere like *that.* At the top, he pulled into the Texaco — but the man who owned it now was his old shortstop, Brian Behnke, and Behnke himself was standing at the pumps.

"Fill her up," Frank said. Still dabbing at his face with the rag.

"Jesus, what happened to *you?*"

"Never mind," Frank said, but he stumbled on the running board trying to climb out, and Behnke caught him by the arm.

"You'd better clean up. Use the men's room. Holy shit." Behnke grinned. "What's the other guy look like?"

"No other guy." Though he *had* been in a fight, in a way.

"Ran into a door, huh?" Behnke had put on weight since his playing days. He never tanned, just turned red — his jowls, the tops of his ears under the cap with the Texaco star. He eyed the Hawaiian shirt. "I like the style anyway, bud. It's colorful."

"Check the oil, too, why don't you."

"Hey, don't bite *my* nose off."

"Sorry, man. I'm just…"

If Frank thought he was sweating before, it was twice as hot in the narrow metal stall, smelling of urine and disinfectant. A steam bath. Water popped from his skin. He pulled out a wad of paper towels. There wasn't just blood on him but grease — from the rag. What a mess. The shirt was ruined. Splotches of blood drying on it like scabs. He ran water and poured gritty Boraxo soap into his hands and scrubbed himself as best he could. His nose was cut on the fleshy part outside one nostril; more blood seemed to be coming from inside. He wet some towels, folded them, tilted his head back and tried to stop the flow with pressure. He closed his eyes to keep the sweat out. He could hardly breathe — and how could blood clot when he was swimming in his own juice?

Frank had time, standing there, to remember. Too much time.

Had it been Jamison there at the crew dispatcher, or somebody else — a handy excuse to run? Dazed and humiliated, he couldn't be sure.

Either way, his gun had misfired.

Just like Dyke's.

And it came to him, as he left the restroom, that for five whole minutes he'd forgotten about the bruise. Did that make Ross right?

Damn.

Once he remembered about it, of course, it hurt like crazy. He limped over to Behnke, who had the hood of the truck up. "You're a quart low," Behnke said.

"Ten-forty, then." Frank turned and went to the machines at the front of the station. He bought a Coke and two packs of Chesterfields.

It seemed almost cool outside. Sweat had stuck the shirt to his ribs. He opened the Coke and drank it, and by then the hood had been lowered. Behnke tossed the empty oil can into a drum and wiped his forehead with a rag as dirty as Frank's. Behnke had eyebrows so blond you almost couldn't see them. He gave Frank a different look — not amused, simply curious.

"I heard you got hurt up there," he said, waving to the north. "Fred told me."

At least he didn't say *hit in the ass.*

"Yeah."

"As bad as he said? You shouldn't be out walkin' around, bud. Much less leadin' with your schnozz like that."

"Tell *them*," Frank said bitterly. "*They* think I should."

Behnke perked up at that. He wanted the story. And Frank discovered that he wanted to stay there and tell it, even though Behnke usually wasn't much of a listener. He paid for the gas and oil: only eighteen dollars left in his wallet. Another obstacle. Should he go back to the bank? Ten minutes ago he'd seen his chance and taken it, appalled and thrilled by the enormity of his crime, knowing that if he paused even a second too long he would chicken out on that too. He'd seen an opening, like a halfback spotting a momentary gap in the line, and bolted for it. But all it took was an empty gas tank, a little soap and water — he still had to hold his nose up so it wouldn't start bleeding again — and something like sympathy...

Damn.

He had just enough momentum left to drive off and leave Behnke unsatisfied.

Down in the canyon, a train made a mournful sound.

Frank knew he ought to stop at home. Change his clothes, pack, collect his guns and tools... but he knew he couldn't. He would be trapped there by having to face Connie and the kids again. *Keep moving.* But where, for God's sake? He turned east off Florence and bumped down a steep little street under a dark tunnel of trees, beside a bank of moss and ferns that never dried out. He crossed the tracks after the caboose of a northbound freight passed by. Eric Riemersma's crew. That meant Jamison's was third out. Two other crews would be called on the North End Pool before Frank had to make himself available. *(Had* that been Jamison? The more Frank tried to remember, the more he doubted it. A mirage...) He rattled over a bridge and turned north on River Avenue, where the green wall of Girard Ridge came right down to the water.

Nobody around. Frank parked beside the river. It was shady here. A good place to hide for a while and try to think.

The bruise stung angrily now. His nose throbbed. He got out and leaned against the truck and lit a cigarette, looking west toward the big highway bridge.

After a while, he noticed an old man and a boy come through the willows and start fishing on the far side, maybe a quarter-mile away.

No, not a boy. Frank recognized the red-checked shirt, the black cowboy hat.

Annie.

He stood and watched her as she sat on a rock and watched her line. She never looked his way.

He lit more cigarettes. The breeze off the river eddied the smoke.

The noon whistle blew.

By then he'd been crazy, he would figure, for a little more than an hour.

13.

John didn't see Clyde Carter come, or see him and Annie leave. He was lying on his back in the fort again, eyes closed, thinking of that trip to Sacramento when he'd gotten the cap gun. He'd gone to the dentist there, too — Dr. Chenoweth, who didn't believe in novocaine. "Unless it's something serious," his mother said before they left Dunsmuir. "I agree with him. Drugs are dangerous. You shouldn't use them unless you have to. *You* don't need anything for just some little cavities,"

John looked at her dubiously.

"You aren't a crybaby, are you?" she teased.

"No."

"So there. *I* don't use any novocaine, and it doesn't hurt me much."

"Can't we go to the dentist here."

"Dr. Chenoweth has taken care of your father and me for years. Think of this: when I was a girl, they didn't even *have* novocaine. You just had to be brave… Anyhow, we trust him. He's a good dentist. And since we're going to be down there anyway…"

But it *had* hurt, as he'd known it would. It was as close to being tortured as anything he could think of, and he hadn't been brave at all. Dr. Chenoweth's office was in a nine-story building — a skyscraper — and the elevator that lifted John up to the seventh floor seemed to leave his courage behind in the lobby with his stomach. He remembered the waiting room with its shiny brown leather chairs, its medicinal smell and the view out a window to the blank brick wall of another building, with a sign painted on it: HOTEL SACRAMENTO… Then he was in the dentist's chair, with wads of cotton in his mouth, and tubes sucking, and a trickle of water in the basin (like blood, he thought); and the drill buzzed and whined into a hot point of pain while little bits of his teeth (it felt like) dropped on his tongue and the very air inside his mouth smelled and tasted like scorched iron. Dr. Chenoweth's face, with its glasses, its clipped gray mustache and its high, tanned forehead — as smooth as the leather on the chairs — showed no emotion except for a faint impatience.

"I can't do it while you're moving so much," he'd say. "You want me to drill a hole in your tongue?" And finally, laying down the drill with a sigh: "OK, let's take a break. I'll see somebody else for a while… You can spit."

So John would be left alone, sometimes in the dentist's chair, sometimes back in the waiting room, where he fell into a kind of trance, memorizing the pattern of the paint flaking off the HOTEL SACRAMENTO sign. It was time enough to grow impatient himself, to imagine that he *could* be brave when Dr. Chenoweth called him again… But when Dr. Chenoweth did call, it seemed like no time at all. Back in the chair, John could fool himself for maybe thirty seconds that the drill didn't hurt as much as before. Then time, which had compressed itself into nothing, would stretch out so far that five minutes seemed like all afternoon…

"Your little sister doesn't make as much fuss as you do," his mother scolded him. "Dr. Chenoweth said you were about the *wiggliest* boy he'd ever seen."

But no matter how much he'd wiggled, or how miserable he'd looked, they hadn't let him go until the cavities were all drilled and silver was crimped into the holes in his teeth.

* * *

And that was it, he thought now, pressing his back harder against the ground. Torture wasn't just being hurt. It was the way time stretched out; it was being helpless and naked. The Gestapo wouldn't even let him rest, the way Dr. Chenoweth had.

Voices echoed in his head:

Ve haf vays to make you talk…

Death is better than dishonor.

You aren't a crybaby, are you?

The Scout was dumb.

He felt the ants tickling; he thought of Apaches staking people out over anthills. He tried to think of everything except how weak and slow his father had looked, climbing into the truck. He thought of snow —

how an Indian kid his age might lie out there hunting, his skin tough because he'd never had to wear a shirt. Waiting for deer. He'd have to try it sometime, some winter. He shivered again…

But it was hard to think of snow in the drowsy warmth and pine scent of a July day. He pressed down still harder.

Ah. Finally. An edge of pain, like a thin, sharp rock digging into his right shoulder blade. He tensed himself, tried to be brave…

Then he heard a whoop.

Gary!

He looked out and glimpsed Gary and Jimmy coming up the street by Curly McPherson's house. No sign of Freddie. They had their guns drawn and were looking up toward the woods. He realized that they'd given up trying to find him; Gary had yelled to tell him where *they* were, if he was still in the war.

John felt suddenly guilty; the shock of it seemed to blend with the pain of the rock-edge under his back. *Jeez*, he thought. I lost track of time. *They must think I quit — ran out on them.* He straightened up to move, and as he did so, he automatically reached down to touch the rock — and stopped again as his fingers felt something he didn't dare believe.

An arrowhead?

Yes.

Half buried in the pine and fir needles, the blackened, rotted oak leaves and sticks. The duff, his Cub Scout handbook called it. The duff of the forest floor.

The first one he'd ever found.

Awestruck, he held it in his hand and rubbed off the dirt: a chip of obsidian, black glass, from the great glass mountain out near Medicine Lake, where the Hillers had gone camping once with his father's Sacramento friends the Joneses. The Indians here must have traded for a lump of it. Then they'd heated it, maybe, to flake off smaller pieces, and finished it with bone tools. That's what his schoolbooks said. Then they'd shot it... at a deer or a man?

Gary and Jimmy had disappeared behind his house.

John climbed out of the fort. The blood had drained from his head; branches whirled in the sun's glare. He slipped the arrowhead into his hip pocket and felt it there like a lucky charm, beating against him like a heart (or maybe it was his own blood beating). His fingers still felt the old, cold touch of the stone, the touch of the long-dead people who had made it, a breath of air like their voices. *They were real*, he thought. *They really lived here. Just like me...* And he thought (with only a little of that sense of watching himself, smiling at himself, that he'd had at the den meeting): *It's because I was brave that I found it. It's a sign, like an Indian boy would get.*

He moved north again, planning to circle down on the other side of Thelma Hoffman's house. Even up on the top of the brink he could smell it, hear the dogs barking inside.

Why doesn't she let them out? he wondered.

He came out above the corner of her house, at the edge of the woods. He drew the cap gun — after the arrowhead, it had never seemed so silly.

Time seemed to slow down… but with excitement, not with pain. John looked north past the Sykeses' house, up the length of the canyon, and saw what he knew would be there (and felt a deep, quiet joy in knowing it, the way a compass needle always knew which way to point): the eastern half of Mt. Shasta, the bigger of its twin cones, more than fourteen thousand feet high. A dozen miles away, it stood out just as clear against the blue as the mountains close by. A single lens-shaped cloud hovered over the summit; its shadow darkened part of the slopes of gray volcanic rock, tinged with pink and purple. Only a few patches of white were left, in the hollows. One was a glacier; it curved around a ridge near the top like a question mark. What was it asking *him?* John wondered. The Indians, he knew, had worshipped the mountain. Their gods lived there.

At the same time he saw Mr. Sykes setting a box down in the dust of their yard. Their house, gray-brown shingles, looked as if it had never been painted; one end was propped up on posts against the slope, and John could see daylight under it. Mr. Sykes was showing his kids a bow-and-arrow set. He hadn't shaved; his T-shirt had holes in it. But he was laughing as he stood next to Jackpot and held the bow so that Jackpot could draw it with his good arm. The arrow flew over the box, into the woods. One of the younger kids — the boy — ran after it. *He shouldn't do that,* John thought. He almost yelled: *They might shoot again!* The arrow might be lost; it might have broken against a rock. It looked like a cheap set anyway, and John knew that the Sykes kids would break things even faster than he would... But in spite of all this, he wished his own father were a little more like Mr. Sykes, who didn't seem to get mad, just stood there and scratched his head with a dirty hand. *Nobody's scared*, John thought. Though he knew his own father was better. *No excuse,* his mother had said about the Sykes kids' teeth. But John wasn't sure what was worse: having your teeth get all black and snaggly, like Jackpot's, or having to sit in Dr. Chenoweth's chair.

The Indians weren't scared, he thought. *They didn't have any dentists, either.*

The dogs in Thelma Hoffman's house barked louder, as if they could smell him outside.

Jackpot's second arrow hit the box, and the Sykes kids all cheered. Watching it flash, John felt exultantly that it was an answer to the mountain's question. He'd get his *own* bow and arrows...

He wanted to be an Indian.

Then Gary and Jimmy came around between the two houses, guns at the ready — the way Ronnie Knudson said he'd done in Korea.

John wanted to do it right. He crouched behind the trees at the edge of the bank and waited until they were out in the open. "B'dam! B'dam!" he yelled, so that they'd know they'd been ambushed — that he *would* have killed them if this was for real. It was close enough range. *If I was them,* he thought, *I'd die. Even if it was Japs that shot me. After all, I deserve it. I was patient. I outflanked them...* But he knew they wouldn't think of it, and though the steady current of joy never stopped flowing through him, he felt a faint resentment as he dashed down the bank. He wasn't sure how the Japs charged — they yelled "Banzai!" or something, and waved swords — but he didn't have his sword, so he just ran zigzagging toward them like an infantryman, yelling, "B'dam! B'dam! B'dam!", even at top speed able to dodge the dog poop that littered the ground on Thelma Hoffman's side. (Bullets zipped past his cheeks; the wind was keen…) He ran almost up to Gary and Jimmy before he staggered, grabbed his side, twisted and fell in the dust.

"Gotcha," Jimmy said. "Dirty Jap."

John lay on his back, heart thumping. The warm dust against his skin felt soft as flour. He touched his pocket; the arrowhead was still there. (Jackpot's third arrow went *thunk* into the box.) The sun shone red through his eyelids; when he opened them, the sky was so high and blue that he almost wanted to cry.

There, he thought. *Now they've seen how I died, maybe they will too. And then it'll be* really *real…*

Jimmy poked him with his gun barrel, laughing. "You think we really killed him?"

"Don't know about them Japs," Gary said. "Maybe just playin' possum. Want to make sure?"

John thought they might kick him or something. He scrambled to his feet, and felt as dizzy as he had at the fort. "I found an Indian arrowhead up there," he said.

Gary squinted; he didn't seem to hear. "Where'd you go? We thought you'd quit."

"Up there." John waved vaguely. "I'm not gonna tell you where my hideouts are. You gotta find me."

"No fair just hidin'," Jimmy said. "It's supposed to be a war."

"If it was, I'd have got you. You'd be dead," John said. "I'm not kiddin'. I found an arrowhead. I'll show you... Where's Freddie?"

"I don't know," Gary said.

"I left him behind to keep you guys busy."

"He must've gone home," Jimmy said.

"Never saw him," Gary said.

"I guess he didn't want to be a Jap," John said.

"Well, *somebody's* gotta be a Jap."

14.

The noon whistle blew.

His mother came out onto the porch. "John-*ny!*" she called.

"I'm coming!" he called back.

It was hot on the street. They looked for Thelma Hoffman on her porch, but she wasn't there. Sometimes she sat out in a rocker, with her swollen feet in fuzzy slippers up on the railing — seldom saying anything, just watching the kids play, sipping something that looked like iced tea.

"Whiskey," Gary had said once. "She drinks whiskey." But John wasn't sure. When his father drank whiskey, he used a little tiny glass, like the cowboys in the movies. A shot glass, he called it. Thelma Hoffman drank out of a tall glass with ice cubes in it.

John checked: his father hadn't come home. No truck. Just the sky-blue Chevrolet sedan his mother drove, parked in front of the retaining wall.

Gary was looking at it too. "Your pa like Chivies?" he asked. That was how he said it — the twang again.

"Yeah."

"My pa says a Chivy's good for speed, but you want it to last, you're better off with a Ford."

John didn't know what to say. He still didn't want to make Gary mad. Mr. Grissom worked in a garage, so he ought to know. But John thought *his* father ought to know what was a good car too.

"My dad *likes* 'em fast," he said.

His mother called down. "Hey! Lunch is ready."

"Do you want to eat lunch with us?" John asked suddenly. He wanted to change the subject... and he still felt a little guilty about hiding from Gary and Jimmy all that time. Just looking for his father's truck had somehow taken the joy away; he couldn't imagine being an Indian now. "My mom won't mind."

"We'd better git on home," Jimmy said.

"She made biscuits this morning. And my mom makes the best biscuits in the world."

"What are you *doing* down there?" his mother asked.

"Can Jimmy and Gary eat with us?"

"I guess so." His mother's coppery hair was pinned back severely, except for one loose strand that fell over her forehead. She wore an apron; she leaned on the railing so that her elbows bent toward each other a little. "If it's OK with *their* mother."

"Gary," Jimmy said in a low, worried voice. "We're supposed to help Ma out. Remember?"

"It's OK," Gary said.

"No, it ain't. We'll git in trouble... I ain't picked up them toys yet."

Gary was already climbing the steps. "We got plenty of time," he said. "But if you want to, go home. I don't care."

Jimmy paused at the bottom, eyes full of foreboding.

John clumped up past him. "Look!" he told his mother. I found an Indian arrowhead."

"Really?" She started to smile. He dug for it in his pocket, but as he reached the porch he heard her gasp. The freckles on her face seemed to expand with indignation. "How come you have your shirt off? Didn't I tell you —" She pulled the wadded shirt from his belt; a cloud of dust puffed out and she sneezed. "What have you been *doing?* You're *filthy*, from head to toe." She held the shirt at arm's length by her thumb and forefinger and shook it, then dropped it to the floor. "Just filthy," she said. Cleo, who had been sleeping beside the door, lurched up, chain collar jingling, toenails clicking. His mother took John by the shoulders, the way Mrs. Ordonez had, and turned him slowly around, swatting the dust from the back of his pants, while Gary grinned. "What were you playing — cowboys and Indians?"

"GIs and Japs," Gary said. "He was a Jap."

"Is that why he's so much dirtier than you are?" To John she said: "You know you have leaves in your hair? And *ants.*"

"I was up in the woods. That's where I found this," he said, holding out the arrowhead, almost in despair. How could he explain the joy of finding it —

or how he'd *had* to flop full length in the dust if he wanted to die right?

"Lemme see that," Gary said, finally interested. John turned to him and Gary made a grab for it; then they were wrestling — strenuously but not quite seriously, because his mother was there. Gary's hot, sweaty arms had him in a hammerlock and were bending him down toward the floor when Cleo stiffened and growled.

Gary let go. "Hey, does she bite?"

"No, she's a good dog," John said, surprised. Still clutching the arrowhead in his right hand, he caught Cleo's collar with his left. He almost couldn't hang on, she pulled so hard, claws scraping on the boards. A low, tense rumble came from her throat.

"You shouldn't play around like that in front of her," his mother said. "She thinks Gary was really trying to hurt you."

"She *looks* like she bites," Gary said, edging away.

"I never saw her like this before," John said. "Honest. She never bit anybody." He was embarrassed for her, but also secretly glad to see Gary scared for once — to have Cleo try to protect *him*, even if he didn't need it. "Take it easy," he murmured, stroking the smooth top of her head. "Good dog. Good doggy."

"Well, whoever wants some lunch —" his mother said. "Where'd Jimmy go?"

"Home, I guess," Gary said. He sounded calm enough now, even scornful. "Jimmy's kinda shy."

No, he isn't, John thought, with a little of the same resentment he'd felt charging down the hill. His ears still throbbed where Gary's arms had squeezed them. He thought: *You shouldn't call Jimmy shy just because* you *got scared.* But that made him wonder. If Gary *could* get scared, then why wasn't he more afraid of his dad? Why hadn't he gone home, the way Jimmy had?

Connie Hiller looked concerned. "Well, he doesn't have to be shy around *us*. You're always welcome… as long as your mother isn't expecting you or something."

"It's OK," Gary said.

"You sure? All right, then… Whoever wants some lunch has to wash up *thoroughly* and put on some clean clothes." John knew she wasn't talking to Gary. "No, just leave that shirt right there. Don't bring it inside. I don't know why I even bother to do laundry."

* * *

He laid the arrowhead on a bookshelf above his bed. (That was one reason the Hillers were different. Nobody in the neighborhood had so many books: shelved, piled and in boxes, in every room.) But first he'd sniffed it, put his ear close to it, hoping to hear again the faint whisper of those Indian voices. Nothing. Here it was just a rock. There were too many other whispers in the hot, airless house, too many smells, too delicate a balance between comfort and fear. In the bathroom, where he scrubbed himself, he saw the hairbrush his father spanked him with — yellow plastic against the white porcelain of the basin, stained with rust; a wet-pipe smell. And in his and Tommy's bedroom, where he put on clean jeans and a T-shirt, his father had torn out half a closet wall, leaving the bare studs. John could smell plaster dust, the heat of the power saw cutting (like the tooth dust and the heat of the drill in Dr. Chenoweth's office); he could hear the menace of the electricity crackling through the wire — and something else. He could feel the work itself, something heavy and dark in the air that made it hard for him to move or even breathe — the same way he'd felt trying to get the other Cubs to make armor; something that told him: *You can't do this. Ever. It's hopeless even to try...* Next door, the dogs still barked.

15.

Annie and Clyde crossed the bare dirt past Dr. Malevich's house, near where the bulldozers were working on the freeway. There wasn't any shade. It was hot. Then they looked both ways to see that no cars were coming, and crossed Highway 99. They followed a little street down to the tracks. A freight train was just disappearing around a bend. They walked along the ties — big hunks of wood stained with black tarry stuff, sunk into the gravel. She stepped only on the wood, as if she were playing hopscotch. Even here it was hot. The sun burned down on her cowboy hat and her red-checked shoulders. She could see her shadow — short and fat; she kept stepping on it, as if it couldn't get out of the way. The tops of the rails shone. Big spikes nailed them to the ties. There was a hot, cindery metal smell. She and Johnny had put pennies on the rails once and let a train run over them to see what happened. They weren't supposed to do that, but they did. When the train had gone, the pennies were flattened and bright and the pictures on them were rubbed out. They weren't any good as money anymore, Johnny said.

"Here we go," Clyde said.

They were almost to the highway bridge. Clyde led her on a path down to the river. Annie scampered past him. It got cool, suddenly, and she could smell wet rocks and plants. A swarm of golden bugs no bigger than specks of dust swirled around her head. She sneezed and brushed them away. Then she came through to the river, and the concrete arches of the bridge far above, and the bridge's shadow. The river made a noise like people clapping, except it never stopped. It was all one noise, but she could hear the separate people in it, too. She looked back and saw Clyde still slowly picking his way down the path. "Hurry up!" she called. Clyde was old. But even when *she* was old, Annie promised herself, she wouldn't be slow.

Clyde gave her one of those rare smiles. "Got nothin' but time here."

Long green grass hung from some of the rocks like hair, swaying in the water. Annie saw willow trees and water plants with big leaves and stems, like rhubarb. She saw a wild blackberry bush, but the berries weren't ripe yet. Most were green, a few red. None black. She saw some kind of tree that, when the breeze off the river blew, the leaves flipped over and turned from green to white, then green again. *How did that happen?*

Clyde had her sit on the biggest rock. It was gray and had scabby, mossy things on it. He baited her hook with a salmon egg. "No point in casting here," he said. "You'll just get your line snagged in all this stuff behind you. Just underhand it out there." She looked at him. "Just *toss* it, like a softball."

So she did. She let her feet hang down almost to the water, but not quite. It was nice and cool here. Under the water, the egg looked white instead of pink. It moved down with the current until the line was taut; then she pulled it back. Over and over. It was kind of like rowing, she thought. Meanwhile, Clyde put on his waders and walked out to where he had room to cast into riffles of white water. Annie was jealous of him. She wanted waders too. *How come I have to stay on this old rock?* Clyde moved knee-deep out into the sun, so that his hair shone white. She looked at the rutted back of his neck.

Soon Annie got used to the noise of the river, and could hear other sounds over it. She heard birds, and trucks roaring on the bridge, and sometimes a clocking sound as the current rolled rocks against one another on the bottom.

Time went by.

The noon whistle blew.

They took a rest and Annie ate her sandwich. Clyde drank coffee from a thermos and ate soda crackers. She drank river water from her cupped hands, so cold the roof of her mouth ached.

She felt disappointed, once again. Every time she'd gone fishing, she'd expected to catch a fish right away. Every time, she'd imagined it so clearly that it *had* to be true. Drop her line in. The fish — a big one, just waiting for her — would strike; her rod would bend; the reel would spin with a ratchety sound. Set the hook. Pull it out. But it never happened that way. Instead, she just sat on a rock until her tailbone was sore.

"Patience," Clyde told her. "That's the most important thing for a fisherman. Or woman. Patience."

"But where *are* the fish?"

"Oh, they're there. Lyin' low, this time of day, but they're there. That's why I took you to this deep hole here. They're takin' a siesta here, the fish, till it cools off in the evening and they come back up."

"Is this the wrong time of day?"

Annie had a first, faint suspicion then. Someday she would know that this wasn't *real* fishing — just something for little kids. But later still she would decide that Clyde had been as nice as he could be.

"Not necessarily," Clyde assured her. "Early morning and evening, that's good. But you'll get all the moskeeters out then. They'll bite you. You don't want that."

"No." Annie shuddered. "Skeeters!"

Another little smile. "Well, let's get at it, then."

Clyde gave her a new salmon egg. It was slippery and fishy-smelling. Annie had learned how to twist an egg onto a hook without tearing it apart or pricking herself. It wasn't easy, though. She dropped the egg into the dark green-brown pool and watched it get smaller and smaller as the current took it away.

Clyde waded out again. The water chuckled around his legs. Where he was, downstream from her, the river was bright and shallow and fast-moving, with gold and brown spots in it from the rocks underneath. Clyde was using one of the flies from his hat. Annie had watched her father tie flies. He had a little vise that screwed onto the edge of a card table and held the hook; then he'd wind colored thread on it. That was supposed to be a bug's body. And the thread held the feathers that were supposed to be wings. The flies had names, her father had told her. *Nymph. Royal Coachman. Gray hackle red. Or red hackle gray.*

Annie hummed the names. What kind did Clyde have?

Then, looking past him, she saw, far away, on the road on the other side of the river, her father's maroon pickup truck. And her father, standing beside it.

* * *

Annie did remember the day when he had cracked her and Johnny's heads together. But she remembered it only as a vague dark spot, like the spot she'd see after she squinted into the sun and closed her eyes. She remembered being whipped — the stinging and burning of the willow switch on her legs. But she didn't think about either now. She was glad he was watching her, and proud. *See? I'm fishing!* She stood up on the rock so he could see her better. She straightened her back. She could see the shadow of her cowboy hat on the water.

Then something jerked.

"Hold on there!" Clyde shouted, splashing toward her.

Annie whooped.

16.

The house had seemed empty minutes ago. Now it was packed. Connie Hiller had to get Johnny cleaned up and into fresh clothes; she had to calm the dog, who had growled at Gary Grissom, nearly bitten him, maybe; she had to corral Tommy, who was caught up in all the excitement and was running from room to room, shouting. Now she had to set an extra plate for lunch. She took the fourth plate down from the cupboard again. Then she set out the sandwiches and soup bowls and glasses of milk. Johnny wanted to eat biscuits, too. He'd been bragging about them to Gary, apparently. So Connie set a plate of *them* out, though only a few were left over from breakfast — misshapen ones she'd baked from the last scraps of dough.

"Of course they're cold now," she told Gary. "I could warm them up — but that just makes them harder, I think."

"That's OK, ma'am," he said. Gary fascinated her a little. She hadn't seen him so close up before. The same age as Johnny, the same size, but altogether different — tanned and gritty-looking and somehow *adult*, with those strange pale eyes: a little man in a boy's body. And he had those Southern manners. "They sure taste good."

"I'm sorry it's just tuna sandwiches. We weren't expecting company."

"That's OK, ma'am."

He could have washed *his* hands, Connie thought, but it was good to worry about something besides Frank. She thought of Annie. Had a single sandwich been enough? If Clyde had so many pockets, maybe she should have given her more. She would fix a snack, maybe, when Annie came home. Tommy sat in his high chair, tomato soup staining his bib, milk on his chin, a smear of banana on one cheek. The two older boys were wolfing their food down, and Connie felt a twinge of envy: It would be years before *they* had to worry about their weight. Even Frank hadn't gained much yet... but wasn't that the point: *not* to think about Frank?

"It sure tastes good, ma'am," Gary said. "You sure are a good cook."

"This isn't cooking. This is just opening a can and slicing some bread." Connie smiled. "But I'll tell you what, Gary. It makes a cook feel good when she sees you men cleaning up your plates."

Men. The word hung in the air. Johnny shot her a pained look, and Connie understood it instantly. Once in a while this happened between her and Johnny — they were alike, in a way. She had never called *him* a man, not by himself — so just like that, he was wondering if she liked Gary better. So silly! The things Johnny let himself stew about! Sometimes she wished she could shake the silliness out of him. But she understood.

"You were playing war?" she asked.

"GIs and Japs," Gary said. "My pa fought the Japs."

"He did?"

"He was on Iwo Jima island. There was *big* fightin' there, he said. The Japs were hidin' in caves, and our guys had to go in after 'em with flamethrowers. It was the only way, Pa said. They wouldn't surrender, even when we had 'em beat."

"War can be terrible," Connie murmured.

"They started it. The Japs did."

She remembered. Her last winter in Oakland, her last as a single girl. When the news of Pearl Harbor came over the radio, she'd driven down to the shore of the bay, not knowing why, and stared across the grim gray water at the Golden Gate, through which the Japanese fleet might come steaming any moment. She saw the whitecaps blown up by the wind; even inside the car she was chilled. What she felt wasn't fear, exactly, but an emptiness, a void. *Everything's going to change, but into what? Nothing about life is ever going to be the same.* And she felt that way now. What was Frank...?

"Still," she said, "we did terrible things too. Like the atomic bomb. All those women and children who didn't —"

"My pa says," Gary said firmly, and Connie was startled to find that this little boy was *arguing* with her, in a grown-up way, as Johnny never could. "My pa says the A-bomb was a blessing from the Lord. They'd've had to land in Japan. Him and his buddies. My pa was all ready for it, he says. Him and his buddies who were gonna get killed. My pa says he went right down on his knees there in Okinawa, where they were gettin' ready, and thanked God for the A-bomb. Because it saved more lives than it took. That's what my pa says. It was a sign."

"Does he talk about this often?" she asked.

"No, ma'am. He don't talk about it much at all. The war. But when he does, we sure listen."

I bet you do, Connie thought. That explained some of Gary's odd maturity: He was parroting the words of adults.

At that moment Tommy distracted her. Red soup drooling from his mouth, he began banging on the arm of the high chair with his spoon. He was talking to himself again, and pressing his hand against his mouth. 'Yay, Tommy," she heard him say.

"Be quiet," Johnny hissed at him.

Connie understood this, too. He was embarrassed by Tommy, just as she was, no matter how hard she tried to fight it.

"What's wrong with him?" Gary asked.

"Nothing's wrong with him." Connie included Johnny in her glance: *Don't you dare.* "He's just fine."

Everyone shut up for a moment. Even Tommy.

"I just meant to say," she said, "that I guess we *had* to fight, but war's so terrible, even when it's just play… I hope neither of you ever has to go for real."

That should have ended it, she thought. But Gary, like a little bull terrier, wouldn't let go. And right then

Connie decided that she didn't like the boy. It was unfair, of course. She had too much on her mind today. He was only a child. But still...

"It's because we've sinned," he said solemnly.

"What?"

"We've let Satan loose. We gave him the power to make war because we listened to him. That's what Pastor Johnson says."

"Well, maybe so."

"It's the truth, ma'am. You ought to come to our church."

"We have our own church, Gary," Connie said — although that was stretching it. She had been raised as a Congregationalist, but there was no such church in Dunsmuir, so she went to the Episcopal services. Frank never attended church, though he said he believed in God. He insisted that organized religion was a con game; ministers were liars and frauds. (Again, why so *angry?*) "But thank you just the same."

"Are you saved?"

Gary's face flushed in spite of his tan. Connie thought: No, she didn't like him, but she had to admire him, somehow.

"Don't you think that's our business?"

"No, ma'am. It don't make any difference what church you go to if you ain't saved. That's just Satan talkin' — tryin' to deceive you." Gary swallowed; his Adam's apple pumped. "Besides, some of them other churches are just the Devil's work anyway. Pastor Johnson says they don't believe in the Bible anymore. All this evolution, how we come from monkeys..."

Connie knew Harold Johnson. She had taught his younger sister, Alice, her first year at the high school. She saw him now and then downtown, at the S&J or the bank. A pursy little man, she'd always thought, with a doughy, jowly face and a string tie. Pleasant enough. But how remarkable that this boy should invest him with the authority of an Old Testament prophet.

A thunderer.

"Pastor Johnson says all this schoolin' don't mean anything if you don't have faith. Like *him,*" Gary said, pointing to Tommy — and now she knew he'd gone too far. "If you come to our church, Pastor Johnson could lay hands on him and heal him, even if the doctors can't. I seen him do it, lots of times."

"He isn't sick," Connie snapped. "Whatever gave you the idea he was?"

"I thought —"

"Well, he isn't. There's nothing wrong with Tommy."

And she glared down at Gary, hands on hips, until he lowered his eyes and fidgeted. *Darn* you, she thought, while Tommy, her sweet boy, seemed oblivious to it all, whispering to himself and banging the spoon.

Then Connie was sorry. Gary *was* just a child, and a guest. She was breathing hard; the sweat under her dress had gathered to beads, trickled down her sides.

She remembered one of her stepmother's maxims: *Horses sweat. Men perspire. Women glow.*

Well, she was glowing now, for sure.

"Gary, tell me," she said more gently. "This idea of inviting us to your church… was that your parents' idea?"

"They talked about it," Gary mumbled, his face even redder.

"But you just decided to ask, right now?"

"Yes, ma'am."

"Well, tell them we appreciate it… their concern. But you can't force things like this. If we ever *do* go, it'll have to be when we're ready. Not before."

* * *

Later, washing the dishes, she asked Johnny: "Have you been talking about Tommy? To the other kids?"

"No."

"You must have said *something*. Or Annie. But probably you, if Gary knew."

"You said… it was OK if we talked about him."

"I said you shouldn't be ashamed. It's not his fault he got so sick when he was just a baby. Three days old… I guess there's no way to keep it a secret. It *isn't* a secret. But I wish you wouldn't…" Connie raised her hands out of the water and held them there, uncertain of what to say next. She wore rubber gloves; soap bubbles sleeved her freckled arms to the elbow. Detergent was hard on her skin. Like the sun. That was why she wanted Johnny to wear a shirt. *We aren't the kind of people who tan. We burn.*

"Mom, what did Dad do in the war?"

Connie knew he was changing the subject, but let it go. "Why do you want to know?"

"Well, Gary… he was talkin' about *his* dad."

"He worked on the railroad," she said. "Right here in Dunsmuir."

"I mean in the Army. Wasn't he in the Army?"

She lowered her hands, peeled off the gloves and reached for a towel. "They wouldn't let him. They needed trained railroaders for the troop trains, all the freight they were sending up and down the coast. They'd call him up for the draft and the SP would get him deferred, every six months. Then they'd call him up again. It nearly drove him crazy."

"Oh," Johnny said, clearly disappointed.

And maybe Frank should have gone, Connie thought now. *He's always felt he missed something. A man's thing. A chance to prove himself, to see the world. An adventure.* But she remembered how she had felt at the time: *We just had a baby! We're just starting out! Why do you want to leave us and maybe get yourself killed, when you don't have to?*

"He wanted to go," she told Johnny. "Or at least he wanted to end the suspense. It was driving us *all* crazy. Finally he went and volunteered — didn't wait for the draft. But the Army didn't want him so much after all. He was twenty-seven, twenty-eight then. He was a father. They wanted young, single men more… And the railroad still managed to hang onto him."

"Oh," Johnny said again.

The towel squeaked as she dried the glasses.

"If he *had* gone, he might not be here. Or Annie or Tommy either. Ever think of that?" She smiled. "I'm sure he was doing just as important a job here as Gary's dad. Or anyone. Then, the year before you arrived, when I went back home to Oakland when your Uncle George was sick, your dad worked baggage on the Oakland Pier, where all the soldiers were coming and going. They'd throw these big duffel bags at him — a hundred pounds, *two* hundred, some of them weighed — and he'd catch them and turn, like this, and stack them in the baggage carts." She was stacking the dishes in the cupboard. "If you ever wondered how your dad got so strong, that's one reason. But all that twisting… it didn't do his back any good."

The same poor back that boxcar hit.

She turned back to Johnny, and he was still so droopy-faced that she said: "Don't look so *serious*. Not everybody gets to be a hero… Why don't you show me that arrowhead you found?"

17.

Maybe he'd known earlier, Frank Hiller thought. Even as far back as when he'd hung up on the Trainmaster instead of saying something. Something he couldn't take back.

Maybe he'd known when he picked this stupid shirt out of the closet.

Or thought he saw Jamison at the crew dispatcher.

All the time, he realized now, even when he was crazy, he'd been protecting himself. Leaving himself a way out.

Frank wrestled with this idea. He stood and smoked and watched Annie and Clyde Carter stop fishing and eat, then pick up their rods again.

The lump in his gut wasn't squirming anymore with terror and hope. It just sat there, heavier and bitterer every minute. Like a rock. He had let the old man down, and his grandpa too. His moment come, and already it was gone. He was on his knees, beaten like them — only worse; it seemed that he'd hardly fought. And right then, Frank began the long task of persuading himself that he *hadn't* chickened out, just grown up. He'd put his family first, not run off from his responsibilities like some asshole. That's why he'd hedged his bets all along. Frank would come to believe this, but it wouldn't be easy for him, or quick. It would be like busting up that granite boulder jammed against the back porch with nothing more in his hands than a crowbar. Knocking off little chips of it. Dust.

The boulder was inside him now. The bruise was part of it, part of the same pain.

He still blamed Connie for letting *him* down.

She *cared*, he'd thought as he lay in bed and she poured the lotion over him.

But it wasn't the kind of caring that did him any good.

The kids, maybe. But not him.

And he still cursed the SP and Ross. They had no right, he thought. No right to do this to him. *They* were the assholes.

All Frank could do now was knock off the first chip. He remembered taking her brother, George, barely recovered from his illness, still hobbling on a cane, his knuckles white, to this same stretch of river. George didn't have to climb much here. He could almost stand on the road and cast.

Frank had been wrong about that. Her family *had* had some hard times.

He watched Annie.

And it would seem to him, after enough of the boulder had been chipped away, that she was the main reason he'd stayed. How could he leave his little girl? He'd said something to Annie when he stormed out of

the house. Something mean. He couldn't remember —
but he was sorry for it now.

Frank admired how Annie never looked at him.
Not once. She was concentrating, by God. Fishing for
all she was worth. Good for her. After a while he tried
to beam his thoughts in her direction — tried to get her
to turn, to wave. That usually worked. And maybe she
did see him finally. He thought so. But she wouldn't
admit it, even then. *Damn*. She'd been sitting on a big
rock; now she stood up. Her back straight. Her line,
invisible until then, catching the sun.

Frank smiled.

Yes, that's what caught him, he would think in
years to come. That wisp of iridescence in the air,
binding him to her, as strong as spider's web.

Monofilament.

18.

"Isn't it beautiful?" his mother said. "People used to find them all the time, they tell me, but not so often these days. You should take it to school and make a report on it."

But the arrowhead was still just a rock. In John's bedroom the hot sunlight through the yellow-brown windowshade made the air seem heavy, as if he were under water. The room still had its vague menace. He felt guilty — for what, he wasn't sure. Getting so dirty? Inviting Gary for lunch? Wishing his father had been a soldier? *Something.* He had to do something. He shoved his head up under her arm, pressed it to her side and hugged her around the waist. He closed his eyes; she smelled of detergent and perfume and a warm, familiar smell — herself.

He remembered the argument that morning.

"I love you, Mom," he said.

"Well, I love you too," she said, startled, and hugged him back. He opened his eyes; it was all right.

* * *

Where I grew up, he would tell somebody, sometime, *bears used to come down out of the woods, right to our house, before the freeway got built.* They were black bears. John had never seen them — only heard them a couple of times, at night, like the boulder crashing down. But Cleo could smell them — a smell like an invisible current of terror that raised the hairs on her back like electricity. The only other thing that scared her so much was a thunderstorm.

Now he and the dog lay side by side again on the back porch, in the long peace of a summer afternoon, and the only smells were of pine lumber, dog poop, of course, Cleo's own smell and the scent of the trees above the bank, which sweetened the outdoor air even on the hottest days — which, like his fear, grew fainter and fainter but never entirely disappeared. He wore the cap gun again — "You'd wear that thing to school if I didn't make you take it off," his mother had said — but he was thinking about how to get that bow-and-arrow set. Sell Christmas cards door to door? He'd seen an ad for that in Boys Life. A recurved fiberglass bow, Port Orford cedar arrows... It sounded like an awful lot of trouble, though. The dog whimpered in her sleep; her hind feet twitched.

"Chasing rabbits," he said. That was what everybody said when a dog dreamed, but as far as John knew, Cleo had never chased a rabbit. Only ducks and geese and quail and pheasants. She was half Irish setter and half Chesapeake Bay retriever, with curly hair on her body and smooth flaps for ears. A bird dog. Her ribs rose and fell; her muzzle lay flat on the boards. Her nose was black. He remembered how, two weeks ago, she was sleeping just like this on the living-room floor and he'd tried to throw darts as close to her nose as possible without hitting it, like a knife-thrower in a circus. The first one stuck three inches away. The second one… just flopped on the carpet, but a dark-red drop of blood suddenly shone on her nose. And her eyes opened wide. He still felt sick inside to think about it. Her eyes hadn't looked hurt or accusing at all — just surprised. Which made it even worse.

Now Cleo stretched — she'd heard his voice — and those brown eyes opened again. Still nothing. No sign that he'd hurt her; no sign that she even remembered — except in her dream, and that was the bears, more likely. Maybe he was the only one who remembered it now. She hadn't been able to tell anyone — wouldn't have, probably, even if she could. Her tail thumped. She loved him. (Look at how she'd growled at Gary!) And he loved her…

But if he loved her, how could he have done it?

We've sinned, Gary had said.

That was true. John knew he had… But did that mean he had to join Gary's church?

"Hey," he whispered and petted her, stroked her all along her side, but his new uneasiness wouldn't go away. He was trying to tell her with his touch that he wouldn't ever hurt her again. But that meant reminding her that he *had* hurt her. It wasn't that he was afraid she wouldn't trust him anymore. She would. That was the difference between dogs and people. But he wouldn't be able to trust himself. No matter how gently he touched her now, he would always feel himself holding back from what he *could* do. Had done. In some strange way, being nice to her was just the other side of torturing her. Not something different. Because he knew... that although her teeth were sharp, her jaws strong enough to splinter the bones in his arm, she was helpless. Because she loved him. The way only an animal could.

"Good dog," he said.

Still, he knew, Cleo loved his father more. Frank Hiller didn't spend hours fussing over her, the way John did; he just gave her an occasional word or a pat on the head. But he took her hunting. He was proud of Cleo, and let her know it — proud of how this half-breed bitch, runt of the litter, that he'd picked up free from another railroader down in Gerber could outhunt his friend Bob Chapman's hundred-dollar pure-bred Irish. How without any training at all, just by instinct, she knew how to work up slowly on quail so they wouldn't flush with the hunters still out of range. "That big red goes lollopin' in there like a race horse — I thought Bob would have a heart attack, yellin'." How one bitter morning at Tulelake she'd swum through a knife-edge of ice that cut her legs to retrieve a Canada goose that turned out to be only winged. "You know how big a honker is. She can hardly get her jaws around him, and he's whalin' away at her, right in the face, with the other wing. But she brought him in. She has guts."

John would hear the pride in his father's voice, and for a moment Cleo's glory would warm him too. "Good dog," he'd tell her when she came back from the field — muddy and footsore, with ticks on her, exhausted and triumphant. But the thing was, she seemed to know she was good, beyond any praise John could give her. Her pride belonged to the men's world, closed off from him. (When he got a real gun...) Because what Cleo loved best, John knew, wasn't his own kind of shamefaced gentleness, but his father taking out his shotgun to clean it: unzipping the case and putting oil on round white cloth patches and ramming them down the gleaming barrels. An instant before, she might have been asleep, dead to the world, sprawled and snoring by the stove, but the sight of that gun would electrify her — like the smell of the bears, only this time with joy: like what John had felt finding the arrowhead, but even greater, he thought: more joy than any person could feel.

And it really was his father she loved, John knew, not just the hunting. *He* wouldn't throw any darts at her, at least.

19.

Annie nearly fell off the rock. She'd hooked a trout without even trying. The rod creaked and the reel whirred and the fish danced on top of the water. She pulled, and the fish pulled back. She could feel its silvery strength pumping up through the line. She was scared it would break loose. But Annie was stronger. She jumped down to the shore, hanging onto the rod, and pulled again, and suddenly there it was, flopping in the shallows at her feet. She dropped the rod (without realizing it) and scooped the fish up with her hands and threw it onto the land. It was slimy and shockingly alive. Clyde came in beside her as she chased it over gravel and little pools and clumps of grass. It had lost the hook — free. She was shrieking.

"It's getting away!"

"Now, hold on… hold on."

The fish wiggled, impossible to catch, and she thought it would crawl into the bushes and escape. Or get back into the water. But then it slowed down.

Gasping.

She could hear Clyde's hoarse breathing in her ear.

It'll die, Annie thought suddenly. The wet fish, as it lay there on its side, with a leaf sticking to it, was beautiful. Dark black-speckled green on top, rainbow colors in the middle, a silvery white below. Its gills gaped red as it tried to breathe. Its mouth opened and closed. And she felt an unexpected, terrible sadness. Catching fish was one thing. But she'd never thought about having to kill them.

Put him back, she wanted to tell Clyde. *Please! Let him live. I don't care.*

But Clyde had gripped the trout in his big chapped hand. He whacked its head on a rock, once, twice. Then it lay still.

Annie felt sick, but Clyde was smiling at her.

"Your very first, by golly. A nice little rainbow there."

"Is it dead?" she asked.

"Sure thing. Better get hold of your rod there, before it floats downstream. And your hat, too."

"My hat?"

It had fallen off, and she ran to get it. Clyde picked up the fish, wrapped it in wet grass and put it into the creel. By then Annie felt better. The sun warmed her wet hands and feet. A dribble of water from the cowboy hat tickled her neck. She could feel a grin growing wider on her face, stretching out both her cheeks. *I did it!* She remembered her father then. *He saw me! He saw me catch a fish!*

But across the river, he and the truck had gone.

* * *

Well before Clyde came clumping up the front steps, Annie had run back and told her mother.

Tommy, all excited, trotted up to look at the fish. He tried to pet it. He made noises as if *he* had caught it and people were cheering. Cleo — let inside again — sniffed at it, and sniffed at Annie too.

"How big is it? Can you measure?" she asked. So her mother went and got the ruler. The fish was just over seven inches long.

"Is that *all?*" Annie said. When she had fought it in the water, when it had flopped on the shore, it had seemed so much bigger.

"Good eatin' size," Clyde said. "What you call a pan-size trout."

"Can I eat it?" She turned to her mother. "Can you cook it for dinner?"

"I suppose so," Connie Hiller said. "But you'll have to clean it."

"Aw, Mom."

Clyde actually chuckled.

"That's what I used to tell her Uncle George. Anyone who catches a fish has to clean it… Are you sure you don't want something? I can make some iced tea."

Clyde shook his head. "Martha'll have lunch." That was Mrs. Knudson, his sister.

"Well, all right, then." Annie had the funny feeling that her mother wanted Clyde to be gone. "But thanks again for taking her. You're a very patient man."

"No trouble," Clyde said. "No trouble." He took off his canvas hat and scratched his head. "She's a good fisherwoman. Better than her brother is, even if he's older. He lets his mind wander. Doesn't pay attention. But Annie here, she's got the stuff."

"Still," Connie Hiller said. *She's mad*, Annie thought. *But why? I caught a fish!* It seemed as if Clyde would stand there and talk forever, which was exactly what her mother didn't want.

"Now that she's caught one," Clyde was saying, "she'll be hooked for sure."

Tommy kept grabbing for the trout. Annie loved her little brother. He was sweet most of the time. He followed her around and hugged her. His gray eyes were so deep and clear. But now she pushed him away, and he fell. Cleo jingled and barked. Tommy cried.

It was horrible, when everybody should have been glad.

* * *

In the kitchen, later, her mother showed her how to clean a fish. "Just this once," she said. "Then you're on your own." She was trying to be nice now, Annie could tell, but she was still mad about something. And not just Tommy.

Her mother laid the trout on a cutting board on the counter. It was dull now, with the grass picked off it, and almost dry, though it still felt heavy and cold. The green part looked almost black; the rainbow colors had faded. One eye — where Clyde had slapped it against the rock? — was torn loose.

The fish was really dead.

"See? You cut here," her mother said. "Straight up from this thing."

"What *is* that?"

"It's what a fish pee-pees with. Or poo-poos."

It looked like a belly button, Annie thought. A little circle thing with a pinhole in it.

"Does a fish poo-poo?" she asked.

"I *guess* so," her mother said. "I hadn't really thought about it, to tell you the truth. Fish eat things. Bugs. So I guess they'd *have* to, don't you think?"

Annie giggled.

Her mother took a knife and slit the fish's belly from the circle thing up to the gills. "Now comes the hard part," she said. She put down the knife and hooked her forefinger under the throat of the fish and pulled until something snapped. The sides of the fish's head — its cheeks? — fell apart. Then she reached into the opened belly and pulled out the fish's purple guts.

"Eeuw," Annie said.

"At least they come all in one piece. Trout aren't bad."

With her fingernail, her mother scraped black stuff off the fish's backbone. Then the inside of it was clean — pink-white, with rows of tiny ribs. Her mother ran water from the faucet through it. "OK," she said. "Then we put it in the fridge and that's it, till dinner."

"I don't know," Annie said.

She wasn't sure she could use that big, sharp knife. She might cut herself. But she also meant… what was it?

The sun had moved west by now. Light slanted in through the back window. She felt a little of the sadness she'd felt on the riverbank. She could smell it. When she was sad in the future, Annie wouldn't remember the dying fish with the leaf stuck to it, or the dead fish on the counter with its torn-out eye, or Tommy's face when she'd pushed him, or her disappointment that nobody had cared as much about catching the fish as she had, or that slant of yellow light. But she would smell all those things at once, somehow.

"Don't let Johnny eat my fish," Annie said. "*I* caught it."

"Don't worry, dear. It isn't big enough to —"

"I *mean* it! It's *my* fish." She knew Johnny would be jealous of her. He hadn't caught any trout yet. And he was older.

"OK, OK," her mother said.

But her mind still seemed to be on something else.

Then Annie remembered what had happened that morning — how she'd heard angry voices right here in the kitchen, and come in, scared but curious, and there was her mother with her face flushed and her mouth pressed tight and her father with a big vein sticking out in his neck. They shut up when they saw her. But they still *looked* mad.

"I don't even know where your brother is," Connie Hiller said. "Out back, I think. Or at Hughie's. I wish I knew where your *father* is. That's the question."

"I saw Dad!"

"What? You did? While you were fishing?"

"Over there," Annie said, pointing vaguely in the direction where the maroon truck had been.

"What was he doing?"

"Watching me. He saw me catch it! I think he did. He was just standing there by the truck."

"Where did he go, then?"

Annie shrugged. In all the excitement when the trout hit her line, had she glimpsed the truck moving away on that road across the river, back toward the middle of town? Or was she making it up? She pointed again — south.

"You sure?"

"No," Annie said. She shook her head. "Maybe." She had hoped this news was what her mother had been waiting for. For a moment, it seemed to be. She hoped it would make her mother happy. But it didn't.

20.

Frank Hiller did drive south. He doubled back on the same road, which the river would wash out in a few years. Even now, between the point where he'd entered it and a point across the river from the roundhouse, it was only a single lane of crumbling asphalt and dusty potholes. Barely enough room for the truck's wheels. But he'd rather go this way than back downtown. He drove along Butterfly Avenue, with its old two-story frame houses where Dunsmuir's Negro families once had been forced to live, and most still did. Bright-colored laundry on lines. Junk cars. Kids. The street was on low ground; it often flooded in a wet winter. Then Frank headed down South First Street, with Girard Ridge on his left and the river on his right. Through the trees on the riverbank he could see the SP yards: lines of rust-red boxcars, switch engines, the web of rails. Long shimmering arms of steel. The Octopus, reaching out for him.

And the SP would have him, he knew. That was decided. But not quite yet.

Let 'em wait.

He stopped again where South First began to curve back west toward the highway. The street crossed the river and the tracks near where a creek came in, shallow in its bed of round white stones. Connie and the kids used to park there sometimes and wait when he went out on a South End Pool trip; he'd wave from the caboose; they'd wave back. He could see Castle Crags from here — gray spires and domes of granite south of Mt. Bradley, with sun and shadow tracing every line of them. Frank climbed out of the truck and stood. He winced. He spread his feet to lower himself a little — tried to get as comfortable as he could — and rested his elbows on the hood. The metal was hot. He smoked more cigarettes. *Might as well smoke 'em all.* Over the steady sound of the river, he listened to the chugging and banging from the yards — that whole SP world that, for an hour, had wavered and become unreal. Now it would have to be real again.

But not quite yet.

It seemed to Frank that this might be the last free afternoon of his life. Free even though in truth he was already caught, like the last few Apaches in a James Warner Bellah story he'd read in the Saturday Evening Post: riding, twisting, running out of food and water, slitting their horses' veins and drinking the blood, to elude the cavalry one last time. And just because he couldn't get away, he let himself imagine what it would be like if he could.

Just start up and go. I've got gas. The canyon had only two exits, north and south. He didn't know north so well. So he'd probably head south, back into the

Sacramento Valley, all that yellow grass, where the sky and the earth expanded to their full width. Big puffy white clouds, air crawling with heat. He'd pass through Del Paso Heights. But when Frank thought about it, he knew damn sure that his mother would never approve of his leaving his family; and his father... well, the old man had lung cancer — *from cigarettes just like these*, Frank thought grimly but with a certain defiance, too, watching the smoke curl up: *As if anybody cared* — and wasn't in any shape to deal with this. Only Ralph, he realized with some surprise, might be willing to hear him out. His brother the engineer, with his narrow lips and coldly logical mind. Ralph would listen quietly, nodding. As if everything Frank told him he'd already known a long time ago. *Even though Ralph hasn't done any living at all, himself.* Understanding but offering no comfort. Frank longed even for this, but then he thought: *Hell, no, I won't stop. I'll just keep moving.*

He remembered the trip to Tempe with Bud Jones; it seemed to him now that this was the happiest he'd ever been, though it hadn't seemed that way then. They'd been on their own, he thought. Two young bucks. Free. What could be better than that? In the mornings, when the desert air was briefly cool, they'd get out of the Model A and yawn and stretch and play catch by the side of the road. The spiny bushes throwing long shadows. The hills, all rocks, sharp in the early light. Birds. Lizards. The feel of their muscles unstiffening and the smack of the ball in their gloves, back and forth, the rhythm of it. The smell of the dirt. Ahead of them a cheap but good breakfast at some diner: bacon and eggs and hashed browns and toast and coffee. And then driving on.

All we needed was a little more money. Then we could have stayed around. Maybe changed that coach's mind.

But this time, Frank knew, he wouldn't stop in Tempe or anywhere else. He'd drive clear to Mexico. Find himself a job. Meet some pretty *señorita*, maybe.

He spent quite a while imagining this woman — what she would look like. Smaller than Connie. Slimmer, anyway. Long dark hair, dark eyes, dark nipples. A shy yet incandescent smile. Mostly he thought of her skin: how it would be brown and warm, almost hot; how it would never feel cold when he touched it, even in the winter — what winter they had in Mexico. A warm *señorita* to lie beside. That was enough. Who cared if she had an education? Who even cared if she spoke much English? She would be smart enough, Frank thought; he wouldn't be attracted to her if she wasn't. Maybe it would be better without so much talking. They could understand each other...

But the trouble with this line of thinking was, it kept going. Sooner or later there would be more kids. *Lots* of kids; she'd be Catholic. Mouths to feed. He would have to go to work again — serious work, not just enough to keep them in tortillas and beer.

And then the trap would close again.

What could he do? Frank didn't know much Spanish. He supposed he could work at a gas station, but what would that pay? Damn little. Mexico had railroads, of course, but he wasn't sure that the SP couldn't reach across the border and blacklist him even there, the way it had blacklisted Dyke in that novel. Who knew? Even if the SP couldn't, he thought, what would life be like as he and the woman and the kids grew older — him still a brakeman, working the same crazy hours for less money, fewer benefits, no insurance if he got hurt again?

He was thirty-eight already.

Frank remembered what his grandpa had said: *That's what the sonsabitches want. To turn us all into Mexicans. Stoop labor.*

He'd be doing that to himself.

21.

What energy the ordinary kid had! John would think.

Later that afternoon he took a pick and shovel from the porch and started digging in the bank behind the house.

He wanted to dig a hideout. An underground room, like some kids had built in a book he'd read. Only they'd dug it in a flat English meadow and put the sod back on it for a roof. His plan was to dig straight in from the bank, maybe twenty feet, and run an escape tunnel up to the woods.

The thing about books, though, was that they never told you how hard it was. The surface of the clay was dry and cracked. When John broke through that with the pick, it got darker and redder; a couple of feet in, it was damp enough to stick to the shovel. In the winter, springs oozed out of every square yard of the hillside; the clay slid... He dug out rocks and chopped through the fringe of tree roots that hung down from the top of the bank. He got tired. Still, it felt good sweating in the sun. Inside, the tunnel was nice and cool. A good place to hide. If he made some kind of door — a flap of canvas, maybe — he could curl up in there like a hibernating bear. Nobody could bother him. Maybe then he could have visions, like an Indian. At least get rid of that sick feeling in his stomach...

Clean living?

He wondered what that was. He'd read about it in a Hopalong Cassidy comic book. Hoppy rode into a town where people kept disappearing, and a man named Hiram Fleer, who owned a wax museum, made statues of them, one by one, and charged money to see them. John remembered his name because it reminded him of Fleer's bubble gum. Of course it turned out that Hiram Fleer had killed those people; he'd soaked their bodies in a huge tank of molten wax and stood them up stiff so that the visitors to his museum *thought* they were statues. Hoppy found out when he sneaked into the museum at night and held up a candle to one of their faces; the wax melted right off. Then Hiram Fleer jumped on Hoppy and almost shoved him into the boiling tank. Hoppy was an old guy; his hair was white. But *a lifetime of clean living* — that's what it said — gave him the strength to slip Fleer's hold and throw him into the tank instead.

Just like magic.

John figured it probably just meant not smoking cigarettes or drinking whiskey. Stuff like that. But maybe it meant something more. Like Gary's church. Or like an Indian purifying himself so he could stand pain. Or like his father, knowing he didn't have to pet Cleo all the time to make her love him...

"Hey there, prospector," his mother said.

She was looking up at him, a basket of laundry on her left hip, shading her eyes with her right hand. The sun was in the trees now; the shadow of the bank reached almost to her feet.

"Come down here a minute. What are you digging for?"

He told her.

"I don't know." She bit her lip. "I'm worried it might slide down on you when you're in there. You'd be buried alive."

"It won't cave in," he said, remembering the book.

She shook her head. "It might. I don't think you ought to take that chance."

"Aw, Mom."

"I'm sorry," she said. "You've done all that work. I didn't know what it was, or I'd have stopped you earlier. You were just working away like a little beaver — almost two hours, did you know that? Why can't you put that much energy into something useful? Here, you can help me with the laundry."

"Aw, Mom." *That wasn't work*, he wanted to say. *That was fun*. But if she thought it was work… "I've already got it in so far. I can't quit now."

"Yes, you can. Come on."

He threw down the pick, too hard, and she gave him a look that meant business.

"And put that away… You're all *dirty* again! I just washed your other ones. The least you can do is help me hang them up."

It was true. He'd tried to be careful, but, climbing down into the sunlight, John saw that his arms and pant legs were smeared stiff with clay. There was grit in his hair and down his neck.

"I could just cry," his mother said. "I know you aren't looking forward to when school starts, but I am... Don't touch them. Just hand me the clothespins."

The clotheslines stretched parallel to the house and the bank, from the porch to a post near Thelma Hoffman's house. Following his mother as she hung the clothes, John looked down at the bleached dirt, pebbles, footprints, and felt hypnotized, all the energy draining out of him. His arms ached. He seemed to plod in slow motion. When they reached the far end, he heard Mrs. Hoffman's dogs yap louder, heard the whining of cats. Even Cleo, who had ignored them, came jingling over to sniff.

"Why doesn't she let 'em out?" John asked.

"Maybe there's something wrong," his mother said.

The sun slanted on the gray, peeling boards of Thelma Hoffman's house, rotten where they touched the ground. The smell of dog poop was powerful here. "Are you *sure* I can't dig a hideout?" he asked.

"*Yes,* I'm sure."

Then Annie came out on the porch. She waved and yelled. "Johnny, I caught a fish! You wanna see my fish?"

They turned. The basket was empty now. "That's right," his mother said. "Your sister caught a nice trout."

"Well, *I* found an Indian arrowhead," John yelled back at Annie, but he knew that didn't sound nearly as good as a fish. "I bet Clyde caught it," he said, climbing the steps. "He just let you pretend it's yours."

"Did not!" Annie said.

"Clyde said she caught it," his mother said, "and I believe him."

"It's *my* fish!"

John knew she was telling the truth. He just didn't want to admit it, after all his work on the hideout had been wasted. How come Annie was so good at things? Baseball. Fishing. She was a girl, wasn't she?

Now he had to go inside and look while his mother opened the refrigerator and Annie showed him the fish on a plate.

"Aw, that's just a little one," he said. "No bigger'n a bullhead."

"Is not!" Annie said, and she looked ready to cry — or fight. "Don't you try to eat it, either."

"Is too!"

"That's *enough*," his mother said — so sternly that it would have surprised John if she hadn't been in such a bad mood all day long. "Both of you. I can't take any more of this. Quarreling. Just get out of here for a while. Go play over at Hughie's or something. I don't care."

22.

Tommy needed his nap — all of a sudden, after so much excitement. Connie Hiller laid him or her and Frank's double bed, on a small rubber sheet. He still wet the bed more often than not. She lay down beside him, watching him sleep. Were Tommy's eyes *too* deep-set, she wondered for the thousandth time, were his lips *too* loose as he breathed in and out so peacefully, or did he look like any other four-year-old? Connie never could be sure. She laid a hand on his forehead. Warm but not feverish. Tommy grunted without waking up. *What kind of dreams does he have?* she found herself wondering. *Just like ours, or something strange and wonderful?* She edged away and stretched out on her back, on top of the bedspread, her arms and legs wide, so that no two parts of herself touched. Even holding herself still, she was sweating again. The house was at its hottest now, in late afternoon, when the outside air was already beginning to cool. Connie could smell herself; she could smell Frank — the lotion she'd put on him — even with the sheets changed.

Before long she felt itchy and drowsy. Her head ached.

Alone with Tommy in the morning, she had longed for somebody to talk to — though she probably wouldn't have talked about Frank. At lunch, surrounded by chattering kids, she had felt even more alone. Now as she stared up at the unfinished ceiling — bare beams and wires, spider webs and pads of insulation — Connie felt herself sinking into a despair she'd known only once before.

That was four years ago, after Tommy had been born, gotten so horribly sick and recovered — only days, really, since she'd floated into the depths of a benign universe and thought: *Why do we struggle? It's all so simple.* So much had changed — and so quickly, before the smell of that forest fire up by Black Butte had even blown away. It hadn't been so bad, Connie thought, when there was still a chance Tommy might die; fear had aroused her then to a desperate struggle. It was only when the danger was over and she and this pale, quiet baby, shrunken to half his birth weight, were back on Shasta Avenue that she lost all her strength. She lay on her bed, just as she was lying now. Her limbs heavy, unwilling to move. The very sunlight through the window somehow darker. Connie had heard of postpartum depression, but she'd experienced none of it with her first two babies. In fact, she hadn't ever quite believed in it, as a legitimate complaint. It made no sense. Only an unnatural mother, she had always thought, wouldn't be delighted with a newborn. But that fall, even when Connie forced herself to get up and care for Tommy, she moved around the house in a stupor. The railroad was busy then; Frank was seldom home. She couldn't keep up with the cooking and scrubbing and ironing. The other children roamed wild. So her stepmother came. Connie would have preferred Henrietta, but *she* was pregnant again. Anybody but her stepmother — though, to be fair, Nellie Ames Weldon had turned out to be a good grandmother for Annie and Johnny. More relaxed, more fun-loving than in Connie's own childhood, so that the kids enjoyed her nervous sparkle. If she *had* changed — and Connie hadn't spent more than holidays with her for several years now — what was there to fear?

She soon found out. Her stepmother came with the fall rains — in Dunsmuir, sometimes, it could rain for a solid month. Clouds hung deep in the canyon; the leaves fell; the black branches of the oaks dripped. The light was gray. Her stepmother looked the house over, and everywhere she looked, it changed. Connie felt like a child again, seeing everything through the older woman's eyes. The peeling paint, the muddy back yard. Threadbare carpets, unwashed linen, dishes in the sink. The *squalor* of the place, like some hovel in darkest Appalachia. *Tobacco Road.* Connie didn't have the energy to argue that it hadn't always been such a mess — and that Frank had plans to fix it up. Instead, her stepmother made *her* believe it was hopeless, as anyone would have known who wasn't foolish enough to go and live in the middle of nowhere with a railroad man who was gone most of the time.

Not that her stepmother blamed Frank. *He* was working hard enough. She blamed Connie for lying down on the job. "You think it was easy when I married your father and came into a house with two girls I didn't even know? I had no experience with babies or children at *all,* but I was expected to take charge. And I did. You think that was easy? *Nothing* about life is easy. I thought you'd learned that already. A woman's life, anyway. Now this baby, he *needs* you, and why you think you can take time off now, after what *he's* been through, I can't for the life of me…"

Chin up.

As far as Connie knew, Nellie Ames Weldon had never needed more than six hours' sleep in her life. She had never been depressed. She took charge again, mouth pursed with disapproval. She spat orders. Her skinny arms and legs — her right wrist had a wen on it the size of a robin's egg, which fascinated the children — were a blur of action. The dog slunk away. In next to no time, she'd whipped 305 Shasta Avenue back into shape. When she left after five weeks, Connie thanked her, weeping. But not from gratitude. No. Those were tears of humiliation. Connie hadn't grown up after all. She was still thirteen: too clumsy and too big (the tallest in her eighth-grade class, boy *or* girl; she'd never forgotten that); too careless and absent-minded, and worst of all (she'd always suspected) too blatantly… well endowed. All the nights her stepmother was in Dunsmuir, Connie had gritted her teeth and curled up in bed, trying to shrink herself. She'd pulled the blanket up over her breasts, full and sore, and the rest of her, still flabby from Tommy's birth. She was still an oversized child, drying supper dishes in the kitchen in Oakland. Nothing in between had ever happened.

When her stepmother found cold dishwater in the tablespoons next morning, she made Connie and Henrietta drink it. *It won't kill you. But it'll make you remember.* Connie remembered, all right. The awful taste. The shame. The ingenious cruelty of it — if they complained (and they never did), people would only laugh.

Had her father known?

Surely not. But what if he had?

Connie would never think ill of her father, and she didn't now. He was the soul of kindness. He always would be. But just for this moment, lying beside Tommy, worrying about Frank, she wondered if, just maybe, that kindness had its limitations. If, in regard to her stepmother, it hadn't been a form of... weakness?

Would he have stood up to her, condemned her? Connie couldn't imagine it.

That's just lovely, Nellie.

And she felt a faint stirring of rebellion, which she promptly quashed. For if her father had been weak — which she wouldn't admit longer than it took to say the word — so was she. Had she ever stood up to Frank when *he* disciplined the kids?

No. Not even when he whipped Annie with that switch.

Frank was horrified afterward. Those welts! "My God, I didn't mean to... I didn't think I hit her that hard," he'd confessed to Connie, on the point of tears himself. No, he wasn't a cruel man. She'd been sure of that when she married him.

And wasn't it best if parents agreed — if they kept a united front?

That's what she always told herself. Some spanked their children — that's how Frank had been raised — and some didn't. Did it really make all that much difference?

No, Connie would think when this day was over, and for most of the days to come. *It doesn't. Not really. We've done the best we can. The kids are fine.*

But at this moment, when even thoughts of her father failed to bring her the usual comfort, a new and disturbing idea occurred to her: of a *chain* of weakness. Her stepmother had diminished her while her father looked away. Then she had looked away while Frank did what *he* wanted. For there was never any question of whose system of punishment would prevail. He had always seemed so... certain.

I'm not supposed to be their buddy. I'm supposed to be their dad.

Once she'd told him, about Johnny: "That boy's afraid of you. Afraid of his own father. I don't know why, but he is."

It seemed a shocking thing to say — Connie had expected it to shock Frank. But he just shrugged and shook his head and said: "Maybe so, Mouse. But what can *I* do about it?"

She had no answer to that. It was just a matter of personality, she'd come to think. Frank and Johnny were different, that was all. She had to hope it wouldn't always be that way.

Annie, she felt, was more resilient. A tomboy. Good at sports, like Frank. More like him than Johnny was, to tell the truth.

And a girl, besides. Exempt from the demands fathers made on sons.

Meanwhile, Connie tried to help. If Frank was stretched under the truck on a piece of cardboard, bolting in some heavy, greasy part, she sent Johnny out to hand him tools. If Frank was sawing boards on the back porch, she sent Johnny out to learn how you measured first with a steel tape, then drew a pencil line to saw by. All the things George had done with *her* father. Didn't boys like that? Of course they did. And she was sure Johnny would have liked it too, if only Frank hadn't been so... *angry.* The boy had inherited some of her clumsiness. His gaze would wander; his hand would slip. Frank would yell at him, and Johnny would steal away as soon as he could.

Before long, he didn't want to go out there at all. But she made him.

"Of *course* he wants you," she would say as brightly as she could. "And he needs your help. He really does."

Because Johnny was a boy. He couldn't be a baby forever.

That's how Connie usually thought, and how she would think again. It wasn't the fault of the spanking — what little there was of *that.* It was Johnny himself. He had to get tougher.

But not now. Now she lay in a misery of sweat and shame; her head throbbed. She remembered how Johnny had sneaked up after lunch and hugged her.

Poor kid. And she remembered what Frank had said in front of Annie. It seemed to her that nothing had changed since four years ago when Nellie Ames Weldon came and the rain fell endlessly outside and the walls smelled of mildew and she cowered in this same bed, certain of her worthlessness as a mother. As a wife. As a human being.

When Tommy woke up, she was crying.

She carried him into the bathroom and wiped her eyes with a towel and found the bottle of aspirin. Then she carried him into the hallway and phoned the crew dispatcher again.

No, they hadn't seen Frank. But his crew was third out now.

23.

Almost everybody was at Hughie's clubhouse: John and Annie, Gary and Jimmy, Hughie and his brother Walt, even Jackpot Sykes. The others were climbing onto the roof, screaming and swinging from the branches of the willow trees like monkeys. (What would Pastor Johnson say about that?) At first John was nervous around Gary, whose face with those pale, squinty eyes didn't show whether he was mad or not. *And maybe he* should *be mad*, John thought. *I invited him in, after all.* Now and then he glanced across the street to see if his father's truck had returned.

He took off his shirt again.

He knew he wasn't supposed to. His mother had said so; Gary had heard her. But if he disobeyed, maybe Gary would think that he was brave — that they were both on the same side, even. Maybe Gary wouldn't feel so bad about what she'd said to *him*.

Whose side *was* John on?

He didn't know. All he knew was, it excited him to take his shirt off, with everybody watching... just because he *wasn't* supposed to.

Then he was swinging in the willows too. And screaming like Gary.

Ten feet above ground, John jumped for a branch and slipped. He barely caught it with one hand, then with both. Kicking wildly. An explosion of fear. The branch cracked but held. The shock of relief came just as a cloud drifted over Mt. Bradley from the west. A thunderhead. It only half blocked the sun; it just formed a bruise-dark background for the green-and-gold light shining through the willow leaves. At that moment, as if through a magnifying glass, he saw how every scratch in the smooth gray trunk revealed the moist green inner bark, the white wood; he saw cedar branches nearby — not leaves, not needles, but a network of scaly fingers — glowing like velvet. In the sudden coolness he heard bird calls that must have been going on all the time. John shivered. There were goose pimples all over his skin. And then, unexpectedly, the joy came back. He was an Indian again. He felt the strain of hanging from the branch run like fire down his arms into his body. He remembered the fort and his thoughts of torture, but that wasn't all of it; there was something else his body longed for, something he couldn't even name…

He wished Julie Land still lived there.

* * *

Then they went down past the blackberry bushes, picking a few berries that were ripe, and wound up at Hughie's sandbox, pouring in water and floating chips of wood. Hughie looked worried, the way Jimmy had looked when Gary climbed the steps of the Hillers' house. "We'd better turn it off," he kept saying. But nobody listened to him. Gary just grabbed the hose and turned up the water higher and sprayed it until the sandbox became a lake, with big waves running.

"Stop that," Hughie said.

"It's a hurricane!" Gary yelled. "Hurricane!"

"My mom says —"

But nobody listened. Hughie just wasn't the kind of guy anybody listened to. He was as tall as Gary, but skinnier — his ribs showed, and his chest was as pale as John's. His eyes and hair were dark. Over his right eye, running into his hair, was a splotch of reddish purple — a birthmark. Maybe that was it. Because there wasn't anything else wrong with Hughie that John could see, yet everybody seemed to know. Just like they knew about Gary, the opposite way. Even when Hughie got mad, like now, he didn't scare anybody.

Then Gary turned the hose straight up, so that it seemed to be raining. "Hurricane, hurricane!" he chanted. Annie squealed. Sand was stuck in a circle to the seat of her jeans. Hughie grabbed for the hose and water flew everywhere, rattling against windowpanes and the faded peach-colored siding of the house. Gary sprayed him in the face. Walt ducked. Jackpot Sykes hooted, his limp arm flapping.

"I'm gonna tell my mom!" Hughie yelled. John couldn't tell if he was crying or not, with all the water dripping from his hair.

"She's not your mom," John said scornfully — still riding the good feeling he'd had in the willows, still on Gary's side, joining the laughter. "Your mom's gone."

Then Hughie's grandmother was right behind him. She had burst out the back door. Her face was white with powder, her mouth thin and red; her upper lip (he thought at that instant) was wrinkled like the cowcatcher on an old locomotive. She threw up her hands as if shooing away a flock of birds. Then she rushed to the spigot — knocking off the lid of the garbage can so that it rang, spinning, on the walk — and turned off the water. She looked up. Her red lips opened; her eyes, outraged, were focused on him, John. She was saying:

"You shut up. Get out of here!"

John's throat clenched.

"Filthy kids. All of you. I *told* you not to play with water."

"We didn't do nothin'," Gary said.

"You," she said to John. "Don't you *ever* talk like that. I don't want to see you around here anymore."

She reached for Hughie, who was as slippery as a fish.

* * *

Then they were running, east of Jackpot's house and north of Dr. Malevich's, to where the bulldozers had been working on the freeway. Dirt was piled up in long ridges. The prints of huge treads — like tanks'? — seemed to be hammered into the ground, deeply shadowed. The men had stopped working for the day.

It was quiet. Little red flags hung from lines of wooden stakes.

"They'd make good spears," Gary said.

He didn't seem to be bothered at all. But then, it wasn't really because of Gary that Hughie's grandmother had gotten so mad. It was mostly John's fault.

"What happened?" Annie kept asking. "What did you do?"

"I didn't do anything," John said. "She's crazy. Old witch."

But he knew what he'd done. What he'd said... He just didn't know why.

Children can be very cruel, his mother had said.

But he hadn't meant to be cruel. It was just that... he'd felt good for a moment.

Every time I feel good, he thought, *something happens*.

We've sinned, Gary had said.

But now Gary was yelling "Ungawa! Ungawa!" and jumping up and down. Jimmy had found some half-gallon milk cartons in Dr. Malevich's garbage. He lined them up on one of the ridges of dirt. They were supposed to be African natives now, spearing their enemies. Or lions.

"Ungawa!" they all yelled.

The cartons were hard to hit, though. The stakes weren't balanced right to throw. Dully, John remembered that he'd used the same kind of stake to make his sword. *Death is better than dishonor*. It seemed so stupid. He glanced down at his chest — it was sunburned now, but still sickly-looking — and wished he could put his shirt back on. But then he wouldn't look like a native.

"Where's your bow and arrows?" he asked Jackpot.

"Broke 'em," Jackpot said, showing his rotten teeth. He didn't seem to care. "All three of 'em."

"The arrows? Jeez, already?"

Jackpot shrugged.

I thought so, John thought. The dirt didn't look much like Africa, either. More like a reddish-yellow desert, striped by shadows and glare. His stomach felt queasy again. He saw how the bulldozers and scraped an angle from Rodley's Ford dealership north to the bridge over the river, bypassing the S turn on Highway 99. He remembered the big truck that had flipped over on that turn in the spring. That's where they all flipped over, after they lost their brakes on the long grade down from Mount Shasta City. This one had slid all the way off the road into somebody's front yard. It rested on its side in a haze of dust, some of its double wheels turning slowly, the surprisingly thin metal skin of the trailer torn open. John saw the driver climb out of the cab, a little blood on his forehead, and argue with a policeman who had just driven up. John was too far away to hear them, but he saw the driver step forward suddenly and throw his arms out. Then the policeman punched him in the jaw — *bang!*

Knocked him down.

Now John thought about how hard it must be to punch somebody in the jaw. In real life, not the movies. With his sweaty face moving and his jaw just a slippery point your fist had to hit if you didn't want him to hit back.

John wondered if *he* could do it. What he would need. Practice?

Clean living?

But his mother had been angry at the policeman, Mr. Brettschneider. "He had no right," she said. "The man was probably in shock. He might have been injured. Who knew? And Pete Brettschneider had his gun and his nightstick — it's not as if he was in any danger."

It was only when she spoke that John had remembered how much the driver's face, thin and yellow, had looked like Ronnie Knudson's.

His father had just said, "They ought to straighten out that damn turn. Brian down at the Texaco was telling me, one of those truck drivers told *him*, 'Mister, we hate to drive through your town.' At the bottom of the hill like that, no runaway lane, no place to bail out."

But how could anybody hate Dunsmuir?

Then he saw Freddie Ordoñez coming from the direction of Hughie's house. Freddie hesitated on the edge of the dirt, as if afraid to join them. His shadow stretched out. He had something in his right hand, the bright pink of mercurochrome. A squirt gun? John turned to wave him over before he disappeared again. He wanted to tell Freddie he was sorry... for leaving him back in the woods, for going along with the Jap business. He remembered how Hughie's face had looked when Gary squirted him with the hose. Had John made Freddie's face look like that? The same way

Gary's face had looked for a minute or two in the Hillers' kitchen? The way Cleo's face had looked when John stuck her with the dart? Or Annie's face when he claimed she hadn't caught the fish? Or Hughie's grandmother's face...

It all whirled together in that sick place in John's stomach. It was all his fault.

He remembered the truck driver's face at the moment the fist hit it.

"Hey!" he shouted.

John took two steps, and the next thing he knew he was running between the trees in Hughie's back yard, the low sun flashing through them like spokes. Later he would wonder if he'd set a world record for the 100-yard dash, with nobody there to click the stopwatch. What had happened to him seemed to unreel backward. He thought he saw, for the first time, Curly McPherson walking slowly up through the poison oak to his house, a gray-headed man in overalls, carrying a black lunch box. But he would never be sure he hadn't imagined it... Then he saw little Walt trotting after him for a while, looking gravely interested. Then Annie's shocked mouth, like an O. And finally the spear clattering away after it had stuck him in the leg.

Had it?

Then he was on the street. Then flying up the front steps to his house — as smoothly as on those escalators in Sacramento; his feet never seemed to touch.

24.

"It was Jimmy," Annie said, still breathless. "Jimmy Grissom did it."

"I don't know," John said. "I can't remember."

He knew he was in big trouble. He'd gotten hurt, and that meant a trip to the doctor, and that meant a doctor bill to pay. He was even dirtier now — his mother grimaced as she tried to pull off his jeans. And if Hughie's grandmother ever told her about what John had said, it would be twice as bad. His father might use the hairbrush then. A good thing Frank Hiller wasn't home yet. No truck.

"It's your fault as much as Jimmy's," his mother said. "Playing with such dangerous things… Johnny, sit still. At least take that darn gun belt off."

She unbuckled it and slid the jeans down to his knees. The hole was in the middle of his right thigh. There wasn't much blood — just what looked like yellowish lumps of fat inside. Around it, the skin was paler than usual, and faintly mottled.

"Would you look at this?" she said. "The point didn't even go through the cloth. Just sort of stuffed it down in there."

He was in trouble — but, he realized, he was safe, too. He'd gotten hurt; his mother wouldn't punish him on top of that. Not now, anyway. And she was still waiting for his father to return. Or call. *Something.* John sensed that her mind was mostly on that — not on his spear wound. Any other time, that would have bothered him — he was just a kid! He'd been stabbed! — but now it helped.

"Does it hurt?" his mother asked.

"It stings a little."

"I'll call Dr. Reed. I'm sure it's going to need stitches. And maybe a tetanus shot, too."

"Does *she* have to watch?" John said, meaning Annie. It embarrassed him, sitting in the living room in just his shorts.

"Oh, for Pete's sake," his mother said. But she told Annie, who pouted: "Go see what Tommy's up to." And then to John: "I'd better take you down there. Let me get some gauze."

"I can't go swimming again?" he asked.

"Probably."

He remembered when he was seven years old — they'd just moved from Sacramento Avenue — and he and his mother were walking downtown to buy the family's season ticket for the community pool next to the ballpark. It cost five dollars. She had stayed on the sidewalk while he cut across a vacant lot. He tripped over a root and fell on some trash and broken whiskey bottles. The hard clay scraped his right hand. It seemed on fire, unbearable. Crying, flapping it in the air to cool it, he ran to his mother, who looked at him with sudden intensity and grabbed the *other* hand, which hadn't hurt at all. Then he saw. His wrist gaped open; inside were red and bluish cords. His mother fumbled a handkerchief out of her purse — in seconds soaked with blood. He heard her breathing. "Hold it up," she said harshly. As in a dream, they were right across the street from Dr. Reed's office. She held his left hand up as they jaywalked; he was still flapping the right hand. In Dr. Reed's waiting room he felt dizzy, and wondered if they'd have to wait a long time on his maplewood chairs by the magazine rack, but the nurse knew right away they were in a hurry...

Now his mother taped the gauze to his leg and dialed Dr. Reed. When she was done, she said, "Put your shirt on," but she didn't ask why he'd had it off again.

* * *

Dr. Reed was ready for them. He used the same oddly curved needle and the same blue-black thread: three stitches in John's leg, the same as in the wrist. He said the same thing about swimming: "Not until we get those stitches out, at least. There's too much risk of infection. You've got the whole town swimming in there — no telling what kind of crud." Dr. Reed had a forehead as high as Dr. Chenoweth's, but instead of being smooth and impassive it wrinkled up like a sheet of corrugated roofing tin as his eyebrows lifted. He had a dry way of talking that made John's mother laugh. She liked Dr. Reed; he'd gone to Cal too. "That man has no bedside manner at all," she would say, "unless you're *really* sick." John liked him OK, except during physicals when Dr. Reed checked him with his shorts off. "Bag of worms," he'd always say, fingering John's left testicle. It hung lower than the right one, and seemed shriveled, and inside were the outlines of bluish things like those John had glimpsed inside his wrist. Dr. Reed never said what it meant. Just "bag of worms."

But this time, though John had to take his pants down, Dr. Reed didn't say it. He just leaned back, crossing his knees and lacing his hands over the top one, and amid the sharp smell of antiseptic and the gleam of his chrome-plated instruments, and asked, "How did this… ah, puncture happen?"

When John didn't answer, his mother said: "Playing African natives. I think."

"African natives." Dr. Reed nodded. "That'll do it every time."

* * *

Years later, his mother would tell John something else about Dr. Reed: how when Tommy had gotten so sick just after he was born — so sick he might die — Dr. Reed had broken down and wept in front of her. Still a youngish man, not so many years out of medical school, a Dunsmuir boy who had come back to practice in his home town. Connie Hiller had never seen a doctor cry before or since. She didn't blame him, as far as John could tell. She believed he'd done everything a doctor in Oakland could have done. And it wasn't exactly that he seemed to feel guilty about it, but from then on Dr. Reed took a special interest in how Tommy was getting along. He would often praise her: "You're doing a terrific job with him." She would protest that she wasn't doing anything any other mother wouldn't do. "Still," Dr. Reed would say.

Today all John noticed was how, before they left, Dr. Reed took his mother aside and spoke to her quietly, more like a friend than a doctor.

"How's Frank?" he asked.

She looked quickly at John to tell him: *Don't say anything.*

"Better, I think. It's an awful bruise. I —"

"I'd like him to come in and let me take a look at it again. At least before he goes back to work."

"That's the problem," Connie Hiller said. "They keep *calling* him. They won't let him alone to heal up. I wish —"

Dr. Reed frowned. "That's not good," he said. And it seemed to John that he was about to say something more — something bad about the Southern Pacific? — and changed his mind.

"Frank gets so *angry* about it," she said. "I can't help but worry."

"That's only natural," Dr. Reed said. But he spread his hands and shrugged as if to say nothing could be done. "Please. Have him get in touch."

John still held his breath, but that was all.

They drove home. His mother was silent; her hands gripped the wheel tightly. The sun had gone over the western mountains, but Girard Ridge still had a band of light on it. The air through the rolled-down windows was cooler. The hole in his leg didn't hurt much — it never would, even with the stitches in it. The sunburn on his chest was beginning to hurt more.

And there, in front of the house, as if it had never left, was his father's truck.

25.

Time sneaked up on Frank Hiller. It had seemed he had all day to stand and smoke and watch the switch engines in the yards put together a new train. Almost a hundred cars, with a second locomotive at the rear to help push them up the Cantara Loop grade. Tim Frulan's crew. Another of the old masters. After this freight headed north, Jamison would be second out... and it *was* Jamison he'd seen by the crew dispatcher, he knew now. No matter how blurred his sight had been. He had a lot of explaining to do to a lot of people — he was beginning to realize just how much. He wouldn't live this day down anytime soon, not in Dunsmuir.

Then he noticed thunderclouds moving in. The sun was already going over the crags. At this time of year there were still hours of twilight left, but you never saw a real sunset here, or a dawn; the canyon was too steep and narrow. In winter the shadows fell at 3 p.m. It was good country, Frank had thought when he first came — good hunting and fishing country — but the lack of sky had bothered him. The mountains seemed to close over his head... and never more than now, when his time had run out.

Trapped.

He had to call the Trainmaster. Right away, before Ross' office closed at five.

No way he could go back to the depot, looking like this. And there wasn't a pay phone he could use.

So he had to call from home, and that meant getting there the shortest and quickest way he knew. Straight up the highway through the middle of town.

He was tired by now, and ashamed of himself, as he'd known he would be when he first drove away from the front of the house. *Falling.* If Connie were with him now, he'd tell her how sorry he was. He felt like a fool — going off half-cocked like that, without a plan. But when he climbed onto the truck's seat, he discovered that his back had stiffened up, and the pain made him angry all over again. How had he managed to drive so far? How the hell could anybody expect him to go to work? Once he'd started up and shifted into second gear, he left it there — no more need for the clutch. He half turned to that his weight rested on the side of his right leg, on the edge of the bruise. That way the pain was steady, almost bearable. Up Florence Avenue again, past the stores: he tried not to see any of it. Behnke was still at the Texaco pumps. Neither of them waved. Frank passed the point where he'd turned down to the tracks and the river — completing a circle. He ached in new places, twisted sideways like this. He stank of sweat. On the seat, on the dash, the mirror, were spots of dried blood. Still chipping away at the boulder in his gut, piece by piece, he wondered: *What do I tell Connie and the kids?*

But Connie's car was gone.

And as Frank stumbled up the front steps, he was certain she'd left *him*. Children were shouting somewhere across the street, but the house was silent.

He burst in, panting.

Where did she go? Back to Oakland? She took the kids with her?

For he deserved it, he knew. He deserved to be left alone.

It was a terrible moment, but then Cleo surged up around his legs, barking, and in the back bedroom he found Annie and Tommy with a Dr. Seuss book.

"Where's your mother?" Frank asked.

"She took Johnny to the doctor," Annie said. "She said she'd be right back."

"Johnny? What happened to *him?*"

"Jimmy Grissom speared him. In the leg."

"Speared?" None of this made any sense. "But she's coming home?"

"We were playing natives," Annie said. Then she noticed the blood on his shirt, the swollen nose. "Where'd *you* go, Daddy?"

"Oh, nowhere." He started to wave the question away, but this was his little girl, bound to him by an unbreakable thread of brightness, not Behnke. What *had* he said to her when he left? "I had to go down to the yards. Had to check on things."

Tommy, too, was staring at him.

"I just hit my head on something," Frank said. "Had to stop too fast. Nothing to worry about."

He left them, found a clean T-shirt and put the bloody shirt into the hamper. Then he picked it out and tossed it into the trash. He never wanted to see the thing again, even if it could be cleaned. Cleo stayed alongside, nosing at him until he stopped to pet her. "You missed me, girl? Huh? You missed me?" She licked his hand. For some reason, it mattered a lot that Cleo was glad to see him. How could he have gone off without the dog? It was hard to imagine now.

His back kept stiffening. Frank checked his watch and the angle of the light. He shook his head and sighed, leaned his elbow against the wall of the hallway and dialed Ross.

He knew what to expect. The Trainmaster would accept his apology. But there would be a price to pay. Oh, yes. This was just the beginning.

What Ross said to him, again, Frank never told anybody.

But when he hung up, it seemed much later, the evening air darker, though he couldn't have been on the phone more than five minutes. He was breathing hard. Those dogs had never quit whining next door.

Cleo was beside him — and, surprisingly, so was Annie. Her eyebrows under the cowboy hat were level. Had she overheard? Or was she still mad at him from this morning?

"Look, honey," he began.

"Did you see it?"

"What?"

"Did you see me catch my *fish?*"

Had she caught one? *Damn.* He couldn't remember. She'd been standing up on that rock across the river when he turned away. Had it happened right then?

"You were there!" she said. "I saw you!"

"Sure I saw you," Frank said, but he wasn't sure if she believed him. "Saw you reel it right in there. A heckuva job."

"It's in the fridge. You've gotta see it. Mom said she's gonna cook it for me."

So he followed her into the kitchen and looked at the trout.

"What'd you catch it with?" he asked.

"Huh?"

"What bait?"

"A salmon egg."

Frank nodded. "Well, that's great." His voice sounded strained. He was afraid she could tell he was lying. In the refrigerator was a fifth of Old Crow; he dragged it out by the neck and poured himself a shot. It tasted good — took the edge off all his aches. *Damn.* Maybe that's what he'd needed all along.

"How old were you when you caught *your* first fish?" Annie asked.

"Older than you," he told her. "Don't worry. You're the champ."

But he didn't want to talk anymore. Not to anybody. He wanted another drink, and he would have poured one, maybe, if Connie's car hadn't pulled up outside.

26.

"Well, I called him," Frank said. "I'm going out. Damned if I know how, but I'm going."

"You… apologized to Mr. Ross?"

"I said so, didn't I? Isn't that what you wanted?"

"I wanted you *safe*," Connie Hiller said.

She didn't know what to think. His nose was cut. How had that happened? He had whiskey on his breath. He was still angry… but at least he was home.

Connie had been light-headed with relief ever since she saw the truck out front. Then Annie had run out and shouted, "Daddy's back!" It would have been enough to make her forget how Frank had been in the morning — except that he hadn't changed: He still seemed to be blaming her. *Isn't that what you wanted?* No, she thought. Not at all… but what *did* she want?

Now Frank was lying on his stomach again, on the bed. He had taken off his shoes but not the rest of his clothes. "You might as well," she told him — if he was going to work, he would have to wear overalls anyway. How soon would the crew dispatcher call him? He was second out now, apparently. But Frank only grunted — out of spite, or was he hurting so much? "Do you want me to put something on that cut?" she asked. "You should see Johnny's leg. I had to bandage that up. What a day! I should get my nursing license." She waited for Frank to smile at that, to say *something* that would make things easier, but he didn't, so she went into the kitchen to start dinner. Fried chicken. That was simple enough; the chicken was thawed already, and the children loved it. Connie knew that Frank didn't like chicken much, but she was angry enough herself — how she'd *worried!* She hadn't heard anything from him all day — not to care. String beans and corn on the cob. Those were simple too. But first, before the dew got to them, she had to take down the clothes she'd hung out back. She wouldn't even bother to fold them, she decided — just pile them in the basket. That would get her out of the house for a few minutes. Clear her head.

She wished she'd had time to take a bath.

Horses sweat. Men perspire…

"Go show your dad what happened to *you*," she told Johnny.

He gave her a frightened look, and she remembered what she'd thought an hour or two ago — that she hadn't protected him enough. But that thought was already fading. What harm could *this* do?

"Go ahead," she said. "Show him. Chin up."

* * *

John started changing the moment he saw the truck. All the strength went out of his arms and legs, as if the maroon paint and the dusty tires gave off a killer ray like kryptonite. His stomach lurched. It didn't matter how he'd felt lying in the fort, or swinging from that willow tree — how he'd dreamed about being brave. He couldn't help it now. He was in *big* trouble, with his safety gone — a coward and a sneak, tiptoeing up the steps, hoping his father was back in the bedroom, hoping he wouldn't ever come out.

Had Hughie's grandmother called?

Apparently not. Nobody said anything about that. And his father *was* in bed. Right away, John began planning: after dinner, how to slip past him to his own bedroom, shut the door, pull the covers over his head and pretend to be asleep.

But then his mother said, "Go show your dad what happened to *you.*"

He gave her a look — pleading with her — but it did no good.

His father lay on the bed in his brown slacks and a T-shirt. The Hawaiian shirt was gone. He was smoking a cigarette; as John peered in, he reached over the side of the bed and stubbed it into an ashtray on the floor. Cleo was there, curled up by his father's big shoes. *She loves him,* John thought. *Of course. She loves him the most.* It was dim in the room; his father's body threw a shadow on the wall, and seemed huge. John was still changing. For the first time since the spear had hit him, he felt dizzy. He might throw up.

Would that help, if he was *really* sick?

Frank Hiller raised his head. He said nothing at first — fishing another cigarette from a pack of Chesterfields beside the ashtray, striking flame from his silver Zippo, breathing in so that the end of the cigarette glowed orange. John had seen this so many times. Under the bitter smell of the smoke was a rank, heavy smell of grown man's sweat. John tried to look anywhere but into his father's eyes, but everything he did see — the muscles of his father's back, the creases of his neck, the dark-red scab on the side of his nose — only scared him more.

He wanted to run. But he was paralyzed.

"What's this about Jimmy spearing you?" his father asked.

"It was an accident."

"But you were doing something dumb, right? What'd he spear you *with?*"

"A stake. A wood one. From the freeway." John began to pull down his pants. If he had any safety at all, it was in *proving* he was hurt. "It's got three stitches."

"Never mind. Don't mess with that bandage."

John stopped, bent over.

"It doesn't matter. The *point* is, it was dumb. Goddamn it... *Look* at me. Whatever Jimmy did, it doesn't change the fact. Right? You weren't using your head."

John still couldn't look at him. The sickness rose from his stomach to his throat.

"Right?"

He pulled his pants up, but what good would that do? His father would grab him by the ear now, twist it so that it stung, and walk him into the bathroom where the hairbrush was...

But maybe this time, John realized, his father didn't want to get up. Maybe it would hurt *him* too much.

Lucky.

He let himself think, just for a moment, of what it would be like if his father were like Mr. Sykes. He could ask: *How'd you hurt your nose?* And they might even laugh together a little. At having both done dumb things on the same day.

But what if his father had been in a fight? Not with Mr. Grissom, but with somebody else.

Suppose he'd *lost?* John didn't dare ask.

Should he tell him about the arrowhead?

Instead, John heard himself say, "I saw Curly!", and saw by his father's face that he should have kept quiet.

"So?"

"He never… comes out. I never saw him before."

"He comes out every day, for Chrissake." His father shook his head in disgust. "At least your brother's got an excuse. What's yours?"

* * *

Was it possible to dislike your own kid? Frank Hiller wondered after John had ducked out of the room. He had never put the question to himself quite like that before, but once he did, he decided: *Yeah. Maybe.* It was a hell of a thing to say — he watched the cigarette smoke curl up in the air and form loops, as if it would spell out letters and words, tell him it wasn't so, of course it wasn't — but the boy was just too much like Ralph. For whatever reason, Frank couldn't help being bothered by it. The kid seemed to wear a "kick me" sign on his butt, and even when you didn't give in to the temptation, you were aware of having to resist it. And then when you *did* kick him, so to speak, you felt like shit. So wasn't that Johnny's own fault, in a way?

Frank didn't know.

Hell, getting speared... not that he'd tell Johnny about it, but Frank had done dumb stuff like that when *he* was a kid, and survived. The problem was Johnny himself — how to go on raising him, a boy he didn't understand, probably never would. And Tommy. How to shoulder the burden of them all, his whole family, after he'd nearly put it down.

Like eating potatoes. Nothing but potatoes.

That's how life was going to be, now that he'd called the Trainmaster.

No way out.

Connie was cooking now. Frying some chicken, by God. Frank could hear the sizzle in the frying pan; then he could smell it. She knew he didn't like chicken. *She's still pissed at me*, he thought. This was just her way of rubbing it in.

* * *

The fish on Annie's plate looked totally different now. Smaller. Her mother had rolled it in flour and fried it, so that its sides were crusty and brown. Its single eye was cooked white. She tried to remember how it had looked when it was alive and shiny, wiggling over the gravel. But she couldn't.

The fish was less than dead now. It was food.

"I almost fell off that rock," Annie said, and her mother, as always, took it wrong.

"You be *careful*. I don't know if I should let you... you're so young."

"*Mom.*"

Still, she was the only one at the table eating trout. Everybody else had chicken — and she could have chicken too, if she wanted. That made her special. They were watching her — jealous Johnny, and Tommy in his high chair. The vegetables steamed in their bowls. Her mother served them. Annie was just breaking the skin of the fish, trying to separate the tender white meat from the bones with her fork, when Cleo came out of her father's bedroom and barked. Then somebody knocked at the front door.

It was Jimmy Grissom.

* * *

He wore a white shirt and black slacks with suspenders. Connie Hiller had never seen either of the Grissom boys dressed up before. Jimmy's face was white too, against the dusk outside, the skin stretched tight over his cheekbones. His hair was wet and slicked straight back, so that it seemed as if he'd run wide-eyed through a strong wind. And just as if he'd run, he had no voice left. "My pa says... he already whupped me," Jimmy whispered. "He says... he says you can do what you want."

"Come in, Jimmy," Connie said.

"I'm sorry, ma'am." He didn't look at Johnny, who came up beside her with Cleo. "It was an accident."

"So we heard."

Jimmy shuffled his feet. "I gotta go to church soon."

"You don't want a bite? We've got plenty."

"No, ma'am. We already et. My pa says…"

"Oh, come on in, Jimmy. Sounds as if you've already been punished enough." She called in to the bedroom: "Frank! Jimmy Grissom's here. He came to apologize."

Frank grunted.

"I know you're tired and sore, but he's come all the way up here just to say he's sorry." The sympathy Connie had felt for Johnny was transferred now to this other little boy, who looked so guilty and woebegone, not like his brother at all.

Frank sighed and grumbled, but he finally came out.

"I guess he'll live," Frank said, meaning Johnny. "You play with sharp sticks, that's what happens. I told *him* it was dumb, and I guess Charley told you too, right?"

"Yessir."

"Well, what's more to say? You want something to eat?"

* * *

John was happy to see Jimmy — didn't blame him at all for being speared. All he could remember, still, was the stake falling away and Annie's startled face. Jimmy had made him safe, he thought — had taken the whipping for him. John remembered how Annie had walked bowlegged over to Dr. Malevich's, holding that

five-dollar bill; then how Mr. Grissom had tossed the
toolbox into the trunk of his car this morning, the
muscles like rawhide under his shirt. He must have used
a belt, John thought. A leather belt. Poor Jimmy. *He's
sorer than I am, probably.*

And now Jimmy was safe too, though he didn't
seem to realize it yet, edging over the worn linoleum
into the Hillers' kitchen. A bubble of safety surrounded
him wherever he went. "See the fish I caught?" Annie
said. Tommy was talking to himself, as usual. John's
mother was smiling. Cleo wagged her tail. And his
father, even, was trying to be nice, standing in the
doorway to the hall with his head tilted, giving off that
smell of whiskey and sweat. John had the sudden,
strange feeling that he was spying on his parents — as if
Jimmy had taken his place just when they decided to
show how good and kind they could be. He was proud
of them at that moment — proud of his whole family
— and jealous, too. Jimmy was somebody else's kid.
That's what made him safe.

"Where'd you catch it?" Jimmy asked.

"Down under the bridge," Annie said.

"I wish *I* could go fishing," Jimmy said, and John
wondered: *Hasn't he gone before? Don't Okies know how?*

"Clyde took me," Annie said. "Maybe —" She had
eaten most of the fish already, except for the head and
tail.

John said: "You want a drumstick?"

"Jimmy said he already had dinner," his mother
said. "But how about a little ice cream? We've got
Neapolitan."

CANYON

* * *

Connie Hiller was glad, too, that Jimmy had come. It was a chance for her to make up for getting upset at Gary at lunch. And it surprised her that Frank actually had come out, despite his pain, and talked to the boy. Been civil to him. It was what she'd been waiting for, she realized. The first sign of his old self. Connie warmed to him — now that he'd done what she wanted, called the Trainmaster, she could let herself feel all over again that what the railroad was doing to Frank was worse than wrong. It was criminal. *No wonder he was angry. Who could blame him?* She could forget, at the moment, that he still hadn't told her where he'd been most of the day, or how he'd gotten that cut on the side of his nose. *It's too much. What can they expect a flesh-and-blood person to stand?* A little of her headache had lingered all this time; now it faded at last. She moved toward him, bringing him a plate and a fork so he could eat standing up.

* * *

Annie had no doubt her father had seen her catch the fish. He'd said so, hadn't he? *You're the champ.* And it had tasted so good — especially the skin, with butter and salt on it. She only wished it had been bigger, and that Jimmy could have seen it fresh-caught. Then he would have been jealous too.

Jimmy looked so funny in his starched white shirt; with his hair combed back, the top inch of his forehead was a pale stripe above the tan. Annie was a little in awe of him. What was it like to spear a person, not just a milk carton? Only Jimmy knew. Annie was glad the spear hadn't hurt Johnny much. But why hadn't it stuck? That's what she wanted to know. If it made a hole like that, it should have gone right through his jeans and stuck in his leg, like the hook in the fish's jaw. Shouldn't it?

* * *

Frank Hiller had to respect Charley Grissom. He'd done the right thing, even if it was hard on the kid. That made it easy for him, Frank — he could let Jimmy off with just a word to the wise, and even grin, saying, "He should've kept out of the line of fire." Meaning Johnny. Going to church on Wednesday nights as well as Sundays — that was taking things to an extreme, as far as Frank was concerned. But maybe there was something to it. Those Grissom boys had been taught their manners; you had to admit that.

Connie had given Jimmy a dish of ice cream and tucked a towel in the neck of his shirt for a bib. Now she took the end of the towel and wiped the corners of his mouth. "There," she said. "Was that good?"

"Yes, ma'am." Jimmy shuffled again. "Thank you, ma'am... for everything. But I gotta go now."

"Well, don't let us keep you, Jimmy," Connie said. "Have a good time."

"Yes, ma'am... Sir."

Then Jimmy was gone, and the whole feeling in the house changed back to what it had been before. Frank stood holding the plate of chicken, corn and beans. He looked at the too-big living room with not enough furniture in it, a second-hand couch and a carpet with a worn spot in the middle; then he glanced back at the bedrooms with their unfinished walls. It made no sense to keep working on the house, but he knew he would anyway. They might not have to move for a year or two; the freeway project was so slow. And even though the house would have to be demolished — it was too high above the street to be jacked onto a mover's truck, even if he'd *want* to move the damn thing — he would keep hammering and painting on it. Like the sucker he was.

Twice today he had driven through downtown Dunsmuir and hardly recognized it. Now his own home seemed equally strange. He'd left it — in his mind, anyway. Left it for good. Now he didn't belong in it. But here he was.

Trapped.

Frank limped into the kitchen, where the kids froze with their spoons over *their* ice cream. Only Tommy was still happy, rocking in his high chair — and what a hell of a life *he* had waiting for him, Frank thought. A blessing Tommy had no way of knowing it. And Johnny. Frank fought against the idea that he didn't like the boy. A good student at least. Johnny got the grades... but then so had Ralph, and what good had it done *him*, all those straight As? Just a minute ago, joking with Jimmy, Frank had seen Johnny grin along with them. Brown-nosing. Frank hadn't been able to resist shooting him a look and seeing the grin die. Johnny *asked* for it. That was the truth. And you couldn't do that and survive in this life — not when somebody like Ross would be waiting for you. And there always *would* be a Ross, by God. That was the only exam that counted.

Frank ate his vegetables; he hardly touched the chicken. The greasy smell of it sickened him. He thought of an old family story: about Great-uncle Howard, who had joined the Klondike gold rush in 1898 and been stranded for the winter in a cabin on the Yukon, with snow up to the eaves and nothing but dried fish to eat. Howard Mullahy had eaten dried fish for six months straight; then he'd come home to Yuba City and never touched a fish again in his life. Frank could understand that. He'd *told* Connie about having to clean those coops... just as he'd told her the other stories, about the SP and the land they'd lost. All for nothing.

He left the plate on the drainboard. He opened the refrigerator and took out the bottle of Old Crow and poured himself another shot. *Damn.* Then he took the bottle and the glass with him, heading back to bed.

* * *

Frank didn't get drunk that night. Nor would he get drunk for more than twenty years to come. He would just drink a little more steadily than before. Connie would notice that the bottle in the refrigerator wouldn't last quite as long before another replaced it, but she wouldn't say anything; it wouldn't seem to matter. But in his fifties, his health would deteriorate. He would have his gall bladder removed at the SP Hospital in San Francisco; later he would lose part of his large intestine. Then he would drink more. By then he would be a conductor — as respected by the younger generation of brakemen as Jamison and Frulan had been by Frank's — though a conductor's job wouldn't be what it was: Computers would do more and more of the thinking and train crews would be controlled by radio from headquarters. Nor would Dunsmuir be the same. Interstate 5 would largely bypass the town. Stores on Florence Avenue would close, then stand vacant. (Time was, he would think, when you could stroll down that street and buy a Ford, a Dodge, a washing machine or a good suit of clothes; now you had to go to Redding or Yreka, fifty miles either way, to get such things.) The Commercial Garage, where Charley Grissom once worked, would collapse under snow and never be rebuilt. The population would dwindle. No longer needing a division point north of Roseville, the SP would pull out many of its facilities — the engine shops, the roundhouse. Frank, bored and restless, would do auditing work for his union — the old Brotherhood having merged into the United Transportation Union, just as the SP soon would be swallowed by the Union Pacific. Maybe management would hold that against him. Frank would think so. At any rate, his drinking would be noticed.

After his death, Connie would find a note, penned in his neat, firm handwriting on lined yellow paper. The end of it said: *I had to be Superman. That's what you all expected of me. I had to carry the full load, all the time. I just got worn out.*

* * *

Now she said, "Frank, are you sure…"

"What?"

"Are you sure this is a good idea?"

He was lying on the bed — where she had lain this afternoon and felt so miserable. A dim, sprawled shape, with a red dot from his cigarette. His glass clinked.

"You think it matters now?"

"If you have to go to work —"

"Oh, I *have* to. You made damn sure of that."

It was as if being nice to Jimmy Grissom had taken the last bit of goodwill Frank had in him. Now he was shutting Connie out again. *Your language*, she wanted to say but caught herself. *The children.*

"*I* made you…?"

"Isn't it enough I'm down on my knees? Those sonsabitches are getting away with it? Huh? Now I can't even take a drink — in my own goddamned house."

In the morning, when they'd argued, they'd done it alone, or tried to. Not anymore.

"Frank, please."

"What?"

"Will you *stop* it?"

"Down on my goddamn knees. And you don't even know what that means."

"Frank —"

"Just leave me *alone*, will you?"

So Connie Hiller did — again with that numb feeling as if Frank had slapped her full in the face. She returned to the kitchen: to the crusted dishes, the chicken bones, the basket of unfinished laundry. *Tobacco*

Road. Tommy had wet himself; she lifted him out of the high chair and took him to the bathroom and peeled off his pants and washed him and pulled on his pajamas while Cleo sniffed under the table for fallen scraps of food. "Shoo!" she told the dog, coming back with Tommy on her hip. He was falling asleep again. Boneless, his head on her shoulder. Johnny was in the living room, listening to the Lone Ranger. Annie helped her listlessly, passing plates.

Her despair came back.

The family's broken, Connie thought, even as she clutched Tommy to her.

27.

Earlier that day, John had been hypnotized by the pebbles and dirt in the back yard. Now it was the beige threads of the upholstery of one arm of the couch as he huddled next to the radio. And his skin. He looked at the pores on the backs of his hands, the pattern of the veins; it seemed strange, his skin, as if he'd never seen it before. As if it belonged to somebody else. Or some other kind of animal. He looked at the scar on his wrist; then he glanced down the neck of his T-shirt at his sunburned chest, by now almost as bright a pink as Freddie Ordoñez's squirt gun. The hole in his leg hardly hurt. It just ached a little, below the surface. But his chest stung. It felt hot. That was where the dizzy feeling seemed to come from — the fever — as he overheard his parents' voices.

John tried to listen to the radio, with the volume turned down: *From out of the pages of yesteryear*, and then, as the William Tell Overture faded, the pounding of horses' hooves, the roar of six-guns and the Lone Ranger's voice, as deep as a roll of thunder. It was the same as ever, and yet somehow different. For the first time in his life he was bored with the Lone Ranger; for the first time (with that part of his mind that stood off to the side and watched) he could tell halfway through how the story would end. With a kind of shock, he began to suspect that nothing bad could happen to the Lone Ranger because the story had been written that way, and he wanted to change the story. Give the outlaws a chance. Even the preview of next week's episode, which left the Lone Ranger in a terrible fix — *We got 'im covered, boys! Now let's just see who's behind that mask* — even that was a trick. For every week the Lone Ranger escaped.

Then, as the program ended, he heard real thunder. Just a grumble of it, off to the northwest. It wasn't close enough to make Cleo howl, but it bothered her, John could tell; he heard her feet clicking restlessly in the hall. "Here, girl," he called, and she came into the living room. "Good dog," he said and scrooched off the couch and sat on the floor beside her; he put his arms around her neck. "Good doggy," he chanted, the fever rising. Cleo trembled and whined. John told her he loved her — told her it was just a noise; it couldn't hurt her — but she was deaf to him now, lost to her fear, jerking each time the thunder came.

28.

"Frank?"

He had been lying on his stomach again for a while, and he felt better. The whiskey helped. He had heard another northbound freight moan up the canyon — that meant he was first out. When would the call come? He should sleep all he could. But as it turned out, he wouldn't sleep; the call wouldn't come until midnight, and by then the bruise would be rigid again; he would begin to suspect that his nose was broken. It would be a real chore to drag himself to work — Connie would have to drive him to the depot, as she'd done in those old days, the honeymoon. It would be as hard to climb the steel steps of the caboose as he could imagine, and nothing after that would be any easier.

But now Frank felt better, listening to the thunder and a few big drops of rain. The air was cool, comfortable. Connie came in.

"Frank, those dogs next door... Thelma's dogs. They're still barking. I've heard them all day, but we've just been so... distracted. It's like she hasn't *fed* them or something. Could there be something wrong?"

And when Frank spoke, it was in his normal voice. "Yeah, I heard 'em too, this morning. I wondered what was eating 'em. Maybe you ought to go check."

"I wish *you* would. It's dark... It's creepy over there."

"In the shape I'm in?"

He laughed — the same bitter sound he'd made that morning.

But the whiskey had soothed him just enough. He noticed the desperation in Connie's face, and it wasn't because she was afraid of the dark. No. She was offering this to him — the man's job. It wasn't that she couldn't do it herself.

"You were gone for *hours*," she said. "This is just next door."

Leaving home had given him power over her — over all of them. He saw that. It was why he had felt so good driving off in the truck, despite the shame of it. *Now, damn it, maybe you'll listen. Just once.* If he'd gone clear to Mexico, disappeared, they'd be paying attention forever. Even Ross might have felt bad about it, a little.

Sonsabitches.

Now the only power he had was to stay here, sulking, like a kid who didn't want to get out of bed on a cold morning and go to school.

And that was stupid, Frank felt now. That was childish. Even though he would never get justice from the Southern Pacific, and Connie would never come to him the way he wanted, with her hair unpinned and tears flowing — climbing into bed with him, murmuring, touching him softly and taking the pain away. Those days were over. Yet it had taken guts for Connie to come to him at all, he saw, after the way he'd snarled at her. To ask him — to offer him his place in the family back.

Togetherness.

Because that's what she was doing. Wasn't she?

It was time to knock the next chip off the boulder inside him.

"Well, OK, Mouse," he said. "Just hold on a minute. Let me put on my shoes."

He heard her sigh in relief.

Frank groaned as he swung his feet to the floor. Between thunderclaps he could hear Thelma Hoffman's dogs. Connie was right. They were going crazy over there.

"You ought to take a flashlight," Connie said.

He ignored her — the last of his defiance — even though he knew it was a good idea. He couldn't see well where he was limping through the back yard, through all that dogshit. The air smelled of ozone, though the thunder was fading now and the raindrops were widely spaced. The edge of the storm, nothing more. He turned between the houses and felt something squish under his left shoe. *Damn.* He climbed the creaky side steps to Thelma Hoffman's porch and paused. No light. He knocked on her door. There was no answering voice, but a flurry of animal sounds: yips, whines, the scrape of claws, the thud of little bodies trying to break through the wood and reach him.

"Thelma?" he called.

Nothing. Nothing human, anyway.

The door was unlocked. Frank turned the knob and pushed. It gave way; the dogs scrabbled in a frenzy, and a cat flashed out at his feet.

"Thelma? You there?"

Still no answer. Frank went in, and most of what happened next John would have to imagine, just as he would imagine so much of this day — what went on in his mother's mind, his sister's. All John would know for sure was that his parents argued twice; in between, his father drove off for hours; he came home with a cut and swollen nose. Then he went back to work, though the terrible bruise from the derailment hadn't healed yet. John would remember certain events: He got speared. Annie caught a fish. He would remember *fear*, if not the reasons for it. For what did his father do to him, after all? Nothing, or almost nothing.

We never asked you to be Superman.

When his mother discovered that note among his father's papers, John would still be "finding himself" after Vietnam, just as Ronnie Knudson had done after Korea.

Did we?

* * *

What John would imagine is this: His father went into Thelma Hoffman's living room. It was dark, with the shades and curtains drawn. He couldn't find a light switch. The dogs swirled around him; the cats whipped in and out of his vision. He could feel something crunch on the hardwood floor underfoot. More turds? Dried dog food? Corners of furniture bumped him, and there was a powerful smell — the day's closed-in heat and spoiled canned cat food and unwashed clothes and rotten wood and stove grease and old-lady mustiness, all at once. A faucet dripped. Frank followed that sound. His eyes were still adjusting to the dark; the air seemed to swarm, as if bugs or even bats were circling his head. *I needed that flashlight after all, by God.* In what had to be Thelma's dining room, there was a table with her typewriter and stacks of papers on it, and a window shade raised enough to show an inch of outdoor light. He used that light to lift the shade, and then he saw the switch at the entrance to the kitchen. That was where the faucet was. Still dripping. Plink, plop, plink. Frank turned on the light. The dogs barked louder — he could see them now: a dachshund, a Yorkie mix and a couple of Scotch terriers — and then he saw Thelma. She was lying on the kitchen floor, squares of gray linoleum, on her back with one knee raised, so he could see her fat leg with its purple varicose veins. She was wearing an old blue bathrobe, as if she'd just gotten up in the morning; she must have been trying to make a phone call when the stroke or whatever it was had hit.

Thelma had dragged the phone down with her as she fell. The receiver was on the floor, beeping along with the faint sounds she must have been making all day.

29.

"Creepy, all right," Frank said.

He was breathing hard again, John saw. He had called Frenchy Rubidoux's ambulance service from Thelma Hoffman's phone, and in ten minutes Frenchy had driven up from the south end of town. Frank had tried to help lift Thelma onto a stretcher and carry her down to the street, but his back hurt too much; Frenchy and his partner had had to do it all. Now Frank stood beside Connie and the kids in the flashing red light. She was talking to nobody in particular:

"She had such a hard time. I could cry. Remember when Thelma's mother was still alive? She was out of her head — she must have been eighty-five — and she'd just *curse* Thelma, like a sailor, and Thelma never complained, just took care of her all those years until she died. Do you remember?"

John didn't.

"We'd just moved in... Just *cursed* her. I'll never forget it. Of course, the old lady didn't know what she was saying. But for Thelma... She was really fond of you kids. I hope you know that."

John hadn't known. All he knew about Thelma Hoffman was the fuzzy slippers, the tall glasses of iced tea (or whatever it was) and the smell of dog poop. This new fact about her didn't fit. Now she was dying — everybody felt that, though she was still alive when they slid her into the ambulance. John couldn't see much — just her mottled bare feet and the curve of a cheek. She had a blanket over her.

Quite a crowd had gathered by then. None of the Grissoms — they were in church. And no Curly McPherson. But all three of the Sykes kids were there, with Mrs. Sykes, looking shy or dazed as usual, hanging back. Clyde came with Mrs. Knudson, a bony woman holding an unbuttoned red cardigan over her shoulders. Mrs. Ordoñez came with Freddie and his sisters, Nicole and Juana. The two Lorenzo kids, Paul and Vickie, came, with their perfect skin and long-lashed eyes. Paul couldn't have seen any more of Thelma Hoffman than John had, but he was already concocting the story that would make the rounds of the neighborhood in the next few days:

When they found her, she was all swoled up, and she was purple. She'd already started to rot. Those dogs, they got so hungry, they'd started to eat on her. Swear to God! They chewed off part of one of her arms. She couldn't move. She just had to lie there and watch 'em eat her…

None of this was true, John knew. But in time he would half believe it anyway. It was a better story.

Now some of those dogs were out in the street. Cleo had joined them. They sniffed one another's noses and hind ends; they ran in circles. They acted glad to be outside — just as the people watching the doors of the ambulance slam shut were glad to be alive and well, not like Thelma. The Hillers, especially, were horrified that Thelma had lain so long only a few yards from them. Helpless. Making those little mewing sounds, which nobody had heard. In the days to come, John would think: *All that time I was digging the hideout*, and Connie would think: *When I got to the end of the line there, hanging clothes, I thought about checking on her. Why didn't I?*

The guilt would linger. *Those dogs. They were trying to tell us something, and we didn't listen...*

But right now, John would remember, the Hillers were happy.

The storm had passed. The clouds were gone. The rain had only speckled the ground, but it had released all the smells of the dirt, the scent of the pines and firs and cedars above the cutbank. The air was sweet. The beauty of the country — *their* country — came home to them then. It was part of the awe they felt at what had happened to Thelma. It blew over them like a wind, clean and cool; it made their own problems seem trivial, at least for the moment. Wasn't that true?

Yes. That's what John would remember, anyhow.

As the ambulance drove away, its siren wailing, and the rest of the crowd drifted off, the Hillers still stood there. They looked up (as if they had compass needles in their heads; as if they were Indians) and were surprised. Though it had already seemed like night indoors during the storm, and though the lower ridges, sawtoothed with tree-shapes, were dark, the big mountain, Shasta, was still half-lit against a greenish sky.

The Hillers breathed in. John could hear them — he could hear himself. Then they breathed out. He thought he glimpsed Hughie's grandmother starting to work her way up through the dimness of her yard, past the blackberry patch, and he edged closer to his parents — staying out of the old witch's sight — just as his father put a hand on his mother's shoulder and said, "I'm sorry, Mouse."

Frank Hiller did say that.

John would swear by it, though by then he was truly feverish. His mother reached out to hug Annie, who had taken off her cowboy hat for dinner but had put it back on. The black brim buckled between them. His father encircled him, John, with an arm so strong, so thick and banded with muscle, that neither Mr. Grissom nor anyone else in the world had a chance of whipping him. Not in the world. They all squeezed together. Sweat, perfume, detergent, chicken, dog poop from somewhere. His father's shoe? John looked down. Then they all looked up again. The lower slopes of Mt. Shasta had turned the color of ashes; the tops of the cones were rose and orange and violet, the glacial ridges knife-edged in shadow. The arrowhead whispered from its shelf. The curved patch of snow still asked its question, and for that moment, at least, John felt he knew the answer. *Were they a family?* Of course they were.

FLUCY

by

Michael Harris

For Jackie Cotton

1.

She thinks it's her name. Everyone has always called her that.

So when her kindergarten teacher, calling the roll on the first day of school, says, "Jessamyn Colton?", she doesn't raise her hand and say, "Here!" There must be another Colton in the class.

When the teacher finishes saying all the names and the girl still hasn't heard hers, she feels puzzled, then frightened. Is she in the wrong room? The wrong school? All she knows is that she doesn't dare speak up.

She bends low over her desk, hoping, as always, that nobody will see her.

"No Jessamyn? Then who —?" the teacher says, counting the rows of pupils quickly with a forefinger, glancing down at her attendance book.

The girl rests her cheek on the dark-brown wood and gazes out the window. A wall of something almost as dark and brown has been building in the sky all morning, hiding the mountains. "Like a dust storm in Oklahoma," Mama would say. But this isn't Oklahoma. This is San Bernardino, California, and the stuff in the air isn't dust, Mama says, but dirt. What's the difference? It makes her older sister, Rose Ellen, cough all the time.

She thinks she can smell the dirt through the glass. It isn't a dusty smell, sure enough — it's sharper, stinging her nose, like gasoline. She breathes it in along with the smells of chalk and varnish and floor wax, the cedar of the freshly sharpened pencil in its groove on her desk, the red rubber of the eraser. Her own sudden sweat.

The silence in the room seems to last a long time. Through the dirt in the air, the sun glows an angry copper color, like the bottom of one of Mama's pans, so bright she has to close her eyes.

When a hand touches her shoulder, she jerks and almost screams.

"Whoa, there! Take it easy," Mrs. Macpherson says, recoiling a little herself, then laughing, as if she has touched a spider that turned out to be harmless. "Are you Jessamyn?"

The girl blushes furiously.

"Well? Are you?"

"No, ma'am."

"You *have* to be, dear. You're the only one left on my list."

The girl's eyes, a very pale blue, look right, left, everywhere but back at hers. Mrs. Macpherson wonders: Is this a retarded child they've given her?

"Come on, now. Are you sure you aren't Jessamyn Colton?"

The girl licks her dry lips and nods. "Colton."

"Yes?"

"But not... Jess. What you said. My name is Flucy."

"Flucy? What kind of name is that?" Mrs. Macpherson says.

And instantly regrets it.

Just ten minutes into the school year, and already this child has been singled out. *The girl so dumb she forgot her own name.* The freckled boy across the aisle smirks. The girl two desks behind, with blonde braids, covers her mouth. Some kid in the back row stifles a hoot. All at once, the first-day jitters and shyness whoosh out of the class like air out of a punctured tire — after seventeen years of teaching, Mrs. Macpherson doesn't have to look; she can feel it. Their relief. Here's someone even worse off than they are — someone they can pick on.

It happens so easily, so quickly — and once it *has* happened, there's often nothing she can do about it.

"That's just a nickname, dear. Isn't it? Flucy has to be your nickname."

But what a strange one! It sounds coarse and malicious. Like *floozy*. Who would saddle an innocent child with that?

"No, ma'am."

"You sure?"

The girl, close to tears, nods again.

No, not retarded after all, Mrs. Macpherson decides. Just uncommonly bewildered. But why? Is it possible that this child has never been told who she is?

Mrs. Macpherson has seen some strange cases in those seventeen years, but nothing quite like this.

Yet she can't waste any more time with her. She has another thirty-one of the little devils to ride herd on. Ever since Pearl Harbor, when servicemen started pouring into California, and workers for Kaiser Steel, building ships and airplanes, the elementary schools have been jammed. If anything, it's worse now, two years after V-J Day. Okie kids, Mexican kids, Negro kids, white-trash kids from neighborhoods like Waterman Gardens, where families live in Quonset huts. Once they come and find out it doesn't snow here, they never leave. They stay on, with jobs or without, and have babies. As for this poor girl, she's clean, but it looks as if her parents scrubbed her with a wire brush, and they couldn't — or wouldn't — even buy her a new dress for opening day; the one she wears, faded red-and-green plaid, is obviously a hand-me-down.

"Well, let's talk about it later, OK? I'll mark you 'present' for now. Don't worry." She smiles at the girl, turns and raises her voice. "All the rest of you settle down."

Returning to the front of the room, Mrs. Macpherson is about to write her own name on the blackboard when she yields to an impulse.

"You know," she tells the class, "there's a famous writer named Jessamyn West. Just last year she wrote a book called "The Friendly Persuasion," which you'll all probably read when you get older."

Her intentions, she would swear, are only the best. But the result is to shift everyone's focus back to the girl, who blushes again and droops her head.

A skinny little girl with an uncombable tangle of sun-bleached hair, so that she reminds Mrs. Macpherson of a dandelion gone to seed. Scabs at her knees and elbows, and what look like bruises, vivid blue finger marks, on her frail upper arms. Where did *those* come from? Who can say? These Quonset-hut kids run wild, fall off their bikes, scuffle in vacant lots, throw rocks at one another, do cruel things to animals, all the time making an infernal racket. With people like that, what else can you expect?

2.

One hot September afternoon in 1952, the year she turns eleven and starts the fifth grade, she has a headache. It gets worse and worse, as if the sun is pounding a nail into her skull.

She should ride her bike straight home from school and rest. The Coltons have long since left Waterman Gardens; home now is a rented frame house on Fourteenth Street. But no rest is waiting for her there, only chores — her own chores and the chores her big brother, Spike, makes her do for him. If she doesn't, he'll beat her up. She'd rather ride free as long as she can — to swim at the plunge at Perris Hill Park in Highland, or, on this day, visit a new friend who lives in a nicer neighborhood. It isn't going to last, this friendship — she knows that, even expects it. Her own clothes, next to Patsy's, are shabby, and right from the beginning Patsy's mother seems suspicious of her — this skinny, painfully shy girl whose hair hangs down over her face. But, like diving into the pool, the time she spends playing in Patsy's back yard, on Patsy's swing set, is sweet.

If only her head didn't hurt so much today. She feels faint. The brown dirt in the air — people have started calling it "smog" — seems to swirl inside her eyeballs, making everything blurry.

Patsy's mother comes out the sliding glass door from the kitchen with glasses of milk, starts to hand them to the girls, then reconsiders and sets them on a patio table, out of reach. She peers closer. "Jessie, isn't it? Are you sure you're feeling OK? You don't look so good."

"Yes, ma'am."

"Do you have a fever?"

"No, ma'am."

"I think you do." Patsy's mother, who is small and dark-haired and pretty, like Patsy herself, reaches out a hand, then withdraws it. "You're as red as a tomato. I don't even want to touch you, honey. I think you're sick. You'd better go home." She squeezes her lips together. *"Right now."*

So the girl leaves, gazing longingly at the milk as she passes the table. It looks so cool. But Patsy's mother follows her eyes and says, "No, I don't want you using our glassware."

Patsy, who wears black patent-leather Mary Janes with white socks, doesn't say anything, doesn't even look at her. The girl knows she isn't a friend anymore. Just like that. Patsy has to protect herself now. If her mother is anything like Mama, she's about to get whipped for bringing sickness home.

MICHAEL HARRIS

Patsy said nobody whips her, but who can believe that? They must be sneaky about it — do the whipping when nobody is around to see and hear.

No, it was bound to end sooner or later, the girl thinks as she wobbily pedals home through the heat, and her being sick is probably just an excuse for Patsy's mother to do what she was going to do anyway — get rid of this kid from the wrong side of town.

For the girl *is* sick, not just miserable. She feels faint again. Good thing it's downhill from Patsy's house to Fourteenth Street, so she can coast most of the way.

Inside the house, it seems even hotter.

Rose Ellen lies on the couch, fanning herself with a movie magazine. Her skin is pale because she so seldom goes out. Just this year, at fourteen, she has grown breasts, which look strange because the rest of her is still childlike and undeveloped — or is it just that Mama doesn't seem to approve of them? "Just watch," Mama keeps saying. "Big tits'll draw trouble like suet draws flies." Either way, those breasts embarrass everybody.

"You're late, Flucy. Why don't you open the windows? Mama'll be here any minute."

The girl may be Jessie at school now, but at home she's still Flucy.

"No, she won't. It isn't even five yet." Mama won't come back from her job at Thrifty Drug until six, expecting all the housework to be done. "Why didn't *you* open 'em? Are you *that* lazy? Where's Spike?"

"Outside somewhere." Rose Ellen sits up, holding the magazine flat against her chest. Then she rises slowly to her feet, groaning. "I don't feel too good today, Flucy. You know how I get when it's a hundred-plus and the air's all cruddy like this." As if to prove her point, Rose Ellen coughs, which is both real and fake, Flucy thinks. Her sister *does* have asthma — has had it all her life — but she can make it seem worse whenever it suits her.

"So? I'm sick too. You better help me."

She bangs open the windows, sweeps, dusts, mops and vacuums. Rose Ellen follows her from room to room, helping almost in spite of herself, because the fear is on them now. Why didn't they do the chores earlier? Every afternoon, for some perverse reason, they cut it as fine as they can. When the faintness hits her, like a dull blow to the back of her neck, she has to lie down for a minute or two on the double bed she has shared with Mama ever since Daddy left. Then she hears a *thump, thump, thump*, like her pulse, which brings the headache back. Spike! He's throwing a tennis ball at the side of the house, catching it on the rebound with his baseball glove.

Flucy leans out the window. "Stop that!" The ball has left dirty smudges on the siding, knocked off flakes of yellow paint. She almost adds, *Daddy's gonna kill you*, but Daddy is gone, and Spike grins — he's always able to read her mind. And from then on, whenever she goes to another room, he follows her. *Thump, thump, thump*. Leering in at her with his crooked teeth and scarred forehead like a jack o'lantern or a Frankenstein mask.

Of course, she *would* be lying down again at the moment Mama arrives.

"Flucy, get your lazy butt out of bed! Is the table set for dinner? Doesn't look like it to me. And what about the front lawn? It still looks like hell. Spike?"

Mama's blue eyes and red hair blaze. She is tall and beautiful, though her chest is almost as flat as Flucy's, and rawhide-strong, even after an exhausting day at work. She hardly stops to glare at them, kick off her shoes and rub her bunioned feet before she's in the bathroom, knocking around for the hairbrush.

Daddy used his belt, or willow switches from the Santa Ana River bottom.

"I feel sick, Mama," Flucy says, hardly able to stand back up. Can't Mama tell just by looking at her? Rose Ellen doubles over, coughing — for real this time; fear works on her lungs just as smog does.

"You think you're sick now? Well, you're gonna be a whole lot sicker in a minute." Mama's sweat stains the armpits of the white smock she wears at Thrifty; her voice rises to a screech, like a dentist's drill. "*Spike!* You little shit, get in here! If I have to go out there and drag you in by the ear, it'll be ten times worse."

Oh, why didn't they get all the chores done? It's too late now.

Yet it *could* be worse, Flucy thinks dully. Her sickness numbs her to the blows of the hard plastic brush, which will leave knots and bruises on her arms and back. Mama *is* tired, and without Daddy there to help her corral the three of them, she grabs whichever kid she can and lashes out blindly, then grabs another. Rose Ellen, as always, manages to get the least of it. Spike, even howling with pain, darts Flucy a look she understands perfectly: *If you think this is bad, just wait till I get hold of you. This is all your fault.*

Finally Mama flings down the brush with a clatter on the kitchen floor and stands flushed and panting. "Is it too much to ask? To come home to a neat house? I work my butt off all day to put food on the table, and then there's no table ready to put it on, and the place looks like a pigpen. Huh? Is that too much? Just a *little* help from you all? Spike? Flucy? How about you, Miss Hollywood? Huh? God damn it, answer me. *Is that too much to ask?*"

They are panting too, and too sore to speak. For Flucy, the guilt stings even worse than the pain. Isn't Mama right? Daddy has left them; he lives across town somewhere. The walls of this house are nicked and chipped by things he and Mama threw at each other, and at least a little blood has been shed in every room, but now that he's gone, Mama should have no reason to be angry anymore — as long as they, the kids, do their part. So why don't they? Why can't they live, as Mama says, like civilized people, not like the scrapings of the manure pile?

Sleeping beside Mama — and as deeply as she ever sleeps, Flucy is never unaware of her, just inches away — she dreams of weird black stick men who dance against a white background, as blank as nothingness itself. In the morning the headache is back, worse than ever, and her neck is so sore and stiff (though Mama didn't hit her there) that she can hardly lift her face off the pillow. When Mama calls her to breakfast, she can't get up.

Mama storms back into the bedroom. "Get your fat ass out of bed, Flucy. I haven't got time to mess around in the mornings. You know that."

It's only when she sees that Flucy has to roll slowly out of bed sideways and prop herself, trembling, with her hands on the floor that Mama's expression changes.

"Jesus. Maybe you're sick after all. I'd better take you to a doctor."

But what *is* Mama's new expression? Flucy has learned how to judge her parents' and Spike's moods to a hair, but this one is different. Is Mama angry that she'll have to call Thrifty and miss half a day's work, lose money? Or is this one of those rare and wonderful moments when Mama will feel sorry for her and say she loves her in spite of everything? That's almost too much to hope for, though Flucy hopes anyway.

No, this is different. If Flucy didn't know better, she would say her mother is *scared*. But Mama has never been scared, even when Daddy got drunk and yelled so all the neighborhood could hear that he was going to kill her, the Devil's redheaded bitch.

Yet she sees the same expression on Dr. Goodman's face — a long, pink face with a bristly yellow mustache like one of Daddy's shaving brushes — after he examines her.

First she has to strip to her underbritches and lie on her stomach on the doctor's cold metal table, in the chill of the air conditioning. A nurse covers her with a sheet, but not before Dr. Goodman has noticed her bruises. He frowns and glances over at Mama, who answers so smoothly — "You know how these kids are.

Tumblin' all over the place like monkeys" — that it seems to Flucy that her mother, just for that moment, has managed to make herself believe it. The doctor seems to believe it too. So is it true after all? Flucy can't think — her head hurts too much.

"Never mind that," Dr. Goodman says, as if they have more important things to deal with here. He hums tunelessly, taking a shiny metal hammer with a rubber head and tapping Flucy's knees and elbows. They don't respond. He frowns again. He tickles her under her arms, but she doesn't jerk or giggle. He turns her over onto her back and tickles her stomach with a wooden tongue depressor. Still nothing. The doctor stops humming. He slides his stethoscope under the sheet, an icy touch at her heart.

"I know there's probably nothin' the least wrong with her," Mama is saying, "and I shouldn't have come botherin' you, but the way she was this morning — it gave me the creeps."

"No, you did the right thing," Dr. Goodman says.

He and Mama move away, so that Flucy sees them blurred, out of the corner of her eye. They talk for a long time — it might be only ten minutes, but it seems like an hour. Their voices seem blurred as well. Flucy tries to read their lips, but the slightest turn of her head sets it to pounding. The walls are the same empty white as in her dream.

Mama and the doctor come back. Mama's brilliant blue eyes are red-rimmed now. She grabs the girl's hand to comfort her — or perhaps to comfort herself. Dr. Goodman looks straight at Flucy and speaks. Some of his words are long medical ones that confuse her, but one word she recognizes, and it's enough:

Polio.

Flucy knows what polio is. It means death, or worse. Life on crutches or in a wheelchair, or less than life in an iron lung.

The most frightening thing is that the grownups seem just as scared as she is. Once the word has been said, Mama drops her hand as if it's poisoned. And that's when Flucy sees that the expression on Mama's face is on the doctor's, too. As it was on Patsy's mother's face yesterday afternoon.

All of them, terrified of *her*.

Flucy thinks of the religious people who some-times come to the front door with tracts — Mama just scoffs at them — and talk about *pestilence*, like the the plagues that struck Pharaoh's Egypt in the Bible: the blood, the locusts, the frogs, the boils, the deaths of the first-born. At school they have started having air-raid drills, though Daddy, who used to be in the Army, told her once that radioactive fallout from the A-bomb, silent and invisible, would kill them all anyway. God's punishment for their sins or a nightmare out of the new scientific age? Polio is both.

"She's been sleeping with me lately," Mama says hesitantly, not looking at Flucy. "In the same bed, I mean."

Is it just Flucy's imagination that the doctor edges a little away from Mama?

Dr. Goodman issues instructions: Mama must drive Flucy immediately to St. Bernardine's Hospital and drop her off at Ward D. Then she must go home and stay there. Period. Forget Thrifty. The Colton family will be under quarantine.

Flucy knows St. Bernardine's, a massive building she passes every time she bikes to the pool. It looms up through the smog, wavering in the heat — what a difference from the doctor's office! But Mama doesn't park in front. She drives around to the rear of the hospital, on a potholed gravel road, every jolt of it a fresh agony, between rows of Quonset huts like the one they lived in at Waterman Gardens.

This is Ward D.

"My God," Mama says. "Will you look at that."

It's clearly another kind of quarantine — for people so diseased and dangerous even the regular hospital won't let them in.

Mama stops the car, shuts off the engine but doesn't release the wheel. She leans her head on her hands.

"I'm callin' your father," she says finally. "I know I *told* the sonofabitch he'd never hear from me again, I wouldn't beg him for one single, solitary dime, but this is different. This is just too much. How can he expect me to make ends meet if I can't go to work?" She looks at Flucy as if the girl is supposed to answer.

This is all your fault.

"Well, go on," Mama says.

Flucy pushes open the heavy door, steps out of the car and discovers that the last of her strength is gone. She topples face first. She'll skin her hands and knees — she can feel it before she hits the gravel, feel her palms sting, old scabs rip open and blood run down her shins — but at the last instant somebody catches her. A thin Negro man in white — he looks like one of the stick figures in her dream — has come out of the nearest hut. His forehead knots in concern. He has a mustache too, darker than Dr. Goodman's, and very white teeth. Flucy finds herself suspended in air.

And then a second miracle happens. Mama has dashed around the car in no time at all; she's right beside Flucy now, holding her by the waist. "I got her now," Mama hisses at the man. You can just take your dirty hands off her. Who do you think you are?"

"I'm a nurse," the man says.

"Like hell you are." Mama yells at the other people who have came out behind him: "Hurry up, for Chrissake! Can't you see my baby's sick?"

Yes, Mama is holding her, as Flucy always wished she would. Kissing her and stroking the hair out of her eyes.

It feels so good. She can relax now. Go ahead and faint. It doesn't matter. All her weight hangs from their arms, like Jesus hanging from the nails of the Cross on the covers of the religious visitors' tracts, but she knows they won't let her fall. She sees a flash of sun, a rippling red cross painted on beige corrugated iron. She smells the black man's sweat, Mama's familiar skin and Mama's perfume; she hears Mama's voice telling the nurses and doctors that this is her precious baby girl and they'd better take good care of her or she'll sure as hell know the reason why not.

3.

When she revives inside the Quonset hut, it's cool again. Mama is gone, and so is the black man. Women in ghostly uniforms and gloves surround the stretcher where she lies. They help her to sit up, then, shakily, to stand. They start peeling off her clothes. "All these'll have to be boiled," one says, tossing her blouse into a hamper. Another flings her shoes into a garbage bin. "We'll burn those."

Flucy tries to speak, but her lower lip quivers.

"Look at me, kid," says a tall nurse with a puffy face, who seems to be the boss. "We got no choice. Anything that can't be boiled gets burned. It's the only way to kill the germs."

Then, as if the girl were a sack of spuds, they hoist her up and drop her naked into a galvanized tub of hot, soapy water. Half a dozen nurses converge on her and scrub her savagely with brushes and rags, as if she hasn't ever had a bath before — as if Mama and Daddy haven't been fanatics for cleanliness all her life.

"You'll need two complete scrubbings," the puffy-faced nurse says. They lift Flucy out red and dripping, put her into a second tub and repeat the process, until her skin feels raw, her eyes smart and her nose is full of steam and the smell of disinfectant.

They dip her into a third tub — the water just as hot but clean. Then they perch her on a tabletop and pat her down with the thickest, whitest towels she has ever seen.

All at once, unexpectedly, Flucy is cold. The nurses dress her in a backless hospital gown, but it's no shield against the conditioned air that fans are blowing through the ward; the sheet over the steel gurney they lay her on next can't prevent her from getting goosebumps. Soon she's shivering so hard that it takes her a little while to notice something else:

Her headache is gone.

The nurses, for their part, realize that she's cold. Brusque as they seemed to be during the bath, they aren't really mean, Flucy decides. They aren't *trying* to hurt her. They spread a thick, scratchy wool blanket over her and tuck it underneath. And as they wheel her down the corridor, she looks around with a new feeling — not so much fear as curiosity. This is the first time she has been in a hospital. Always before, when a relative or a friend of the family went in for surgery or had a baby, she was too young to come along. It's an interesting place, she thinks — spotlessly clean, electric with energy, bustling with people, all there to take care of *her*. She doesn't have to do anything, any more than she did when the black man caught her in mid-air. She can let go and drift, growing warmer, into what feels less like fainting than like ordinary sleep.

When the gurney stops rolling, it's in one of the little rooms on the ward. The girl wakes up. Her headache is coming back — the cold must have knocked it out, but not for long. And here's the black man, who must really be a nurse, looking sterner now, not showing his teeth. "Let me lift you up here," he says, indicating a bed that stands much higher off the floor than normal. Except for a nightstand and a straight chair, it's the only furniture.

Flucy wonders if his feelings were hurt by what Mama said. "If you grew up nose to asshole with niggers like I did in Oklahoma, you'd understand," Mama has told her often enough, but this man, she's sure, was only trying to help. *Sorry*, she wants to say, but he might not understand. His hands aren't dirty, just dark, with big veins in them, and pale palms. And stronger than you'd think from his skinny build — she knew that already. He turns down the covers on the bed and lifts her off the gurney as if she weighs no more than a bag of feathers.

"Now, you stay on this here bed and you never get off," he growls. "You hear that, girl? Your feet must *never touch the floor.* Got that?"

Flucy nods, which worsens the pounding.

Yes, the man is angry at Mama, which makes him uncomfortable around *her*. But it can't be helped. He leaves, his back stiff, before she can apologize, and another nurse, a woman, comes in, pushing a cart loaded with tubes and vials, cotton balls and jars of alcohol. This nurse smiles and says, "We're going to be seeing a lot of each other, I'm afraid."

It's true. She is Ward D's "daytime bloodsucker," as she puts it, and she'll come every morning about this time to tie off the girl's arm, use a syringe and draw off a sample. By now, Flucy's headache is so bad that she hardly feels the prick of the needle.

Then comes a young, slender, blonde nurse who has a name: Miss Johnson. She gives the girl a penicillin shot from a bigger needle; Flucy feels that one. "I'm *your* nurse, honey," she says. "The only day nurse who'll be bringing you medicine as long as you're on this ward." She smiles when she sees Flucy glancing around the room. "It's nothing fancy, I know, but it's the best we can do. The Army loaned us a whole bunch of these Quonsets when the situation… got so bad."

Flucy thinks the room is luxurious, like a hotel room in the movies. And it's all hers.

There's a single window overlooking the parking lot where Mama's car was. Flucy looks out, but the car is gone. The window is screened on the outside with a heavy wire mesh. Is it there to protect her, she wonders, or to protect the rest of the world *from* her?

"The doctors are giving you a special test next morning, so you can't eat anything until then," Miss Johnson says. "Here, drink this." She hands the girl a pleated paper cup.

"What is it, ma'am?"

"Oh, don't call me ma'am! It makes me feel old. A sedative, honey, so you can get some rest and lose that awful headache."

She knows about the headache, and Flucy hasn't even told her! The liquid in the cup is bitter, but the girl drinks it gratefully — it's better than another shot.

She sleeps fitfully, because the stiffness in her neck has spread to the rest of her body; when she awakes in a scrunched-up position, unable to move, she thinks she's in the double bed back home and Mama has rolled on top of her. She tries to push Mama away (in silence, as gently as she can, without waking Mama, because Mama might kick or slap her), but her arms are weak, they don't seem to work right, and once she remembers that she's in Ward D of St. Bernardine's Hospital, all alone, she panics. She's becoming paralyzed! Isn't that what happens to people with polio? Will she ever be able to move again?

Yet when they come for her at 7 a.m., the headache is gone, and Flucy feels a sudden, brief hope. "I think I'm OK now," she tells Miss Johnson. "Can I go home?"

Miss Johnson smiles and shakes her head at the same time. "Not hardly. We have to take your blood again, and give you your spinal."

"What's that?"

"The test, honey. You can't expect all those doctors to get up at the crack of dawn for nothing, can you?"

Flucy doesn't know how to answer that. The "bloodsucker" comes, and then the black man to lift her and lay her back down on the gurney. She can't help him — her body just flops, especially her left arm and leg. And there's no way to hide this from Miss Johnson, who sees the flash of fear in Flucy's glance and tries to smile back reassuringly, but fails.

"It won't take long, honey. Nothing to be scared of. We're going to the operating room. We'll find out for sure what's the matter with you, and then we can fix it. Right?"

Flucy knows she's supposed to be brave and answer, "Right," but this sounds worse than a test. "Are you going to… operate on me?"

"Not really," Miss Johnson says. "That's just the name of the room we'll use. Don't worry."

It's a big room at the end of a corridor, lit with a strange cold brilliance; when they wheel her into it, Flucy can see every fine, golden, metallic hair on her arms, every thread in the black man's sleeve, the overhead fluorescent tubes' own reflections in the lenses of the goggles the doctors are wearing. If it weren't so chilly, she thinks, she might be inside the sun. Nothing can hide from this light — not a bug, not a germ, certainly not Flucy Colton; it falls so evenly that there isn't a shadow anywhere. Four doctors bend over her. She sees an image of herself distorted in each of eight goggle-eyes. The doctors themselves are like giant bugs, she thinks, gowned and gloved and masked, with nothing human about them except their voices.

"Here." One hands Flucy a washcloth. "You're gonna need this."

They have her lie on her side — the left, weak side — and curl up with her neck bent forward and her knees up tight against her chest. The doctors' white gowns rustle as they move in closer, and she catches a glimpse of the biggest needle yet.

It won't take long, Miss Johnson said, but it takes long enough. They raise the back of Flucy's gown, she feels cold, rubbery fingers, then something wet, and then they stab the needle into the middle of her spine, about waist-high — once, twice, three times before they leave it there. Miss Johnson will tell her later that they gave her a "local anesthetic," whatever that is, but Flucy — already, at eleven, an expert on kinds and degrees of pain — has never felt anything worse. When they finish, the washcloth is sopping with her saliva and tears.

Back in her room, Miss Johnson says indignantly: "Such high-and-mighties. Why couldn't they do it right the first time? The least they could do is apologize, but do you think they ever would? *I'm* sorry, honey. You didn't have to go through all that."

All that to find out what Flucy knew anyway:

She has polio.

4.

Late that afternoon, before their quarantine begins, her family comes to visit. Including Daddy.

They aren't allowed to enter Ward D. They get gamma globulin shots in the main hospital, to help protect them from her disease if they haven't already caught it. Then they stand outside in the parking lot in the heat and peer at her through the window. Miss Johnson cranks up the bed so Flucy is half sitting and puts pillows behind her back so she can turn and face them.

Even so, they have to crane their necks to see her. Miss Johnson has opened the window, but they don't come very close. It's as if they think Flucy's germs will swarm out through the screen like mosquitoes and bite them.

"No more than ten minutes, I'm afraid," Miss Johnson calls to them. "Jessie is worn out now, and *very* sick. We all want to do what's best for her, don't we?"

"Sure," Daddy says. He looks uncomfortable, Flucy thinks, and no wonder. He's still Daddy, but he's not part of the family anymore. Mama's in charge of it now. Instead of his usual paint-spattered work clothes, he wears slacks and a white shirt, open at the neck, so his Adam's apple sticks out. He looks thinner — is he eating enough now that he's on his own? "We understand all that. But Flucy's our daughter, and we just want to know how long... Is there a doctor there we can talk to?"

"I'm her day nurse, Mr. Colton. I can answer any questions you have."

"How serious is it?" Mama says harshly. "Will she live?"

Mama stands with her legs apart, braced against the wind that flutters her hair and billows the skirt of one of her best dresses, blue to match her eyes, and powders her good shoes with dust. She has hold of Rose Ellen, who seems to be crying.

Miss Johnson winces, since Flucy can hear every word. "It's serious," she says, "but *how* serious, we won't know for a while."

Rose Ellen coughs and tries to wave the dust away. "They threw eggs at our house last night."

"Who did?"

"I don't know. People. Once that QUARANTINE sign got nailed to the front door. And they call us up on the phone and say awful things."

"I'm sorry to hear that," Miss Johnson says. "I wish I could say you're the only ones, but at times like this..."

Mama grips Rose Ellen's arm hard so she'll hush. "People we thought were our friends and neighbors until they showed their true colors."

"It's ignorance, that's all it is," Miss Johnson says.

"You think so? I think it's pure meanness, kickin' folks when they're already down. Well, just you wait. When the time comes, they'll get theirs. Mark my words."

Safe behind the screen, floating on weariness and a tinge of nausea, Flucy can afford to pity them a little, and feel embarrassed. Mama's right — they aren't civilized; none of them know how to behave.

"Don't cry, Rosie," she says. "I'm OK. They're taking good care of me here."

Spike steps out from behind Daddy and hoots. "That ain't on account of *you*, dummy. She's bawlin' 'cause they stuck that great big needle in her skinny little butt."

He grins crookedly and holds his palms apart, fisherman style, to show how long the needle was.

Spike is disgusting, Flucy thinks — the worst of all of them. But still it's funny, what he said. Rose Ellen *does* have a scrawny behind, unlike her breasts.

"Goddamn it, Spike, shut up," Daddy says and almost cuffs him, but Miss Johnson is watching.

"I bet it wasn't half as big as *my* needle," Flucy says. "The one for my spinal."

"Spare them the gory details, honey," Miss Johnson says. She moves past Flucy to the window. "You'll have to say goodbye now. Jessie needs her rest."

"Hell's bells, we just got here," Daddy says.

"*You* shut up," Mama says. "Like you were around when any of this happened. Like you cared what happened to any of us."

"What you talkin' about?" Daddy says. "I'm here now, aren't I?"

Mama doesn't answer him. Instead, she calls out to Flucy: "You hang in there, you hear? Get well soon so you can come home."

"I will, Mama."

"We're countin' on you."

But it's suddenly clear to Flucy that Mama doesn't believe it for a minute, her face is so grim and strained. It isn't just the wind Mama is bracing against; she knows for a fact she's going to walk away and drive off and never see her precious baby girl alive again.

It's more than Flucy can bear. It's true — she's going to die. She has never felt so abandoned and alone. She's about to burst into tears like Rose Ellen when Spike runs up and shoves his face against the screen, germs be damned. "When you get out," he hisses, "I'm gonna kill you for doing this to us."

This is all your fault.

And, strangely, that helps. At least *he* thinks she's going to live.

Spike sticks out his tongue and wiggles it. Then he runs to catch up with Mama and Daddy, and Miss Johnson pulls the window shut. She turns to Flucy with a bemused smile. Miss Johnson is too nice to say anything bad about the girl's family. She just says, "What on Earth happened to that boy's eyebrows?"

5.

"Daddy hit him with a paintbrush," Flucy would have to say if she told Miss Johnson anything about it — which she won't. "And Mama says it must've knocked his brains lopsided or something, because ever since then he's had the devil in him."

But as far as Flucy is concerned, Spike was a devil to begin with. Maybe even when he was born.

Daddy was a soldier when Mama met him in Oklahoma. He was still a soldier when they moved to California, but he left the Army when the war ended — something Mama has never forgiven him for. Why give up free medical care and government housing (even if it was just a Quonset hut) and a job that made use of his electronics training when he didn't have to? But Daddy said Uncle Sam didn't need so many soldiers anymore. After a six-year hitch, he was sick and tired of being told what to do, of spit-shining his shoes and standing for inspections and saluting the general's Jeep and all that, and if Mama thought *she* could order him around now, she had another think coming.

Besides, Daddy said, he could make more money on the outside — maybe open a shop where he could sell and fix radios and hi-fis and other appliances. But he never did. Daddy blamed Mama for that. He said her everlasting complaints — about how San Bernardino wasn't exactly the California she'd imagined when they were dancing cheek to cheek in the Fort Sill canteen in Lawton and he was sweet-talking her, feeding her all those lies about living right next to Hollywood and the beach — were enough to drive any man to distraction, if not to drink. So Daddy painted houses, and he drank.

No excuses, Mama fired back. Daddy had nobody to blame but his own lazy, shiftless self. He'd fouled his own nest in the Army, hadn't he? He'd been a drinker all along — just not as brazen about it as he was now. And shouldn't there be a law to put sweet-talkers like him in jail?

Think of it, Mama liked to tell Rose Ellen and Flucy — sometimes even when Daddy was listening. Here she'd been, one of five orphan kids hired out by their oldest brother, Uncle Joe, to pick cotton or fruit on neighbors' farms outside Lawton just to make ends meet. She'd worn denim overalls and a wide-brimmed straw hat and a boy's cast-off long-sleeved shirt, despite the heat, to protect her skin from the sun and dust. A girl's skin was her fortune, Mama said; once you lost your looks, you never got them back. And a redhead's skin was the most delicate of all. It could burn and peel and dry out and wrinkle before a girl even had a chance to get old. So here she'd been, working all day Saturday in the fields, literally *eating* red dust, then going home to cook supper, take a bath, rub cold cream into her face and fix her hair as best she could. Then, in the upstairs bedroom she shared with her two sisters, she lay awake until she heard Uncle Joe snore.

Uncle Joe had saved them all; Mama knew that. He had hired himself out after their parents died of spotted fever and discouragement in 1933, worked like a grown man, like *two* grown men, and somehow put food in their bellies, snatched their house out of the snapping-turtle jaws of the Cache Creek Savings & Trust Co., which held the mortgage, even though all the land around it was lost. But such a heroic effort had aged him before his time. Uncle Joe had become more like their father than a brother. He didn't smile. He was strict. He wouldn't hesitate to use the belt on any of them, boy or girl, if he caught them shirking — never mind sneaking out at night to go downtown.

"A GI is only lookin' for one thing," Uncle Joe told the girls, "and it's the one thing you can't afford to lose. You see a*nybody* with two legs and a uniform on him comin' down the street, you steer clear of him, hear? A GI's gonna be here today and gone tomorrow, and you can't trust a damn thing he says."

If Daddy *was* listening then, Mama would give him a look. But Flucy also felt that Mama, besides aiming to needle Daddy, enjoyed the story she was telling — at least this first part, the adventure.

Because Mama did exactly what Uncle Joe told her not to do. She put on a dress and eased out the window and jumped down to the dirt yard, landing as silently as a cat. Then, with her sisters or all by herself, she ran out to the highway and hitched a ride into Lawton. The thrill of it was more than worth the whipping she'd get if Uncle Joe caught her sneaking home. No force on earth could have kept her away from that canteen.

If the wind had stopped, for once, and the dust had settled out of the sky, she could see stars as well as the city lights. The air was full of a wondrous electricity — Mama didn't say this in so many words, but her tone of voice said it for her. At the canteen she stood by the wall in her clean but threadbare dress, her dusty shoes; the only dancing she'd ever done was with her sisters in that upstairs room, the radio turned down so low Uncle Joe couldn't hear it. Now colored lights were running up and down the sides of the jukebox, which was playing Benny Goodman and Glenn Miller. Men were laughing and stomping and whirling girls around. It scared her. But every kind of forbidden delight was here — cigarettes, Cokes spiked with whiskey and rum and, above all, the car Daddy drove up in: a yellow '32 Ford V-8. Daddy wore a silk Hawaiian shirt. He was a *specialist*, he informed her, not just a private first class. When he asked her out onto the floor, and later, when he told Mama that he'd put in for a transfer to California and wanted her to go with him, how could any girl say no?

"All that buildup," Mama would say, "and now look at me."

She meant San Bernardino, the three kids and the rented, battered house, eighty miles from any beach.

"I couldn't wait to get away from your Uncle Joe," Mama said, "but he was more of a man when he went to work at seventeen than any man I've ever known since. Next to Joe, they're all just boys. How's that for my bad luck? Turned out Joe was right about GIs after all. I never should have paid any attention to that smooth talk and that yellow car."

Usually, when Mama said that, Daddy wasn't there — because if he was, odds were they'd start throwing things at each other again.

Mama is mad almost all the time, Flucy thinks. Daddy, before he left, was less predictable. It depended on how much he'd drunk and how long ago. Sometimes he was at his worst the morning after, sober but with a headache as bad as hers, maybe. That was when Daddy remembered that he'd been a soldier once. He yelled orders: *Hup, hup.* He wanted the beds made with square corners and the edges of the lawn clipped ruler-straight. And it was on one of those hungover mornings that Spike didn't sweep out the garage well enough to suit him.

Spike was eight then. Daddy picked him up and set him down on his feet in the middle of the back yard.

"Stand at attention!" he shouted. "Don't you move!"

As if he was under a magic spell, Spike stood there, arms stiff at his sides, while Daddy went back to the garage and took his biggest brush out of a can of paint thinner.

"This'll teach you," Daddy said. *"Hold still*, now, or you'll wish you had, by God."

The wooden brush probably weighed two pounds. Thinner dripped from its bristles onto the grass; Flucy could smell it from wherever she was watching.

Daddy stopped at least fifteen feet away from Spike, as if giving himself a fair challenge. He stretched out his left arm to sight by. Spike trembled but didn't move.

Then Daddy wound up like a baseball pitcher and threw.

The brush wobbled in the air, but the same spell that held Spike rooted in place, that kept Flucy silent, that thickened the sunlight and shushed the birds in the trees, made sure it didn't miss.

It made a *clock* sound, as if Spike's head was wooden too.

The boy crumpled where he stood. Daddy ran toward him, yelling, "Get back up, Mister. I'm not done with you. Stand at attention!"

But Spike, who must have been stunned — almost knocked out — began wailing, "My eyes! Mama, help! I can't see!" Mama ran outside from the kitchen with a dishcloth and screamed at Daddy to leave the boy alone. She knelt and wiped away the blood and thinner and diluted beige paint that were running into Spike's eyes and blinding him. Spike had to get twenty-two stitches, and the scars were right where his eyebrows used to be.

Had Mama been watching all along? Flucy isn't sure. Mama always acted as if she'd seen the awful thing Daddy was doing too late to stop it. But Flucy has this little piece of memory that refuses to fit: of Mama at the kitchen window holding a water glass that she'd been drying with that dishcloth, her eyes big and her lips squeezed tight into a red line, just as fascinated as the rest of them.

6.

Afterward, Mama always said, Spike looked too strange to make many friends in school, so it was no wonder he turned into a loner. That was Daddy's fault, not Spike's. But Flucy has her own ideas about that too. Spike never did have friends, though he had followers — other kids, not popular either, who hung around him for some reason, whispering and sniggering and giving Flucy and Rose Ellen sly looks. Spike seemed to hold them all in the same spell Daddy had held *him* in, that morning in the back yard. Yet even before his face got changed into a Halloween mask, Spike had had the same power, Flucy thinks — over her, at least.

It's a mysterious power. Spike is small for his age, not so good at sports. Except in one twisted way, he's no smarter than Flucy or any of the other kids. But that one way makes up for everything else.

Part of it is his uncanny single-mindedness, his patience. Spike would hiss under his breath, "Flucy, Flucy, Flucy," until she ran away with her hands over her ears, and then he would laugh. Or he would reach out his forefinger and poke her arm, over and over. Not hard — it didn't have to be hard. Just never-ending. Or he would stick her with a straight pin from Mama's sewing kit, or jab her in the shoulder with a middle knuckle cocked out from his fist, so it hurt more and left a bruise. Spike would sneak up behind her and yell, "Boo!"; he would step on her toes, trip her, snap her with a wet towel, throw acorns at her.

"Why are you *doing* this? Flucy would ask. "Why can't you leave me alone?"

But she knew why, and Spike's crooked-toothed grin only confirmed it. He did it because he liked to do it. Because it bothered her, Flucy. Because he liked to bother her.

Mama or Daddy could make time speed up whenever they were due home and the chores hadn't been done. Spike made time slow down. Ten minutes of being teased or poked could stretch out like an hour — even longer, because Flucy knew Spike wouldn't quit, as long as he'd gotten her goat. And he always did, no matter how hard she tried to ignore him. Or plead with him: "I don't do this to *you*." Or cry, or fight back. It made no difference. Spike grinned just the same. And if she told Mama on him, and Mama punished him, he'd get back at Flucy later, twice as bad.

Little details of Spike's face and hands cling to her mind like burrs, and not just the scar tissue everyone else sees: a kind of crust on his eyelids, yellow-green moss on his teeth, pores in his nose, calluses on his knuckles. He has a sour, cheesy smell.

Another part of Spike's power is that he knows dirty stuff that other kids his age don't know yet. *How* he knows it, Flucy can't guess. But he does.

Even last year, when Spike was twelve, he was interested in Rose Ellen's body and tried to sneak peeks at her whenever she took a bath. Rose Ellen, though, is older; she can call Spike a "little twerp" or a "midget" and sometimes get away with it — not by fighting but by looking down her nose at him and, if that fails, using her asthma as an excuse to duck out of range. Flucy had no such defenses this June when Spike, freed from school, discovered all of a sudden that she, too, was a girl, and fair game because she "played with herself."

Flucy had had no name for it — the sweet, dizzying sensation she felt when she touched a certain spot between her legs. She had found the spot by accident. Once she started to touch it, in bed alone or when Rose Ellen had turned her back and seemed to be asleep — had Rose Ellen ever found *her* spot? Flucy didn't dare ask — she couldn't stop touching it. But she knew she had to keep it a secret. Something that felt so good *had* to be trouble if anyone found out.

Sure enough. As careful as she tried to be, an afternoon came when Mama pushed open the bedroom door and saw her. And hurried back to the living room to tell Daddy.

"Marv! You won't believe it! Flucy's in there playing with her snatch!"

She heard Daddy laugh — a bark of surprise — and hid under the covers in case he wanted to look too. Never mind the other people in the house. Hadn't the Callahans from next door dropped by for coffee? Flucy isn't sure. The shock of it, the humiliation, blood rushing to her cheeks, was so overwhelming that the

Callahans, who are white-haired, slow-moving and somewhat deaf, remain a piece of memory that doesn't quite fit, like Mama looking out the kitchen window at Daddy and Spike on the back lawn.

What the girl does remember is that word: s*natch*. She couldn't get it out of her head, it sounded so ugly.

"Snatch, snatch, snatch, snatch, snatch," Spike whispered.

He must have heard Mama too. And although Flucy couldn't help touching herself afterward, Mama and Spike and that word had spoiled it.

When Daddy moved out of the house in July and Mama began working at Thrifty, the kids were left alone much of the day. That meant more time for Rose Ellen to lie around and daydream, more time for Flucy to ride her bike and swim at the plunge and wander through the Harris Company department store at Third and E streets, gazing at clothes and toys and candy until somebody told her to leave. But it also meant more time for Spike to be devilish.

He started inviting his followers home, two or three at a time. Never the same two or three — they weren't friends — though they all had the same scruffy, neglected look. Word of the evil and thrilling things Spike knew must have reached them through the grapevine; they came out of curiosity, eager but shamefaced, got a taste of the forbidden and then left. Rose Ellen stayed in the bedroom and could claim she had no idea what Spike was doing. Flucy wasn't so lucky. Spike made her watch while the boys had a "circle jerk" — they dropped their pants and pulled on their peters and got red in the face until clear white stuff spurted out and dripped on the living-room rug.

"Who's gonna clean *that* up?" Flucy asked, worried about Mama.

"You are," Spike said.

"I can't! It's all sticky."

"Yes, you can. Get down and lick it."

"Yuck," Flucy said. The other boys laughed, but she wasn't so sure Spike was kidding.

Oh, her brother was horrible. And the thing was, he was never satisfied for long; he always wanted more. The next time he brought a couple of boys home, it wasn't enough for her to watch while they raced to see who could shoot his "jizzum" fastest. No, Spike wanted Flucy to take off her clothes too, and play with herself the way Mama had caught her doing.

"Spike, no! Please."

"I'll tell Mama I saw you doin' it again. She'll whip your ass."

"What about you?"

"What *about* me? Mama don't know nothin' about me. And you better not tell, Flucy. She won't believe you anyway. And then *I'll* whip your ass."

"That's not fair," Flucy said, but she suspected that Spike was right — telling Mama wouldn't do her any good.

"C'mon, hurry up. We ain't got all day."

Slowly she unbuttoned her blouse and shrugged out of it; then she held it, crumpled up, against her chest. In spite of the heat, she was shivering.

"The rest of it, Flucy. C'mon. You want me to rape you?"

She wasn't sure what that meant, but Spike acted as if *he* knew, and it would hurt.

"Spike, you wouldn't do that."

But she thought he just might, whatever it was.

Flucy silently appealed to the other two boys, who didn't look quite as mean as Spike, though they were all terribly excited. One of them, even smaller than her brother, wore a nylon stocking cap over his shaved head — he had ringworm.

She let the blouse drop and pulled her jeans off over her Keds.

"Panties," Spike said.

That's what he called her underbritches.

Naked except for her feet, she felt herself blush over her whole body, not just her face.

"Now play with it, Flucy. Play with your snatch."

And she did, with her eyes closed to blot out the boys as they gathered closer. It *was* spoiled now, the feeling inside her. It would never be her sweet, secret thing again. But in spite of herself she shared a little of the boys' excitement. They were all looking at *her*. Was this disgusting or not so bad, or both? Flucy had always dreaded being seen — if anything, this was even worse than Mama catching her in the bedroom — but she also had the strangest thought: *I'm the most important person here. Without me, they've got nothing.* She could hear the boys' hoarse breathing; they were yanking their peters again. Then she opened her eyes. That was enough to make them back up, embarrassed. Flucy knew she was helpless — they were three to her one — but she had a power of her own, somehow.

"She come yet?" the boy with the stocking cap asked.

"I dunno. You can't tell with girls," Spike said as if he knew all about it. "Nothin' comes out. Hey, Flucy, you come?"

"No."

"Well, hurry up, damn it."

"I already did," the third boy mumbled.

In the end, because Flucy didn't know what "coming" meant, exactly, she had to make something up — she shook and gave a little moan. That seemed to be enough.

Then, all at once, the excitement was over. The other boys, pulling up their pants, looked any which way but at Flucy. They couldn't wait to leave — they would never come back to Fourteenth Street, she was sure. Even Spike seemed to be wondering if maybe he'd gone too far this time. Flucy hoped so.

But not long before she caught polio, Spike went even further. He brought home a boy *and* a girl. The girl was a year older than Spike and half again as big; she had greasy, pimply skin and black hair chopped off level with her ears. She wore boys' clothes — brown corduroy trousers and a red checked shirt — but Flucy didn't doubt she was a girl: Her breasts were the size of Rose Ellen's, though on her heavy body they looked smaller. Her name was Linda, Spike said. The boy was her cousin, visiting from Buena Park in Orange County. His name was Buzz.

Right from the start, Flucy decided that Linda and Spike belonged together, even if nobody else might want them. They had the same kind of dirty mind. The plan Spike came up with — using sheets and blankets Mama had hung to dry on the sagging wire clotheslines in the back yard, plus canvas dropcloths Daddy had left in the garage, to build two swaybacked tents only a few feet apart — was at least partly Linda's idea. Spike put the tents together with an energy Flucy had seldom seen when he was doing chores. She knew why, too. If she, Flucy, had been the most important person in the living room, Linda, an actual, angry-eyed bad girl, a girl willing to do *anything*, maybe, was the most important person here. It didn't matter how ugly she was. Spike had to keep her happy or the whole plan would fall apart. So Flucy had the rare experience — something she might have enjoyed at another time — of seeing her brother bossed around and apparently liking it. Linda had stolen a pack of her father's Chesterfield cigarettes. Spike had matches. Linda passed the cigarettes around and Spike lit them. Naturally, Flucy and Buzz coughed the most; the other two snickered.

"Can't you get us some beer?" Linda complained to Spike. "I thought you said —"

"We used to. We used to have lots of beer here. Whiskey, too. But Mama threw it all out after Daddy left."

"You drink whiskey?" That seemed to interest Linda.

"I could, if we had any. Why didn't *you* bring some?"

"That's *your* job. You're the man, ain't you?"

"Not my fault."

"Then whose fault is it, Spike? We *need* beer. It's too fuckin' hot."

Buzz looked ordinary enough — bare-chested and tanned, with blond hair clipped so short the top of his skull showed. Flucy wondered how he and Linda could possibly be related.

The four of them stood on the lawn with the weight of the sun on their shoulders. They puffed smoke into the brown sky.

"Well, what you waitin' for?" Linda said. "You think I got all day?"

"Which tent you want?" Spike asked, stubbing out his cigarette.

"Who cares? That one."

Flucy felt dizzy — partly from the smoke, and partly because the excitement was so powerful. It was pulling them away from everything safe and familiar — pulling *her* away like the Santa Ana River in a winter flood carrying broken sheds and tree branches that whirled in the muddy current as her head was whirling now. It was bad enough, what Spike had made her do in the living room. This would be worse. *Much* worse. Somehow she knew now what Spike had meant two weeks ago when he'd threatened to rape her — and what Buzz must be planning to do to her in the stifling darkness of their tent, hidden from all the world. Nobody had told her. She just knew. And once it had happened, then what? Would this awful excitement — like what Daddy had felt, learning over Rose Ellen? —

have carried her so far away that she couldn't ever get back to herself? *We're just kids*, Flucy thought. If Spike had been anybody but Spike, she would have begged him to stop and let her go.

As it was, of course, Spike, being Spike, read her mind.

"No backin' out now, Flucy, or I'll tell *everybody* what you did. You and Buzz go in this one. And get naked."

The tents, each hung from a single line and held at the bottom with rocks, were upside-down Vs, high and narrow. Flucy and Buzz could stand up at the entrance to theirs, but not in the middle. The air inside, with no breeze, was even hotter than outside. It smelled strongly of crushed grass, bleach and paint. Spike leered in at them.

"You can go away now," Flucy said.

"Oh, no. I'm watchin' till you get get your clothes off."

"We will. Just go *away*. Please?"

"Not so fast, Flucy. I think your pal here might be a little chicken."

Spike wouldn't leave until Flucy and Buzz had both undressed. Meanwhile, Linda, from the other tent, yelled at Spike to hurry the hell up.

"Just a second!" he yelled back. "You naked too?"

"Why don't you come over here and find out?"

"Goddamn!" Spike grinned. "C'mon, now," he told Buzz. "Give her a kiss. Let me see."

Buzz leaned forward and touched Flucy's lips with his.

"That's all?" Spike jeered. He started to squawk and flap his elbows chicken-style, but Linda called again, louder, and he finally left.

Flucy and Buzz looked at each other.

She expected him to put his arms around her and kiss her again, but he didn't, even though she could feel the heat of his body — he was standing so close — and remember what his lips felt and tasted like: kind of salty.

"How old are you, anyway?" Buzz asked. It was the first thing he'd said to her.

"Eleven."

"Jeez."

They listened for sounds from the other tent — for Spike's and Linda's voices, or for something else. Sex sounds?

Buzz said, "You sure you want to do this?"

Flucy shook her head, hardly daring to hope. She was sure Buzz was going to get mad at her.

"Well, if *you* don't —" All they could hear was the yapping of the Callahans' dog next door, an ambulance siren and kids shouting a block away. "What's the matter, Flucy? You don't like me?"

"I don't even *know* you." She was still dizzy, and having to stay bent under the roof made her back ache. "Can't we just sit down? Please?"

"OK."

There was a danger to sitting — it was halfway to lying flat. The tough Bermuda grass prickled her behind. But Flucy could fold her legs, get her knees out in front of her and hold her hands over her crotch. Her snatch. That was better.

And Buzz kept his hands over his peter. Was he scared, like Spike said? Didn't he like *her?*

"Eleven years old. Jeez."

"Sorry," Flucy said.

"Not your sorry. That Spike." Buzz smiled wryly. "Your brother said —"

"He said what?"

"He said you were a wild and crazy little bitch. Hot to trot." Those sounded like words Spike would have used, all right. "You'd even go all the way, maybe, if you liked the guy."

Buzz blushed almost as red as Flucy, despite his tan.

"Don't believe everything Spike says."

"I guess not." He sighed. "I guess I was just a big stupe, wasn't I? Came all the way out here for nothin'."

"Sorry."

"Not your sorry! I should've known he was bull-shitting me. Like Linda always does."

Flucy couldn't help asking, "Is she really your cousin?"

"Hard to figure, isn't it? Linda the Lardass."

"Yeah." The excitement had faded away by now. That was sad for Buzz — she could tell — but for her it was a huge relief. "How old are *you?*"

"Thirteen. I'll be fourteen next month."

"That's pretty old."

"Yeah."

They sat for a while longer. Buzz still seemed puzzled.

"Why'd you take your clothes off," he asked, "if you didn't want to?"

"Spike said to."

"You always do what your brother tells you?"

Flucy nodded.

"Jeez. How come?"

"He'll beat me up if I don't."

"Spike? No shit? Hey, you don't have to cry."

"I'm not crying," Flucy said.

But she was, and she couldn't even lift her hands from her crotch to wipe her eyes. Tears trickled down over the front of her, where Rose Ellen and Linda had breasts and she just had pinkish-brown buttons. "You don't know how mean he is," she hiccuped. "He *will* beat me up! What am I gonna do?"

"Hey, hey, take it easy." Buzz reached out as if to soothe her, then quickly covered his peter again. "We don't have to tell him."

"What?"

"Spike. We can *say* we did — all the way, if he asks. But we don't have to *do* it."

"Really?"

"Sure."

"You won't tell him?"

"I said so, didn't I? Piss on Spike. You don't have to do a damn thing. Unless you change your mind. Think you might?"

"No."

"You sure? OK, then. Shit, you're only eleven, anyway. Let's get dressed."

The boy was pulling up his jeans before Flucy had even decided whether she should trust him. Her clothes were wrinkled and full of grass stems, which stuck to her skin where her tears had run. But she wasn't crying anymore.

Then something happened in the other tent.

First came a frustrated groan from Spike. And then a screech from Linda: "Wait! Not *now!* You sorry little fucker! I thought you knew —"

Spike groaned again.

"You didn't even get it *in*, you idiot!"

Buzz and Flucy stuck their heads out. The bright sunlight hurt her eyes; she felt even dizzier. The girl thinks she remembers a headache starting at that very moment. Was that the first sign of polio, right then? Maybe so. In the few days between then and now, it seemed that she heard ambulances all the time, and the city closed the Perris Hill plunge.

The other tent was ominously quiet.

Then they heard Spike's low, choked voice, humiliated as Flucy had never heard it before: "C'mon, Linda. Not my fault!"

"You came on my *leg!* Fuckin' little weenie."

"I couldn't help it," Spike whined. "Can't we try again?"

"Forget it, Spike. I'm done here."

"Linda —"

"Fuckin' little weenie couldn't even get in."

Flucy held her breath. Her temples throbbed. Only she seemed to know how dangerous Spike was right now — how he was going to make *somebody* pay for this.

"How *could* I, all that flab in the way?"

"Shit, Spike. I thought you knew what you was doin'. But you lied to me, didn't you? I bet this was your first time."

"You're a fuckin' pig, you know that, Linda? Just a big fat pig."

The wire that held up their tent jumped and twanged. Then the sheets on one side of it billowed open, and Spike came stumbling out, naked and clutching his clothes. He tripped over one of the rocks that had held down the bottoms of the sheets and landed on his back, curling up like a roly-poly bug.

"What are *you* lookin' at?" he screamed at Flucy and Buzz.

If Spike had been anybody but Spike, she would have laughed out loud. Buzz did smile, watching Spike scramble to get dressed, though he stopped smiling when Linda came out, tucking in her shirttail and glaring at them all.

"Let's get out of here," she snapped. Flucy had never seen a girl's or woman's eyes with so much fury in them, not even Mama's. "I mean it, Buzz. This place makes me sick. Fuckin' *tents.*"

And if Spike had been anybody else, Flucy might have felt sorry for him. What was he going to do now? Even the girl he belonged with didn't like him.

But as it was, Flucy was simply grateful that she'd escaped the worst — for now, anyway. The look Spike gave her after the other two had left was pure murder.

"I suppose *you* had fun," he said.

"Not really."

"Don't bullshit me, Flucy. You did it, didn't you? Was it fun?"

"No."

"Liar."

"It's the truth." And Flucy realized that it didn't matter after all — he wouldn't believe her either way.

"Well, you better clean all this up before Mama gets home." Spike waved at the dropcloths and blankets, the sheets Mama wouldn't appreciate having to wash all over again, the rocks and cigarette butts on the grass. He stomped into the house.

Now, in her room at St. Bernardine's, lying on the cleanest of sheets, the girl thinks about Spike. If she *does* die, Mama and Daddy and Rose Ellen will be sorry. And so will a few kids at school, maybe, like Patsy. And Patsy's mother. The girl wishes she could float over her funeral like an invisible ghost and see their sad faces, listen to all the nice things they'll say about her. *If only we'd known!* But Spike is different. Spike would be sorry only because if she died he wouldn't have a chance to get his revenge. It's weird but true — her brother wants her to live because he hates her so much.

That's what the window screen is really for, she decides. To keep Spike out.

It helped when school started back up last week — they had less time at home alone together. But without

Daddy there, and with Mama so busy, who will be able to stop Spike if he gets another evil idea in his head?

Maybe nobody can.

That's the real secret of his power, the girl thinks. Whenever she's punished, she feels guilty and tries to do better, to make Mama and Daddy happy. But Spike isn't like that. All that matters to him is not getting caught. And if he *does* get caught, grownups can scold him or whip him all they want, make him holler and cry like a baby, but inside he isn't touched. Spike will never change. He's stronger than any of them. Even at eleven, the girl knows this for sure. She doesn't know *why* — it isn't fair. Mama sometimes says that if Spike keeps on the way he's going, he's bound to end up in jail, and the girl thinks this is likely. She used to wish it would hurry up and happen — then she would be safe. But would it make any difference? When he got out, Spike would still be Spike, more dangerous than ever.

She thinks about Buzz, the boy from Buena Park, and about the power she'd discovered she had in the living room — to back up those other two boys with a glance. She doesn't understand that either. Her power is a small one, and mysterious in a different way — she can't trust it, because it doesn't work with everybody. It sure doesn't work with Spike.

And because Spike is the only boy she really knows, she isn't sure what made it work with the other boys. They were nicer, she supposes. A *little* nicer, anyway.

Was Buzz nice? The girl thinks about that. He'd tagged along with Linda and believed the dirty things

Spike had told him, which wasn't so nice. But he was nice enough to her when it counted — in the tent.

And Buzz was kind of good-looking, she thinks, with his smooth, clear, tan skin and his straight teeth and his smile. The girl figures that whether she lives or dies, she'll probably never see him again, so it does no harm to remember what Buzz's lips felt like. Will she ever get another kiss?

7.

What happened between Mama and Daddy was this: Daddy used to drink his whiskey and beer at home, but Mama gave him too much trouble about that — she said it was a lousy example for the children, and a criminal waste of money besides. So he started to drink at taverns after work instead. That upset Mama even more. How could she know when to put dinner on the table, she said, if she had no idea when he was going to drag his sorry self home and eat with the rest of them like the head of a family should? And didn't liquor cost twice as much at a bar as it did at a store? She bet it did. Not to mention the kind of *people* he'd be rubbing elbows with in a place like that — a place kept as dark as night inside because not one of them could abide being seen as he (or *she!*) really was, in the clear and honest light of day. Wasn't that so? They all had something to hide, didn't they? Something nasty. Which meant Daddy did too. "What *is* it, Marv?" Mama would say. "What is it you're keeping a secret from me? Does she have a name?"

Daddy would deny everything, but Mama wouldn't let up. She would practically chase him around the house, firing questions at him, until his face turned a certain shade of pink and he would stop dead wherever he happened to be — this was the kids' signal to duck and scatter — and grab the first thing he could find to throw at her. It might be a shoe or an orange or a bottle of shampoo or Spike's baseball mitt. Then Mama would throw something back. Daddy would lower his head and rush at Mama and try to pin her arms to her sides; Mama would kick and slap at him and wriggle away, and the battle was on. It would end only when both of them were exhausted, and end more or less as a draw — if Daddy was stronger, Mama was always twice as fierce.

As time went by, Daddy came home later and later. Mama had to serve dinner without him; he ate leftovers cold from the fridge.

One night he came in after they'd already gone to sleep. In those days, Flucy shared a bed with Rose Ellen, who didn't like it much — why should Spike, who was younger, get a room of his own just because he was the only boy? What woke Flucy was Rose Ellen having an asthma attack. Choking and gasping. Daddy was right there, she saw — leaning over Rose Ellen, smelling of whiskey; he had pulled up Rose Ellen's nightshirt and was stroking her big, pale breasts. Rose Ellen hadn't screamed or even struggled, but she'd been so frightened that it cut off her air, and the noise of *that* was enough to bring Mama out of her bedroom. Mama was the one who screamed. She lit into Daddy like a wildcat and chased him away. Then she rushed back and slapped Rose Ellen hard for letting him touch her, and slapped Flucy just for being there and not raising the alarm.

This is all your fault.

A pervert, Mama called Daddy. A disgusting sick excuse for a human being. The next morning, and for the rest of his time with them, Daddy couldn't meet anybody's eye, especially Rose Ellen's or Flucy's. Even before Mama announced that she was thinking about divorce, Daddy seemed to have one foot out the door.

Then there was Nona Kessler, who lived across the street. She was a war widow — her husband had been killed at Kasserine Pass in Tunisia, and she got some kind of pension from the government. Nona was at least forty; she had no kids, or they were grown and gone. She lived alone but hardly suffered from lack of company, people said — look at all those men going in and out her front door. The mailman, the meter reader, insurance salesmen, the Fuller Brush man, even cops. They parked their cars or trucks at the curb. Nona, when she opened the door, never seemed to be fully dressed. She wore slippers and wrap-around robes in bright floral prints; only a hand at her throat kept them from flapping open. She would smile up at the man, whoever he was, and take him inside. He might not reappear for an hour or two. All the neighborhood used to watch, including Mama and Daddy. Did the man's hair look freshly combed? Was his coat off, his tie loose, his shirttail out? Did he seem in a hurry to drive away?

"I don't get it," Daddy would say. "Nona's no spring chicken. She's put on a bit of weight lately, and she's a bottle blonde if I ever saw one. So what's the attraction? Are these fellows blind or what?"

Mama would look grim but satisfied, as if Nona Kessler had proved something about men that she'd always suspected. "It's pitiful, is what it is. They're just taking advantage of a poor lost soul who can't help herself. It's a sickness. Nona's been starved for attention ever since she lost her man — it's that simple, if you ask me. She should've gotten married again right away. Now she's just a slut, and who in his right mind would want her? I mean, never mind the drinking."

Mama would give Daddy one of her pointed glances, and Spike would grin — he was the one who snuck over to count the empties in Nona's garbage can.

"I think she's nice. And pretty," Flucy said.

"What do you mean?" Mama said. "Prettier than me?"

"No, Mama. Nona's old, I know. It's just... she *smells* pretty."

Mama snorted. "Cheap perfume. She must take baths in the stuff."

"And *way* too much makeup," Daddy said. "Like she troweled it on."

But that wasn't what Flucy meant. Nona Kessler *was* nice. She had no harm in her. The girl could sense that, bumping into her at the grocery store, where Nona wore a regular shirtwaist and pumps but still, somehow, looked underdressed. Nona smelled of roses. Her voice was vague and whispery; she peered at the girl as if she was nearsighted, but she recognized Flucy and smiled. Once she bought the girl a grape sucker. *No harm.* It wasn't so different, she thinks, from how she feels now about Miss Johnson.

Not long after the business with Rose Ellen, Daddy stayed out past bedtime again. He was repainting the white trim on a brown house just a few blocks away, on F Street, so he'd left the car at home. Well after dark, Mama roused all three children and told them to put on their robes and slippers.

"Where we goin'?" Spike complained.

"Huntin'," Mama said. "We're goin' big-game huntin', that's what. I can't leave you here alone, so hurry up."

They piled into the car — Mama and Spike in the front, Rose Ellen and Flucy in the back seat. They were all still half asleep, except for Mama. Driving away, she rolled down the windows, as if she could sniff out Daddy's whereabouts in the hot July night air, which seemed to crackle with the same electricity as that long-ago air in Oklahoma. "Tobey's Tippo Room," Mama said, angry but happy too, Flucy thought — happy that she could expose Daddy for what he was when all of them could see. "Tobey's Tippo Room," she chanted. "Over on Base Line. That's where he's got to be."

The tavern had a blinking blue neon sign with a cocktail glass on it. The parking lot was full of cars; music thudded out the open door. Mama went in but came right back out.

"Not there, but he *was* there, somebody said. Just a few minutes ago." Mama climbed back behind the wheel and bit her lip. "The sneaky bastard. I wonder where —"

"Let's go home," Rose Ellen said, yawning.

"Oh, no. He's gotta be on foot. Unless somebody gave him a ride."

Mama drove to F Street, where the top of Daddy's ladder showed above the fence around the two-story house he was working on. Then, abruptly, she turned off the headlights.

"Look! Isn't that him?"

A block and a half ahead of them, the tall, slim figure of a man moved down the sidewalk, in and out of tree shadows.

"That's not Daddy," Rose Ellen said.

"Sure it is," Spike said. "Look at him weavin'."

Mama eased the car ahead, no faster than the man was walking. She let him get even farther ahead before she crossed under each street lamp.

"Think you can pull the wool over *my* eyes, Marvin Colton?" she said. "Huh? Is that what you think?"

To Flucy, the rattle of the engine and the sound of their tires bumping over seams in the asphalt, snapping twigs, seemed terribly loud. Even with their lights dark, how could the man not know they were tailing him? He *must* be drunk.

He led them all the way back to Fourteenth Street, as if he really was Daddy and he was going home.

But then, instead of crossing the street to their house, he glanced around furtively and ducked into Nona Kessler's driveway.

"You see?" Mama hissed. "It *is* him! That's your very own fuckin' father creepin' into Nona's bedroom.

259

Didn't I tell you? Didn't I know it all along? Oh, the dirty sonofabitch!"

Mama switched on the headlights and gunned the engine. The car tore down the street until, even with both houses, she hit the brakes and slewed to a squealing, shuddering stop. Flucy glimpsed the man climbing into a back side window of Nona's house. His head and shoulders were already inside. All she could see was his long, thin legs scissoring in the air, like a grasshopper's. Then they disappeared too.

"That's not Daddy," Rose Ellen said again.

"Yeah? Wanna bet?" Spike jeered.

Mama seemed to have no doubt. "Marv Colton's shacked up with Nona!" she yelled loudly enough to wake up the whole block. "I don't care who knows it! And you all *did* know it, didn't you? You all knew and didn't tell me. Well, fuck all of you, too! Every last one of you hypocrites!"

After Mama put the car into the garage, she herded the children inside and told them to go to bed, lickety-split, or else. In a frenzy of rage and exhilaration, she gathered armfuls of Daddy's clothes from the closet and carried them outside and dumped them on the front walk until the closet was empty and windblown pants and shirts and jackets and boots were strewn all over the lawn.

In the morning, all the clothes were gone. And Daddy didn't come back.

Today, after seeing Daddy through the window, the girl is surprised by how much she'd missed him. She hadn't thought she would. But he looked so nice dressed up; he was sober, and until Spike mouthed off he reminded her of the Daddy he'd been when she was little — the Daddy who whistled, told funny stories about the Army, fixed the radio whenever it went on the fritz, polished the car every Saturday and took them fishing along the riverbank. Not the dark, whiskey-smelling Daddy who'd loomed over Rose Ellen, or the Daddy who'd thrown that paintbrush at Spike. Maybe not even the mystery man Mama had followed through the streets — who knew for sure whether that was Daddy? There were too many of him, the girl thought, and which Daddy was real?

8.

Sister Kenny.

The girl hears that name all the time. *Sister Kenny treatments. Sister Kenny says this. Sister Kenny wouldn't approve of that.*

Sister Kenny must be a nun — this is a Catholic hospital. The girl figures she's the boss of Ward D, hidden in an office somewhere but spreading her authority as wide as the wings of the starched white cap nuns wear on their heads.

"When can I see her?" she asks. "Is she ever going to come and see me?"

Miss Johnson laughs, but in that wonderful way she has, with no meanness in it. "She's retired now, I think. She lives in Australia. Way far away, across the ocean. That's where she came from originally. She was just a 'bush nurse' — she wasn't even registered — but she found new methods of treating polio that nobody else had thought of."

"She isn't a nun?"

Miss Johnson pauses, filling her syringe for the penicillin shot. "I don't know, Jessie. I don't think so."

"Then why do they call her Sister?"

"Maybe that's what they call nurses Down Under. It doesn't matter. She's a great woman, any way you look at it. Hold still, now. This'll just take a second."

Afterward, the girl says, "I still wish I could see her. Just once. I thought —"

"Maybe someday, when you grow up, you can *be* a great woman, just like Sister Kenny. Have you ever thought of that?"

The girl hasn't, but that single word vibrates in her: w*hen*, not *if.*

The Sister Kenny treatments begin immediately. Twice a day the girl is wheeled into a room that has big stainless-steel machines in it, like dryers in a laundromat. Army blankets, heavy dark-gray wool, are steamed in the machines and laid damp and hot on her naked body, covering everything but her face. Sweat pours out of her, along with the smell of the massive doses of vitamins Miss Johnson has been giving her. It hurts to move under the smothering weight of the blankets, but the nurses urge her to try — that's the whole point of it, they say: exercise. Back in her room, in her freshly made bed, she feels too exhausted — too paralyzed? — to move at all, and every afternoon there's a moment of despair when just breathing seems too much of an effort. How long can she keep this up? Yet every evening, after a bath and a hot-oil rubdown, she feels better. It's not just her imagination; she can move a little more easily than she could the day before.

Get-well cards arrive from relatives and neighbors, and comic books collected by kids at school. Are these the same neighbors who threw the eggs, the same kids who used to tease or ignore her? The girl doesn't know. Sometimes she thinks Miss Johnson is doing it on the sly, the way Mama and Daddy pretended to be Santa Claus when she was younger.

Still, it's nice. It makes her feel like a celebrity, if only for being sick. The stack of comics on the nightstand grows faster than she can read them. If only it didn't worry her, too — she has spent her whole life trying not to attract attention, and this is like having that operating-room light shine on her all the time.

Sure enough. At the end of the week they wheel her back to the first Quonset with the three galvanized tubs and scrub her all over again, and boil or burn everything she has touched or worn. The cards and comics go into the fire. All that's left is the rubber head of a doll, melted into a grotesque blob. Miss Johnson offers to throw it away, but the girl keeps it, unable to explain exactly why. It's proof that she was right not to get too attached to nice things, which always disappear; it helps her choke down her disappointment. But it's something else, too. It's proof of her survival — a kind of trophy. She isn't contagious anymore, the nurses tell her. She can move out of her private room into the general ward.

9.

Not everyone in Ward D is a polio patient. A tiny "blue baby" is brought in and placed in an incubator close enough so the girl can watch it wriggle feebly, too weak to cry. Two days later it dies — or at least it stops moving and they take it away. But most of the people in the rows of beds here do have polio, many *aren't* getting better, and only now does the girl grasp how big the epidemic is, why the public is so alarmed.

Day and night, she hears what she thinks of as death sounds — ambulance sirens outside, the rumble of gurney wheels in the corridors, shouted orders, and always the wheeze of the iron lungs on the other side of the wall, just a few feet from where she lies. St. Bernardine's has a whole room full of iron lungs with people in them — she got a glimpse inside it when they brought her here. Who knew such a room existed? Not Flucy Colton, who'd gone to school and ridden her bike and come home to Mama and Daddy and Rose Ellen and Spike and the chores, her little world of fear, when all the time this room was here, waiting, less than a mile away, the way Hell waited for bad people to fall into it. The iron-lung room *is* Hell, she thinks. Not the Hell of the visitors' tracts, with flames and devils and pitchforks, or the Hell that Spike could put her through, when time stretched out unbearably, but a clean, quiet place like a factory that makes things and packs them into boxes to be shipped to stores. Only here the things are people — kids like her, some of them; she saw their heads sticking out — and the boxes are metal tubes that they lie inside, that do their breathing for them. If the machines stop, they die. Now and then, she hears one machine stop while the rest go on wheezing. She hears voices. Did somebody die? Did somebody get well? Or did the machine simply break down? She has no way of knowing. One night she dreams that she's in an iron lung herself. There's a sign taped to the outside of it: LIFE or DEATH or STAY HERE FOREVER. She can't see the sign, any more than the thing from the factory knows which store's address is printed on its box, but she knows the sign is there, and she struggles to squirm out of the tube and read it, afraid that the paralysis she thought was going away — thanks to the Sister Kenny treatments — is coming back.

Still, if Hell is just in the next room, the room she's in, strangely, is more than a little like Heaven.

It began with the second scrubbing. There was something different about the nurses, even though they scrubbed her just as hard and destroyed her gifts. They smiled more. They were happy she'd lasted out the week. And now the girl sees signs of this happiness everywhere. Not just from Miss Johnson, but from the "bloodsucker," whose name is Mrs. DeMarco, and the black man, Mr. Wilkins, who shows his teeth again and doesn't seem half as gruff as before. It dawns on her that she has become one of their favorite patients. They didn't dare like her so much when they thought she might die on them. But she hasn't died; she isn't even going to be crippled very badly, they say. Now she makes them feel good every time they look at her, and they pass the good feeling back. She gets chocolate pudding for dessert, double helpings of Jell-O and all the fruit she can eat.

A card comes from Mrs. Greevey, who directs the school chorus: *Best wishes to one of our promising young sopranos! And future soloist??*

Promising soprano? Mrs. Greevey must have made a mistake, confused her with somebody else. The girl loves to sing, or at least loves to stand on risers at assemblies with the rows of others and let the sound of their singing wash over her. But there's no way her voice could have been noticed. She has made sure of that — even in the loudest parts of a song, she has always sung a little more softly than the rest. Mrs. Greevey is just being nice, she knows — especially at the end. The girl can't imagine herself ever singing a solo — putting her voice out there all by itself, where nobody could have any doubt where it came from. *Her.* She would miss notes and forget the words, even dry up into silence, standing there all alone with her fists clenched and her face burning.

Mrs. Greevey must know that too. Still, the girl is delighted to get the card, and she saves it, along with the melted head of the doll.

Miss Johnson says, "Jessie, if there's anything you'd like to have, anything that'd make you a teeny bit more comfortable, just name it."

She's Jessie all the time now. Or Jessamyn to the doctors, who tend to be more formal. Never Flucy.

What can she say? She loves Miss Johnson — loves her scent, her fingernail polish, the way she curls her hair, the dimples by the sides of her mouth that somehow make her smile warmer than anyone else's. If Miss Johnson were younger, she would be Jessie's best friend, or a better older sister than Rose Ellen could ever be. It's bad enough — though it's also wonderful — that Miss Johnson spends more time with her than she should. The open ward has plenty of other nurses, and Jessie's former room must have a new patient in it who needs constant care. But whenever Miss Johnson can grab a minute, here she comes, just to chat. It's indecent to ask for more. Mama has always told her, "Once an Okie, always an Okie. I found that out the hard way, believe me. They're just waiting for you to slip up, say somethin' wrong. Put on airs, get a little too grabby, think you're better than you are, and they'll be all too happy to take you down a peg."

Even Miss Johnson? Her first name is Cynthia, she has told Jessie. "Call me Cindy if you want." But that's too much. Going from "ma'am" to her last name was enough of a leap.

"I don't need anything," the girl says.

"You sure? How about a little radio of your own? We could put it on the nightstand there."

A radio would be unbelievably nice, but it frightens her, the extravagance of it, and she makes sure to give it up before she even has a chance to see it.

"We could leave it here after I go home, so the next kid can have it." Miss Johnson looks puzzled, so Jessie says, "I mean, it'd be *awful* expensive." And then, "We have our own big radio in our house, so I wouldn't need…"

Miss Johnson shakes her head, but in the kindest way. "You're a hard girl to do favors for, you know that?"

"I'm sorry."

"Good heavens, don't be *sorry*. I just mean —"

Miss Johnson doesn't understand her reluctance, and the girl knows why. Somebody as beautiful as she is, somebody everyone loves, has never been a Flucy. The temptation to tell her all about it — to pour it out in great shuddering sobs — is almost too powerful to resist. But it's an ugly story, the girl thinks, and too hard to believe. Miss Johnson would be even more puzzled, or shocked. A Jessie-who-was-Flucy wouldn't be her favorite patient anymore. If the girl knows anything for sure, she knows that.

It scares her that she has come so close to telling anyway.

So she shuts up and smiles through her tears and thanks Miss Johnson, and next day the radio, a green plastic Philco, is on her nightstand, and it *is* nice. She can listen to all her favorite programs, "Fibber McGee and Molly," "The Green Hornet" and the "Judy Canova Show." And music: Doris Day, Tony Bennett,

Liberace, Frank Sinatra, Nat "King" Cole, Patti Page. All singing of love, filling her with a mood that's part dreaminess and part fizz, like the blend of flavors in a root-beer float.

Jessie would keep that radio turned on around the clock if she could.

As it is, she has to switch it off at night, and the death sounds return. She can't help worrying about the patients on either side of her — a plump, black-haired girl even younger than she is who speaks only Spanish, and a man older than Daddy with a shiny, freckled bald head and bushy orange side whiskers who grumbles constantly about not being allowed to smoke. The girl's legs are crippled; she'll have to wear braces. And the man has trouble breathing — not bad enough so he has to lie in an iron lung next door, but bad enough so it's no wonder they took away his cigarettes.

Lying between them, so much luckier than they are, Jessie wonders if they resent her, even hate her. Would she hate herself if she were in their place?

Maybe I can be a nurse someday, she thinks, *and help people like them*.

Not that she could ever be a "great woman" like Sister Kenny and invent new treatments. But maybe, if she worked really hard at it, she could become like Miss Johnson, who *doesn't* have to work at it, who has only to be her lovely, kind self to make patients feel better.

In the daytime, Ward D seems almost homey. Jessie can hear only what she wants to hear. As she waits for her meals, her treatments and Miss Johnson's visits, the radio audience chuckles and the music wraps itself around her like the whirling pink streamers in a cotton-candy machine at the county fair, enclosing her in its melancholy sweetness, and if this isn't Heaven it's close enough.

10.

"Well, *this* is a pleasant surprise," Dr. Goodman says. "The last time I saw you, young lady, I was pretty darn worried — I guess I can say that now."

Jessie wonders if it *is* the right thing to say, with the other patients listening. But she senses that Dr. Goodman is a little unsure of himself here, wearing an ordinary dark suit when the two St. Bernardine's doctors escorting him are in scrubs. They look so much more serious, even without their bug-goggle disguises — though they're smiling too.

"Oh, Jessie here's a champion," Miss Johnson says. "She isn't going to let any dumb old virus get her down. Are you, honey?"

"Where's Mama?"

"Your family's still under quarantine," Dr. Goodman says. "They haven't been able to leave home and go anywhere. But nobody else has gotten sick — that's the good news. And the quarantine ought to expire any day now, if it hasn't already."

"I bet it has," Miss Johnson says, frowning. "So why —"

"The thing *I* want to know," Dr. Goodman says, to the other doctors as well as to Jessie, "is where all this resilience came from. She's just a little slip of a thing." He bends closer. "Do *you* have any idea, young lady, how you came to be in such good shape?"

"I liked to ride my bike."

"Your bike? You rode it a lot?"

"Yes, sir. Every chance I could." Just talking about it brings it back to her: the wind in her face, the blessed freedom of those after-school hours, the two magic wheels carrying her over railroad tracks and up alleys, to the Perris Hill plunge, everywhere she wanted. She misses it terribly all of a sudden — but her mind sounds a warning: *Better not say too much.* Mama doesn't know what she did with that stolen time.

"Maybe that's the answer, then," Dr. Goodman muses, chewing one end of his yellow mustache. "Or part of it. But the *other* question is, how come you caught polio when nobody else in your family did?"

Jessie has a fairly good idea. The plunge. Which Mama doesn't know about either.

Polio germs spread in the water. Everybody says that. So won't she be punished if Mama learns she sneaked out there anyway to swim?

It surprises her, this old fear, because the *real* reason she's getting well, she's sure, is the knowledge that for two weeks now has been quietly fizzing inside her like the music:

Mama loves me. Once I got sick, she proved it.

Last year, in the fourth grade, her class studied California history. They made papier-mache models of the missions and learned how gold was discovered at Sutter's Mill, east of Sacramento. They read about the Forty-Niners panning for gold in creeks, letting the water wash the lighter sand and gravel out of their pans so only the heavy nuggets remained.

Thinking about Mama is like that. No matter what the calendar might say, Jessie feels she has been in the hospital almost forever. A stream of time has washed over her memories of the day Mama brought her here, leaving only the good things, which have solid weight and shine all the brighter because, like gold, they're so rare.

It's true that when she woke up that morning and felt so stiff and sore, Mama yelled at her, "Get your fat ass out of bed." But a minute or two later, when Mama saw that she couldn't even sit up, that she had to crawl, everything changed. Didn't it? That new expression on Mama's face — what Jessie prefers to remember now is the concern in it, not the fear. Or, rather, Mama's fear *for* her, not just fear of catching whatever she had.

Mama gave her a long look, then squatted down, unbuttoned and peeled off her nightgown and dressed her, gently, from the underbritches out, which she hadn't done since Flucy was a baby.

Then Mama half-carried her into the kitchen and propped her up in a chair and shoved a bowl of Cream of Wheat, a glass of orange juice and a slice of toast at her while flipping through the Yellow Pages, looking for a pediatrician. The Coltons didn't have a regular doctor.

"Eat, eat," Mama told her. "You need your strength."

"I'm not hungry, Mama."

"Eat something anyway, Flucy. Don't give me trouble. Not now. Let's try this one — Goodman. He's closest."

Rose Ellen paused, spooning her cereal. "Can you trust a doctor with a name like that? I mean, just because he *sounds* so perfect, it doesn't —"

"Rosie, will you stow it? You eat too. I'm tryin' to talk to the man."

As Mama talked to Dr. Goodman, her face gradually went blank. Toward the end, all she said was, "Uh-huh. Uh-huh. I see," over and over, her voice quieter each time. After she hung up, she leaned back against the wall and closed her eyes.

And opened them to see Spike imitating Flucy — slouching in his chair, rolling his eyes and going all spaghetti-necked and spastic.

"Goddamn it, Spike!" Mama began a move they all knew well — a backhand slap that would knock the boy clean out of his chair — but her heart didn't seem to be in it; Spike was able to duck, though his knife rang on the floor and his toast landed on it — butter side down, of course.

"Pick that up," she told him.

"Mama —"

"You heard me. And eat it, too. I'm not having food go to waste in this house."

"It's yucky dirty now," Spike whined.

"So? That's not my fault. That's on *you*, for tormentin' your baby sister when she's sick. You'd think I'd have gave birth to kids with enough sense to know better. But no. I'm stuck with the likes of you. *Eat* it, I said." Then Mama caught Rose Ellen in a smirk. "And if somebody'd mopped the floor proper last night, you *could* eat off it, no problem. You think when I was a girl in Lawton, I could let the floor get this dirty and not hear about it?"

But, again, Mama's real attention seemed to be elsewhere. It was on her, Flucy. Wasn't it? The girl enjoyed seeing Spike and Rose Ellen get in trouble when she was just an onlooker, safe. Especially Spike. She wished Mama had slapped him good. But it was hard to enjoy anything very much when her head felt about to split.

"Flucy, I told you to eat, and you haven't touched a single bite," Mama said. "What the hell's wrong with you?"

At that point, Jessie thinks now, Mama must have known. She was just talking to keep her mind off it all.

Mama phoned Thrifty Drug and said she had a *very* sick kid and would be coming in late. Maybe not until ten o'clock, or even noon. But she didn't change out of her Thrifty smock. Wasn't that proof of how worried she was? Ordinarily, Mama would never go to a doctor's office in work clothes.

The morning was already warming up. Outside, hanging onto Mama, Flucy found she could walk a little easier.

"He said he wouldn't open up till nine," Mama said as she drove. "I told the sonofabitch he'd better be open when I get there. Period."

"Just don't make him mad at *me*, Mama."

"What you worryin' about, for Pete's sake? He's a doctor. He's supposed to take care of you."

At Dr. Goodman's office, Mama wouldn't let him undress Flucy; she seemed suspicious even of the nurse. Fierce as an old mother lion. And wasn't it nice, didn't it make Flucy feel safer, to have Mama on her side, for once, when Mama was fierce? Of course it did. Mama did lie to Dr. Goodman about the bruises. But then Mama already knew about the polio then — or was afraid she knew. And the way Mama's eyes looked, blinking and bloodshot, after Dr. Goodman took her aside when he'd finished the examination — she must have been crying and forced herself to stop for Flucy's sake. Even a mother lion would cry if her worst fears came true.

Mama did tell Flucy in a rough voice, "Well, go on," when they'd gone around the main hospital and parked in front of the Quonset hut with the red cross on it. But she must have changed her mind in an instant, because otherwise how could she have managed to run clean around the car and catch Flucy almost as soon as Mr. Wilkins had caught her? Mama said some nasty things to Mr. Wilkins — Jessie can't deny that — but Mama was terribly upset, and had no way of knowing how nice Mr. Wilkins could be once you got past *his* rough way of talking. Wasn't that the important thing to remember — how much Mama cared? How she called Flucy her precious baby girl?

Lying in bed, treasuring Miss Johnson's visits, listening to the radio, feeling stronger every day, Jessie finds these nuggets in her pan, polishes them and holds them up to the light. She's going home, everyone tells her now. She's going to walk again — no doubt about it. She won't even have to wear a brace. The doctors predict she'll lose about a half-inch of growth on her left side; her left leg will be shorter than her right, and she'll have do exercises for months so she can stand straight and walk without limping. That doesn't scare her. All that matters is this: *Mama loves me. I know that for sure. She can't take it back — not after I've been so sick. At home, from now on, everything's going to be different.*

11.

What a strange little girl, Cynthia Johnson thinks, smiling and shaking her head — the same contradictory reaction Jessie Colton has provoked in her from the beginning. She would have bet that Jessie would take the radio home after all, having enjoyed it so much. But no. Jessie *wants* to — that's obvious, from the way her eyes linger on the shiny green Philco — but something stops her.

"I better not," she says as Lester Wilkins approaches with the wheelchair.

"It's yours, honey. Go ahead."

She blushes as only Jessie can blush — bright pink from her throat to the roots of her hair. "I better not. It's *really* nice. But don't you think Robert should have it?"

Robert is the patient in Jessie's old room, an eight-year-old Indian boy from the Morongo reservation halfway to Palm Springs. Jessie has never seen Robert — knows only the little Cynthia has told her about him — but she acts as if Robert is somebody special to her, like a kid brother or a nephew. Or maybe Jessie is trying, in the only way she can, to *nurse* the boy. She has confided to Cynthia: "When I grow up, I want to be just like you." Blushing then, too. "I mean, not *beautiful*. I know that. But always nice. Making people feel better."

Cynthia is used to affection, even hero-worship, from children she cares for, but Jessie Colton is the most extreme case she's known — the same girl who refuses to call her anything but Miss Johnson.

Wilkins says, "Why do you have to be so doggone stubborn?"

"*You* tell her, Les. I can't make any headway. It's hers to keep."

"That's right, Miss Jessie. We got it for you, cause you've been such a good patient." For the last time, he lifts her off the bed and settles her into the chair. "Oof! Aren't you the heavy one now! Growin' up and gettin' better, both. You'll be back on your feet in no time."

"You think so?" Jessie asks.

"Think? I *know*, child. Ain't no two ways about it."

Oh, what a happy day! Both adults smile, wheeling the girl down the corridor to the nurses' station to complete the discharge paperwork. Dr. Goodman is there, and so is Dr. Heslov, the surgeon who needed three tries to give Jessie her spinal. It's a shame, at a time like this, to have a cynical thought, but cynical thoughts about doctors have been occurring to Cynthia more and more often lately. Is this Dr. Heslov's way of apologizing at last?

Everyone smiles. They're about to hand at least this one girl back to the community, relatively unharmed. All their hard work and worry have paid off. Wilkins wheels Jessie out of the Quonset and out into the glare of the parking lot. The rest follow him and stand behind Jessie as if posing for a photograph, facing her family: the tan Chevy, the tall, red-haired mother, the frail-looking older sister, the imp of a brother.

The wheelchair has made tracks in the thin crust that last night's rain — the first of the year — left on the ground. The mountains, hazed over all summer, have reappeared, amazingly close, the dun foothills stippled with brush, every rock and pine tree on the crests sharp enough to make you squint.

Like a football player in a huddle, Dr. Heslov rests one hairy hand on Dr. Goodman's shoulder, the other on Cynthia's.

It's as if a small, otherwise imperceptible cloud passes over the sun. Cynthia wouldn't have minded Dr. Heslov's touch a year ago, fresh out of nursing school. But she minds it now, and glances down at Jessie just in time to see a crease appear on the girl's forehead.

"Where's Daddy?" Jessie asks. "Isn't Daddy here?"

"Your guess is as good as mine," the mother says, moving toward them. "That sonofabitch goes where he pleases. You ready to come home, Flucy? Had enough vacation?"

Dr. Heslov grins wider. "At our little pleasure resort here? You've got to agree, Mrs. Colton, we've done her some good."

Dr. Goodman's nicotine-yellow mustache lifts. "A truly remarkable recovery."

As if he had anything to do with it, Cynthia thinks.

"But she's still in this goddamn *chair*," the mother says. "I thought you told me —"

"I said it was temporary," Dr. Goodman says. "There's been some atrophy to the muscles. That's normal. Jessie's been lying down for weeks. She has to get her strength back."

"Don't bullshit me. She's gonna be a cripple for life, isn't she? You just want to get her off your hands."

Nobody's smiling now.

"Mrs. Colton," Dr. Heslov says. "That is *not* the case. You haven't been listening. We've gone over and over this. I know it's all been hard on you, but you have to understand."

His tone of voice is one Cynthia knows well — pitched to silence any intern or nurse who dares contradict him. Even this formidable woman seems cowed for a moment.

Then that little boy with scar tissue in place of eyebrows sticks his face close to Jessie's and says, "They killed our dog."

"What dog?"

"We got her for you," the mother says. She finally bends down to Jessie's level and hugs her. "It's a goddamned shame. The cutest Cocker spaniel puppy, from the O'Rourkes. They wanted fifteen dollars for her, but I talked 'em down to ten. Since you were sick and all."

Is Cynthia the only one to notice? Something odd has happened to Jessie. The girl hasn't moved, but even in her mother's arms it seems that the bones inside her body have dissolved, and with them all the joy she was feeling just minutes ago.

Jessie speaks with an effort: "Mama, this is Miss Johnson, my nurse. You remember her? She talked to you through the window that time you all came. She's taken *such* good care of me. I want to be a nurse too when I grow up."

"Well, that's nice," the mother says. "Someday, maybe." As she straightens up, she seems to make an effort of her own, belatedly embarrassed; her long, handsome face blushes like Jessie's. She shakes Cynthia's and the doctors' hands. "OK, you don't have to tell me. I'm sorry I mouthed off like that. If you want, just say I'm a dumb Okie and don't know any better. OK? And worried sick all this time, I don't have to tell *you*. Truth is, I owe you kind folks more than I can ever repay. But you're *sure* she's gonna get out of this chair?"

"Sure as sure," Dr. Goodman says.

Meanwhile, the boy has started telling Jessie about the dog, with what strikes Cynthia as obscene relish.

"Somebody put ground glass in her food Tuesday night. She puked her guts out for hours and hours, and then she died. Blood all over the back porch. Yaggh."

Jessie flinches.

"That's horrible," Cynthia says. "Who would do such a thing?"

"The same bastards been peltin' the house with rocks and eggs ever since they put up that QUARANTINE sign," the mother says. "Our lovely California neighbors."

"What was her name?" Jessie asks in a small voice.

"Whose name?"

"The dog."

"Happy," the mother says bitterly. "We called her Happy."

The boy says, "She wasn't so happy when she chomped on that glass, I'll tell you that. I was way off in the front bedroom and I could hear her howlin' and pukin' so bad —"

"Shut up, Spike. Just shut your goddamn trap for once."

That silences everybody. The sister, who hasn't said a word, stands a little apart, her face vacant, her arms wrapped under breasts too big for the rest of her.

Finally, Dr. Goodman tells the mother, "Before you leave, I'd like to go over her treatment plan. She's going to need quite a bit of physical therapy, and I trust you'll all —"

Cynthia's shoulder itches where Dr. Heslov's hand rested.

Why didn't the boy go out to help the dog? Or call a vet? Of course the poor animal might have been too far gone; the mother might have felt a vet was a waste of money. But still… Cynthia continues to sense that something is wrong.

Maybe something the hospital can't fix.

"Can I stay here?" Jessie asks in that same small voice. "With you, I mean?"

"What's that, honey?"

"I can help out, once I can walk again. I watched them do everything, Mama. I know how. I can be an assistant nurse. Can't I, Miss Johnson? I won't get in anybody's way. I can sleep anywhere."

"Don't talk nonsense, Flucy," the mother says. "You're coming home."

"Can't I, Miss Johnson?"

Of course it's impossible. Cynthia almost resents the girl for putting her on the spot, making her say so. "It's not all that glamorous, nursing," she says lightly. "You should know that by now, after all you've seen here."

"I *do* know," Jessie says. "But you... the way you..."

"For Chrissake, Flucy, don't bother these people."

"She's no bother," Cynthia says.

And she remembers what Jessie called her: *beautiful*. It's true, she supposes. She has always been pretty. It's a fact of life. A nuisance sometimes, but also an advantage, smoothing her path in all kinds of ways, blatant and subtle; there's no denying it. St. Bernardine's might not have hired her so quickly if she hadn't made such a good impression on the likes of Dr. Heslov. A cute young thing — that's what he still sees, standing next to her. Unaware of how she's changed. *Good Lord*, Cynthia thinks, *if I'm a cynic now, what's the name for what I used to be?* A schoolgirl learning how to get what she wants without even seeming to try, happily half-oblivious to the process herself. And the irony is that it still works — her charm. It heals. She sees this every day. Jessie Colton bloomed under her care — and if that's because Jessie saw in Cynthia what she'd like to become if she lived, well, that gave her more reason to live, didn't it? *Is that cynical?* She just wishes she had the same effect on Robert, the Indian boy, who will need his penicillin shot any minute.

Robert, who isn't responding to the Kenny treatments nearly as well as Jessie did, and is very likely going to die.

Dying children — *they* have changed her. The epidemic is such a crisis that even the least experienced nurses at St. Bernardine's have been thrown into the front lines, working to exhaustion, double shifts week after week. You either hardened to it fast or burned out and quit. Cynthia has hardened. Glamor? She hasn't been out on a date in months; she still rooms with an ex-classmate in a cheap apartment in Highland that neither has time to clean. And none of it matters anymore. That's the strangest thing — she wishes she could tell Jessie this, wishes Jessie could understand. All that matters is the work. Doing it right, saving lives. Flirty, laughing Cindy Johnson has become, to her surprise as much as anyone else's, a real nurse, a serious person. Measuring herself against the best in the field, like Sister Kenny.

Problems the hospital *can* fix — they're all she deals with, all she has time for.

Still, it's too bad that she has to say goodbye to Jessie when so much of her mind is preoccupied with Robert, who needs her more now.

Thank God, Dr. Heslov steps in and, for once, says the right thing.

"All in good time," he tells Jessie heartily. "I'm sure there'll be a place for you here once you grow up and get your certificate. Just drop by and apply."

Dr. Goodman is saying to the mother, "I tell you, this is a young lady with plenty of spunk."

Wilkins starts pushing the wheelchair over to the car.

"Will you write to me, anyway?" Jessie says faintly. "Send a card?"

"Of course, honey," Cynthia says. "I'll do better than that. I'll call once a week. How's that? See how you're doing."

Robert is tugging her back into the building, but as Wilkins lifts Jessie into the rear seat of the car beside her brother, Cynthia can't help wondering:

What kind of family is this?

12.

Oh, I saw that nurse looking at us — that lah-de-dah little blonde who never had to miss a meal or pick a row of cotton in her life — as if she thought we were trash. And that beanpole nigger who lifted Flucy into the car — supposed to be a male nurse, but I bet he wasn't any more than an orderly. And those doctors with their smiles and bullshit. Making me grovel and beg their pardon. As if now that they were finished with her, Flucy would get right on up out of that wheelchair on her own, and it wouldn't depend on me to ride herd on her, day after day, and see that she does her exercises and such.

I mean, we set up a cot for her in the dining room, where she sleeps, and the physical therapist comes, and a "home teacher" from the school district, so Flucy won't fall too far behind. I can't complain about *them*, much as I hate letting strangers in my house. I can't do everything myself, what with bills to pay and Marv gone off to Henderson, Nevada, with some old Army buddy of his, and me working all the overtime at Thrifty I can. Before Flucy got sick, I might have asked some of the neighbor women for help, like folks used to do back in

288

Oklahoma — otherwise, how could any of us have made it through those years? But not now. Not after they hung toilet paper and threw those eggs and knocked over our garbage cans and talked filth over the phone. And poisoned that poor dog, Happy, out of sheer meanness. And not after Nona Kessler showed *her* true colors. No, sir. Not after California showed itself to be what it is — a nest of rattlesnakes. I have half a mind to take us all back to Lawton and let Joe knock some sense into Rose Ellen and Spike. That's what those kids need, both of them. But Flucy can't be moving anywhere for at least six months, and even then, Joe wouldn't stand for it. I know just what he'd say: *I done all the raisin' I aim to do in one lifetime, Dot. I raised you all, and then I raised my own three. That's enough for any man. I'm not raisin' yours, too, just because that Colton feller got itchy feet. I'm tired.*

And Joe *was* tired, the last time I saw him. He's thirty-six and looks fifty. He has the same kind of skin I do, only being a man, he never even thought about taking care of it, and now look at him. The back of his neck is like a red-dirt road that's been rained on and then dried into cracks. He's worked so damn hard and managed to buy back some of the acreage we lost, but it took so much out of him, I wonder if even *he* thinks it was worth it.

Still, it's all I can do to hold on here by the skin of my teeth. Marv says he and his Army buddy, who's a ham radio operator, are going to start that electronics store, finally, and once it gets off the ground he'll have money to send us, but I'm not holding my breath.

What's Henderson, Nevada, anyway, but just a goddamn wide place in the road between Las Vegas and Hoover Dam? Any money Marv makes is going to go for drink, you can bet on that. It's all just talk — him trying to get back at me, show how much better he can do without me.

Truth is, Marvin Colton was a mistake from Day One — he's got no more sense of responsibility than a tomcat.

And Spike's going to turn out the same way, or worse. At least his daddy was good-looking, but Marv made sure Spike wouldn't even have that going for him. I could cry sometimes, seeing what that paintbrush did to the boy's face, but he doesn't even try to make the best of it. Spike skips school and skulks around with that gang of his, and I don't need a crystal ball to know the day's coming when there'll be a knock on the door and a policeman'll be standing there on the front porch, holding Spike by the scruff of the neck and telling me the bad news — he stole something or hurt somebody. He's at a point where I don't know if even his Uncle Joe could control him. None of *us* were like that. We had too much work to do. Spike has that bad seed in him, I'm afraid — his daddy's seed, the Colton side.

And Rose Ellen! Miss Hollywood thinks she can hide behind those movie magazines and I won't know about the Marine in the sky-blue Plymouth convertible honking for her in the back alley. Fat chance. We aren't out on a farm here. We're chockablock in the middle of a city, and our business is everybody else's business. Those same holier-than-thous who used to spy on all the comings and goings at Nona Kessler's house — those same fine, upstanding citizens who treated us like lepers during the quarantine — they're right now dragging Rose Ellen's name in the dirt, and she's stupid enough to think it won't get back to me. My God! This Marine must be twenty or twenty-one, at least. Which means he has to be a loser — otherwise, why would he drive all the way in from Twentynine Palms and waste his time on a girl with asthma who's barely fifteen, even if she hangs her tits over the top of the back fence like a goddamn billboard? Tits big enough to pull her down and into his car just by the *weight* of them. How the Marine first got wind of Rose Ellen, I'll never have a clue. It's like she sent out pollen or something in the air, like the goddamn fruit trees. I don't know if the Marine's actually talked Rose Ellen into going for a *ride* yet, but is there any doubt he will? Like Spike and the cops, it's just a matter of time.

Flucy's the only one of the three who isn't headed for perdition — and that's because she can't go anywhere.

I've been tough on her, sure. Those exercises hurt. Nobody'd *want* to do them. But what choice did I have? Like I told her, "You aim to be stuck in that chair all your life? You think Mama's always gonna be around to take care of you? Huh? Well, I've got news for you, Flucy. You're gonna end up in a Home, that's what, if you don't buckle down and work. People there'll just walk around you, like you're a piece of furniture."

No, the therapist and the teacher I've got no quarrel with. They do their jobs and leave. It's that nurse, Miss Johnson, who pisses me off. For a while there she was phoning Flucy up every week, chatting away for the longest time, the two of them thick as thieves. Putting ideas into the girl's head that only make her unhappy with what she has.

"I should've kept that little radio they gave me," Flucy told me once. "Maybe Robert didn't need it."

"What radio? And who the hell's Robert? We've *got* a radio, Flucy. Don't you listen to it every day?"

Flucy likes to listen when there's music on, and now and then I catch her singing along with it.

"Mrs. Greevey says I'm a promising soprano," she told me. And then she blushed, the way Flucy does.

"Well, that's nice." I've got no quarrel with Mrs. Greevey, either. School is school. But that nurse — she *did* her job, and now it's time to leave Flucy alone.

"Why do you insist on calling her Flucy," Miss Johnson even had the nerve to ask me, "when her real name is Jessamyn?"

"How do I know? It's just what we've always called her, ever since she was a baby. Not that it's any of your goddamn business."

The truth is, I'm not really sure. It goes so far back. Maybe her daddy started it, talking some baby talk, or maybe Spike did it, or even Flucy herself. Who knows where nicknames come from? Why is Spike Spike, instead of Harold, which nobody *ever* calls him? It just fits. And how come Rose Ellen never got a nickname? It just happens that way. Joe used to tease me by calling me Dot, instead of Dorothy, because at fifteen I was already five-foot-nine and strong as a mustang filly, and for some reason it tickled him to think of me as just this little dot, this black speck like I'd make on my arm with the tip of a pencil. I didn't appreciate it much. There were days when I *felt* like a dot, lost in the middle of some cornfield when the wind was blowing a gale and the sky was as dark as the ground and I could hardly tell up from down and I might have been the last person on Earth. But I knew it wasn't so. I wasn't any goddamned Dot. I was Dorothy, which later turned out to be the name of the girl who flew from Kansas to Oz. I knew I could get out of there and lose that name, and I did — even if Oz was nothing more than San Bernardino. I'm Dorothy for good now — and I could change *that* if I wanted. I could go down to the courthouse tomorrow and sign a few papers. I could become Ava Gardner. Or Susan Hayward, who's got hair just as red as mine.

The point being, Flucy can make up her own mind when she's old enough.

"What's your game, anyway?" I asked Miss Johnson. "I bet you don't call up *all* of your patients like this. You've got too damned much to do — or you should have. What's so special about my daughter?"

"Jessie *is* special, Mrs. Colton — at least I think so. She's going to make a wonderful nurse someday."

"Well, that's fine," I told her. "That's just dandy. If that's all you mean. But you *sure* that's all? You wouldn't have anything... well, pardon my French, but I don't believe in beating around the bush. Anything *funny* in mind, would you?"

"Excuse me?"

Oh, Miss Johnson acted all innocent, but she couldn't fool me. A nurse, even a young one like her, knows all about such things.

"OK, forget that. Maybe I'm wrong. But aren't you still getting the cart before the horse? Flucy's just a child. She can't even *think* about being a nurse until she's gone through high school — and maybe by then she'll change her mind. Won't she have to learn all kinds of math for that? I hate to tell you, but numbers've never been Flucy's strong point."

"Mama!" Flucy said, listening in.

"Well, they aren't, Flucy. Let's face facts." I turned back to the phone. "You know she even wants her hair done like yours? That's when you know things have gone too far. You've got the kind of hair lays down nice and behaves. Flucy's is like a haystack — nobody's ever been able to do a damned thing with it."

Just once, Flucy tried to give me some lip. That was when she was already moving around the house pretty good with a walker, and I guess she was feeling her oats. She stopped in the kitchen — I was peeling peaches for a cobbler — and leaned on the aluminum frame and stuck her chin out, like she was daring me. She said, "First chance I get, Mama, I'm gonna go to St. Bernardine's and see Miss Johnson. She must be worrying about me, ever since you told her not to call."

"You think so? I hate to rain on your parade, Flucy, but I bet she's forgotten all about you. You have any idea how many patients she's had since? Dozens. Hundreds, maybe."

"She didn't forget me, Mama."

"You think so?"

"First chance I get, I'm gonna walk right over there, or ride my bike, and find out."

That got my dander up.

"You'll do no such thing, Flucy. These are busy people, and the *last* thing they need is some Okie brat showing up in the middle of their work and botherin' them, now that you've got no reason to. Any more than I'd want you showing up at Thrifty."

Flucy looked like she was about to cry.

"Don't get me wrong," I told her. "I know Miss Johnson was good to you when you were sick. But you aren't sick anymore, for Chrissake. Put that part of your life behind you."

I pointed the paring knife at her — not that I'd ever use it, but just as a reminder that her days of getting off easy were just about over.

"You want to take a hike," I said, "you can hike out to Henderson, Nevada, and see what the desert looks like. See what your deadbeat father's up to. Why not? It's only a couple of hundred miles. Maybe the sonofabitch would let you sleep on the couch and pay for your food and clothes if you were right there in his face so he couldn't forget. But I wouldn't count on *that*, either."

When the day came when Flucy walked by herself again, I'd just come home from work. The house was so quiet it seemed strange. Spike had gone off somewhere with those raggle-taggle buddies of his. Rose Ellen was in her room, reading or daydreaming. Not all of the chores had been done, but I've had to let things slide a little — just for a while, until Flucy's back to normal. No way we can keep the house as clean as I'd like with these extra people traipsing in and out. The first thing we had to do was to paint over part of the outside, where those eggs broke and ran down the walls and the sun baked in the stains. That's just an invitation for people to throw more.

Besides, I've been so damn *tired*. That particular evening I kicked off my shoes and sat down in what used to be Marv's big easy chair and leaned back and closed my eyes. I didn't even feel like starting supper. I sat there and heard Flucy's walker going *scritch, scritch* on the floor toward me. Then it stopped. She said, "Look, Mama."

When I looked, the sun was glaring bright orange through the window and I couldn't see much more of her than a blob.

"Watch now, and catch me," Flucy said.

"What you talking about?"

"Just look."

She was all excited — I could tell — and trying with all her might to hold it in. She was maybe ten feet away from me, between her cot and the dining-room table.

"Can't it wait, Flucy? I was just takin' a nap here, before —"

"*Watch*, Mama."

And she let go of the walker. She took one step, then another. I was scared she'd fall, but she didn't. Then another step, her hands held out in front of her like a blind person's, to keep her balance. When Flucy got to where she blocked the light from the window, I could see her face, and she had on the biggest grin.

"Catch me, Mama," she said.

And I caught her.

I held Flucy in my lap, as heavy as she is now, while she breathed in and out as if she'd run a mile race. We were both laughing — a long time coming, this day was. We had a right to be proud.

"You know, Flucy," I said after a while, "you're the best kid I got."

And she sighed and relaxed, and kind of settled down into me, like she used to do when she was little — like I'd reminded her, finally, of what she should've known all along: *This* is her home, by God, nowhere else.

Made in the USA
Las Vegas, NV
13 February 2022